Angela Dracup was born and educated in Bradford, Yorkshire, and read psychology at Sheffield and Manchester Universities. She is now a chartered psychologist and has worked with various education authorities assessing the needs of children with learning and behavioural problems. Her first novel was published in 1984, since when she has written several novels for the adult and teenage markets. She is married with one daughter and lives in Harrogate, North Yorkshire.

THE ULTIMATE GIFT

Following a heart transplant, Kay becomes disturbed by a menacing and recurring dream. Convinced that her new heart is carrying messages from its previous owner, she determines to discover the truth about his death. When she finally meets the donor's family, Kay is horrified to find herself triggering off further heartbreak in their lives. However, the charismatic family head, Majid, agrees to help her unearth the dark secret that marked the end of his cousin's life. But as she discovers the shocking truth, Kay finds herself in terrifying danger. Will the donor's killer seek to put a final end to the heart that survived?

ANGELA DRACUP

THE ULTIMATE GIFT

Complete and Unabridged

ULVERSCROFT
Leicester

First published in Great Britain in 2000 by
Robert Hale Limited
London

First Large Print Edition
published 2002
by arrangement with
Robert Hale Limited
London

British Library CIP Data

Dracup, Angela
    The ultimate gift.—Large print ed.—
    Ulverscroft large print series: mystery
    1. Heart—Transplantation—Patients—Fiction
    2. Suspense fiction 3. Large type books
    I. Title
    823.9′14 [F]

    ISBN 0–7089–4634–8

Published by
F. A. Thorpe (Publishing)
Anstey, Leicestershire

Set by Words & Graphics Ltd.
Anstey, Leicestershire
Printed and bound in Great Britain by
T. J. International Ltd., Padstow, Cornwall

This book is printed on acid-free paper

Prologue

The water just beneath the boat was vodka clear, tinted duck-egg blue. A spark of excitement surged within her at the prospect of sinking down into its depths, penetrating its opaque shadowy secrets.

She wriggled her body into the lime-green diving suit, eased herself into the jacket then braced herself for the weight of the tank. He laughed as she fumbled with the Velcro fasteners, stepping forward and wrapping them securely around her waist. He handed her the fins. There were just the gloves and the mask to put on, and then she would be ready.

Behind his own mask his eyes smiled. Inserting his mouthpiece he walked to the tip of the stern.

Her heart began to beat more insistently, as though to remind her of its presence; that vital organ, hidden and silent, constantly alert, ceaselessly active. It was not fear her heart was registering, simply a buzz of energizing anticipation at the prospect of possible danger. For the first fifteen years of her life her heart and spirit had been held

1

down, pegged out and helpless like Gulliver on the sands in Lilliput. The pain of breaking free had been cataclysmic, had almost broken her resolve. But she had learned how to heal herself, had hardened her heart and allowed her spirit to fly.

He stood with his back to the stern, then simply allowed himself to fall in. She followed him, stepping forward into the water, her body slicing through its trembling, sunlit crust.

There was the dizzy sensation of free floating, of soft weightlessness, of a curious dangerous freedom. This was a silent, private, unearthly world with only the thoughts in her head for companionship, and the steady beats of her heart to remind her of her essential being.

The sun's beams penetrated the water for a few feet and slowly faded as she went down. The greyish blue turned gradually to a dense avocado.

She could not see him ahead. He would have shot down like a bullet. He liked speed and danger and taking risks. Sometimes she was tempted to emulate his daring.

Swimming downwards, following the line and looking around her, she found herself in the company of glimmering schools of fish. Black bream she recognized, dragonets and tiny painted goby fish. He had a good knowledge of marine life and had been pleased to teach her about it. And she hungered to learn.

She hung on to the line, kicking out her legs, watching the shimmer of the fish in the thick green water; an enchanted deep-sea aquarium for the eyes of the rich and leisured — a company to whom she had never guessed she might belong.

Happiness had been building in her all week, but this particular day had been the best. A day that had already brought affirmations of love, and promised all manner of wonders still to come. Thinking of him she shivered with pleasure.

When she reached the anchor, he was not there. Of course not. He would have become impatient waiting for her. He would be hiding himself somewhere, teasing her, planning to surprise her with a sudden reappearance.

She swam back to the line, her eyes searching the watery gloom, willing him to come. A long shadow passed overhead, and she was suddenly aware of the strength of a new current, pulling at her body, lifting her away from the line so that she was horizontal in the water. A stream of white bubbles appeared and then the black-clad figure of an unknown diver. Alarm kindled. This was unexpected; this was somehow all wrong.

The diver swam up close. She struck off from the line, fighting against the current, trying to rein in the dramatic leaps of her imagination.

She felt arms pass around her waist.

And now there was nothing for her heart to register except the pureness of fear.

Part One

1

Kay was in the cinema when her bleep went off. The film was active and violent, its soundtrack booming with gunfire and the low thunder of urban traffic. No one noticed as she left her seat and made her way up the aisle to the dimly lit corridor beyond.

Going through into the foyer she placed herself in the corner furthest from the ticket office, slid her mobile phone from her bag and punched out the prescribed contact number at the hospital.

The expected and familiar voice of Sister Sylvia Marshall came down the line, clear, resolute, positive. 'Hello there. How are you, Kay?'

'Fine, fine.' Her voice felt strangled in her throat. There could only be one reason for this call.

'No infections?'

'No.'

'No other problems?' Sister Marshall went briskly through the necessary preliminaries.

'No.'

'That's good. Now, Kay, we've just gained information on an organ that seems to be suitable.' The words were delivered with the calm detachment of the experienced professional.

Kay found her hands shaking, the palms moist. She clutched the phone more tightly.

'We'd like you to come in right away.'

'Yes.' The word came out reed-thin and breathless. She straightened her shoulders. Take a grip Kay. 'I'll be there in around an hour. I'll contact Ralph right away.'

'You know to get back in touch instantly if there are any transport problems? We can easily send an ambulance for you.'

'Yes.' Kay looked around the foyer, watching people queuing to get tickets, ordering popcorn, selecting chocolate bars. Suddenly the routine predictability of ordinary life seemed incredibly precious.

'Kay, are you sure you're all right?' Sylvia Marshall's tone was less crisp now, more kindly.

'Yes, sure.' Her glance focused on a woman with spiky black hair who was studying a poster for a forthcoming film. A film Kay herself might never see. Her heart gave a struggling, painful lurch in her chest. She had the impression that the world was dissolving away.

'Is it looking . . . ?' Kay stopped, hesitating. 'Does it seem hopeful this time?'

'We're always hopeful,' said the transplant co-ordinator, staunch and unswervingly optimistic.

* * *

Ralph was involved in negotiations with a client when Kay telephoned his office.

'I'll go and get him right away,' said the receptionist who took the call.

Kay heard the faint note of excitement in the young woman's voice. She had seen no point in keeping the danger of her condition a secret and the staff at Ralph's firm knew that she was desperately ill, that she was waiting for life-saving surgery, that without it she would die. That she could die anyway during the transplant operation, or in the critical early days following. Or whenever, if some small thing went wrong.

She had the impression that she was viewed as a beleaguered and heroic figure.

But as she stood in the hallway beside her packed case, listening for the sound of Ralph's car in the road, she felt anything but heroic. The nerves in her body were tense with apprehension. Fear scoured her insides. Before the life-threatening virus had taken hold of her, cutting a black swathe through her hopes for the future, Kay had never felt true fear. Now it stalked her most of the time.

She wandered back into the sitting-room. Beside the black Steinway grand piano that had belonged to her mother, Kay's cello stood against the wall, silent and abandoned. She reached out and plucked a string experimentally. The resultant twang was dull and lifeless; she had not played the instrument for weeks. Playing a musical instrument used up huge reserves of physical energy, and her reserves were swiftly running out.

She picked up her book of crosswords, looking at an easy-seeming clue which had so far eluded her. Five across, 'selection', three, two and six letters.

She tapped her pencil against her teeth.

There was the sound of a key turning in the front door. And then Ralph's voice. 'Kay! Where are you? Come along, come along!'

He appeared in the doorway, a big, bluff, dogmatic man. Kay moved towards him. For a brief second they clung to each other, rocking together like lovers.

In the car Ralph was uncharacteristically silent, concentrating on weaving through the rush of early evening traffic.

Kay glanced at his profile. The physical solidness of him was reassuring, proclaiming his robust health and his sure grip on life, despite the approach of his seventieth birthday.

Ralph Denham-Porter was Kay's stepfather. She had never known any father but him, her natural parent having died when she was two. He was one of life's success stories. He had built up an estate agency business in the 1950s, refused to sell out during the bank take-overs in the 1980s, and was now at the helm of an independent company doing very well selling prestige properties to rich clients. For relaxation he dealt in oriental antiques. 'Pin money', he called this little hobby. 'A spot of dabbling to spice up my old age.'

Ralph was the last person Kay had expected to take on the care and welfare of a sick stepdaughter. For all his life he had taken care of his own needs and wants with a self-centred egoism which bordered on the brutal, even though laced with a winsomeness no one could resist.

But, curiously, when she became ill, this solipsistic man, who had cringed throughout his visits to her mother as she lay in hospital, uncomplaining and brave as she neared death, had freely and wholeheartedly offered his support.

Most of her friends were taken up with building high stress careers or having babies. She shied away from sharing the seriousness of her illness with them, did not want to burden them with anything so heavy. It was her live-in lover Luke whom she had automatically looked to for help, and at first he had been tender and sympathetic. But when the full implication of what was happening to her kicked in, he had regretfully packed up and moved on.

'The stinker,' Ralph had exploded when he found out. 'I suppose the modern parlance is 'young shit'. Let the little turd go, sweetheart. Your old daddy'll look after you, never fear.'

She hadn't believed it. She had thought they'd have to pay someone to do the donkey work. Driving her to hospital appointments, shopping for her when she started to feel exhausted all the time. God knows what else. But old Daddy was coming up trumps.

Kay had not been prepared for invalidity. She was just twenty-nine. She was a university teacher. In her spare time she played cello in a string quartet who were gaining a reputation on the amateur perform-ing circuit. She was young and living life to the full. Living in the present: looking no further than the next few months; the next year.

Her life had seemed utterly secure, like a house with the alarm set, the doors locked. But the thief of her well-being had been silently standing by, measuring out a countdown in heartbeats, waiting for the moment when it would slide into her life, changing it forever.

The virus that had crept up on her had at first seemed harmless and innocent. A simple dose of flu. Everyone she ran in to seemed to be coming down with headaches and coughs. It was that season of the year; damp and misty with the smell of decaying leaves rising up from the parks and pavements.

She cancelled her university teaching appointments, stayed at home for a few days, drank fresh fruit juice, and expected to feel better. After a couple of weeks, puzzled to find the return of her normal energy elusive, she had visited her GP practice.

The various doctors she saw on her initial visits had smiled at her across their desks, had seen a determined, athletic-looking young woman whose medical history could be fitted on a postcard and had prescribed hot drinks, patience and paracetamol — eventually a course of antibiotics.

And then she was given an appointment with Ruth Gregory, a keen, young locum doctor who had scented danger with the assurance of a well-trained bloodhound. She had checked Kay's pulse, measured her blood pressure, listened carefully to the rhythm of her heart. 'I think it would be useful to have an electrocardiograph reading,' she decided. 'Right away.'

In the treatment room the practice nurse rubbed brownish grease on Kay's chest and placed a number of concave rubber discs against her skin. Black leads linked her to a small machine placed just behind the couch.

Soon the machine began to disgorge a thin stream of paper. Dr Gregory ran it through her fingers, scanning and frowning. Kay saw that two vertical lines ran down its length. They resembled the sketched outline of a series of alpine peaks.

Prickles of anxiety rippled over her scalp.

'This is an irregular pattern,' Dr Gregory concluded quietly. The addition, *I'm afraid*, was implicit in her tone but not spoken.

Kay stared at her. 'What does that mean?'

'I'm not entirely sure.' Dr Gregory looked once more at the spiky pattern on the paper. 'I'd like to get a consultant's opinion.'

Kay was astounded. She had once broken her leg whilst skiing, but she had never had any serious illnesses, never needed the attentions of a surgeon or specialist physician. She was a fit, strong, vigorous young woman. Her job was challenging and satisfying and she was a successful amateur performer with a string quartet.

14

'A consultant?' Kay echoed.

'A cardiologist,' Dr Gregory said.

'You want me to see a *heart* specialist?'

'Yes.'

Oh, God! 'But why? What's wrong with me?'

'That's what we need to find out. Most likely nothing. But your reading is showing a definite variation from the normal rhythm and I think we need to follow things up — just as a precaution.'

She referred Kay to the cardiac unit of the nearest major hospital. Her consultant was a sinewy, arctic-eyed man called Raymond King. He was quick and thorough and not a man to mince words. A few minutes into the consultation Kay had a clear, sure intuition that a wedge had been irrevocably driven between her and the normal ordinary lives enjoyed by other people. She knew this even before King began to spell anything out. She sensed it in the inscrutability of his face as he examined her. In his gravity and coldness.

Before offering his diagnosis he laid his hands slowly on the edge of his desk and asked if she had brought a relative or friend with her.

The question had taken Kay by surprise. King was aptly named. He had a distant and grand demeanour. Questions about friends came incongruously from him.

'No.' Her heart banged in her chest. 'Why?'

'Sometimes patients get confused when confronted with complex and difficult information. It helps if someone else is there to listen and fill in the gaps for them later.'

'I came on my own.' She struggled to maintain her calm. 'Just please go ahead with what you have to tell me.'

Quietly, dispassionately he told her that she had a condition called viral myocarditis. Kay flinched to hear the stark medical terminology, even though it meant little. King showed her a diagram of the human heart, explaining that the myocardium was the muscular substance of the heart and that the term carditis indicated that the tissue was inflamed.

As he moved his finger over the diagram and continued to speak she found herself unable to focus on his words. Certain phrases leapt out from the rest. *Possible failure of the heart muscle. A likelihood of the need for major surgical intervention.* Confusion and disbelief overwhelmed her.

She breathed in deeply and forced her mind to absorb King's words. He was right, she should have brought a friend.

'How can a virus be the cause of all you've been telling me?' Kay demanded. 'I'm really

16

fit. I go running. I swim. I work out at the gym.' Every particle of her being appealed to him, begging him to do something to stop all the fear and horror which were raging inside.

'Certain strains of virus are not responsive to conventional, known treatment,' he said. 'And as regards your fitness, I have to tell you that some viruses thrive best in healthy tissue.'

'Isn't there anything at all that can be done to get rid of it? Knock it on the head?' She had watched medical programmes on TV. Seen doctors and scientists who could work miracles, do anything.

'I'm going to prescribe some medication,' he said carefully.

She seized on those words. Hope sparked within. Drugs, elixirs, cures. 'Could that clear everything up? Is that possible?'

'I'm afraid it's very unlikely. The primary illness seems to have reached an irreversible stage.' He made it all sound preordained, as sure and lethal as a cut from a razor-sharp scalpel. He took up his pen and tapped on the table with it. 'I'm going to start by putting you on a course of medication which should reduce the inflammation of your heart muscle.'

This icy, factual decision making seemed to carry a ring of doom.

17

'What will happen to me?' she asked, her voice seeming to strangle in her throat.

'As the muscle begins to fail you could experience pain in the epigastric region. Here,' he explained, pressing his hand against his own body, just beneath the breastbone. 'You will most likely have to deal with breathlessness and general fatigue.'

Kay felt all of those symptoms instantly. She noted that King had said 'as' not 'if' when he spoke of her heart failing. She met his steady gaze and felt it as some sort of accusation.

'And if my heart goes on failing,' she demanded, echoing King's own brutality, 'What's the bottom line?'

He did not immediately answer which she found worse than anything. 'Would my life be in danger?' she asked.

'Yes.'

'I could die?'

'Yes.'

A wall of fear rose up before her, cutting her off from normal everyday life, from the future she had taken for granted. 'No! Can't anything be done?'

'The best option would be to have a transplant.' King offered his professional opinion in the solemn yet pragmatic way that the service manager at her garage informed her of the need for her car to have a new battery.

Kay's hand flew up to cover the place beneath which her heart lay. To have her heart removed and to have someone else's heart inside her. How could she begin to get her mind around that? She thought wildly of horror films seen late at night, recalled scenes of blood dripping from crude operating tables, of the way in which organs transplanted into unwitting patients made sinister changes to their personalities, suffused them with evil and turned them into madmen and murderers. No! That was just crazy melodrama.

'The operation itself is not especially complex from a technical point of view,' King said. 'It usually takes around two hours. But there are substantial risks, mainly concerned with the body's natural response to reject invasive foreign tissue.' He paused. 'Is this too much all at once?'

'Probably,' she told him.

'You need time to think things over,' he said. She saw him glance at his watch, a reminder that he was a busy man and that she had had her allotted few minutes of his precious time. Maybe heart transplants were commonplace to him. All part of the working day. The arrogant, callous bastard.

She got up and moved to the door.

'Have I explained enough for now?' he asked.

She shook her head. She simply wanted to escape. To go somewhere quiet and hide herself like a wounded animal.

'How long have I got?' she demanded abruptly.

'The virus can affect the heart muscle quite swiftly,' he told her.

'Months?' Kay looked at him uncertainly, already knowing the answer. 'Weeks?'

He nodded.

She swallowed. 'What about there being a — suitable heart available? Soon enough, I mean?' She was totally overwhelmed with horror. She imagined herself slowly dying as her heart was silently strangled by this malevolent invading virus.

'Procuring a suitable organ is always problematic,' King said carefully. 'But with a heart, the only real medical concerns are size and blood group match. If the blood group of the recipient is one of the common ones there is no necessity for tissue typing. And fortunately for you, your blood group doesn't present that problem.'

Procuring an organ. The full force of her situation kicked in as she realized that she was now waiting for someone to die so that she could live. How was she going to deal with that? This is all so *unfair* a voice inside her protested.

She left King's office in a perplexed and trancelike state, only half remembering what had been said to her, yet at some deep level having a total understanding of all the awful implications.

At home she struggled to be normal. She made herself a cup of tea, but the moment the hot liquid touched her lips her stomach suddenly heaved and she had to lean over the sink and be sick. As she straightened up she felt her heart beating very fast, very oddly.

She took some deep breaths, packed her music and her cello into the car and drove to the recently created metropolitan university where she worked as a tutor in the music department. She sat and drank coffee with colleagues in the senior common room, holding on to her secret, forcing herself to put aside the recently detonated anxiety, to join in the daily group ritual of solving *The Times* crossword. Later, in the practice room with two keenly striving students, she hugged the warm wood of the cello between her legs, and was temporarily comforted.

For the rest of the day she was cheery and brave, her conscious mind working frantically to deny everything that King had said.

But in the night her unconscious howled with protest and horror. She dreamed of being pursued by an invisible attacker, of there being no escape. She tried to run but her legs were filled with lead. She woke up with her heart slamming itself against her ribs, her throat choked with the fear of death.

In the morning she called Ralph. She had planned to break the news as unemotionally as she could. But when she heard his deep gruff voice she went to pieces and began to sniffle and babble incoherently.

He banged down the phone and drove round to see her right away.

'We'll get a second opinion,' he said.

'No, Mr King knew what he was talking about.'

'These consultant chappies,' he insisted, 'they have to watch their backs. Everyone's getting sued nowadays. It makes sense for them to paint the picture on the black side and tell you the worst. That way they can't be accused of not having warned you.'

She smiled and shook her head. 'No.'

They sat in silence for a few moments until she broke it by wailing out, 'Ralph, I don't want to die!'

He put his arms around her and held her very tight. When she pulled away from him his eyes were moist and red-rimmed.

She managed to drag herself through the harrowing weeks that followed during which she had no choice but to become a sick haunter of specialist clinics. She was repeatedly examined, talked at, advised, counselled. And all the time the illness was working away inside her, grabbing at each breath she took, wearing her down in body and mind.

From an initial horror of the whole notion of having a new heart placed inside her, she became desperate for an organ to be found and for the life-giving surgery to take place.

She got to know other patients in the same situation. She learned of the various hopes and fears they all shared. She also came to understand, through the hospital network and from her own experience, that Raymond King was one of the most respected surgeons in the field. If anyone could open you up, cut your heart out and put you back together again whole, King was the one. And when you got to know him he wasn't the iceman he pretended to be.

'It's all going to be fine,' Ralph commented as they made their way through the rainy, glistening London streets. 'Are you feeling OK, girl?' He patted her knee.

Her stomach felt like it used to as a small child when she had to play the piano at school concerts (she did not get her cello until she was ten) and hadn't learned the piece properly. Only much, much worse. She gave a sharp, hollow laugh.

'That's the spirit,' he said.

'If I die,' she told him, 'I want you to remember me as I was before all this started.'

Ralph had been a rocklike, imperturbable figure throughout her illness. She hated to think that he might carry a memory of her as the flawed and diminished human being she felt she had become.

'You're not going to die,' he told her.

'We have to face the possibility.'

'We're not even going to consider it. Now let's talk about something else.'

He began to tell her about a man who'd brought a Chinese figurine to show him. 'Chap said he'd found it at the back of a wardrobe when he was clearing up his dad's house. Tried to persuade me it was Shang Dynasty. Timeless and priceless. You know the spiel. Some people!'

She stared through the window at the luminous dark blue sky and the sparkle of the falling rain and felt a savage stab of love for the beauty of the world, the seasons and the changing weather. Loss and grief seized her.

'Nice little figurine,' Ralph burbled on. 'A dancing girl. Very charming. The thickness of the red paint decorating the gown gave it away, of course. Neat, canny copy. Early 1800s. But a fake.'

'Mmm.'

They both knew this wasn't working.

A woman with a walking stick stepped out at a crossing. Ralph slammed on the brakes, bringing the car to a shuddering halt. 'Bloody geriatrics!' he raged. 'Pardon my French.'

They went on in silence. There were signs for the transplant unit at each major crossroads now.

'Hope they've got things sorted out this time,' Ralph muttered under his breath as he swung the car out at a T-junction. She knew he had been preoccupied with the same thoughts as hers, remembering the night two weeks before when she had been summoned to the hospital in just the same way as on this current evening. A suitable organ had been identified. The harvesting team had set out to collect it and bring it back to the unit. Kay had been prepared for the operation, had signed all the appropriate forms, had been all ready and waiting in the anaesthetic room, trembling under the thin surgical gown. Waiting, waiting. Endless. Fear and excitement had stripped her innards bare. And then it had turned out that the heart was not suitable after all . . .

'Well, at least we should know the worst

soon,' she said, aiming for black comedy cheeriness. 'A heart can only last four hours, body to body, and after that it's unusable whatever its condition.'

'Christ, what a bloody awful thing to have laid on you,' Ralph exploded. 'Pray God they don't make another fuck up.'

Kay pardoned his French.

The transplant team was waiting for her at the hospital. They seized on her, wrenching open the car door as it drew to a halt. They crammed her into a wheelchair. Kay felt the blood singing and buzzing in her veins. Voices swirled around her, telling her that everything was set up. The organ had arrived. It was A1 perfect. They'd take a blood sample from her right away, get her into X-ray. Blah, blah, blah. How long since she'd eaten? Did she have any infections? Had she been taking her antifungal tablets regularly? Good girl! Everything fine! And Mr King was all ready to go.

She looked up at Ralph's face, grey and creased with anxiety as they wheeled her away.

Bless you, goodbye, she thought, just in case. She was beyond fear now, just slushily sentimental, on the edge of tears.

As she lay on the table looking up into the anaesthetist's reassuring face the solution to clue five across came to her. 'Act of choice.' She exclaimed triumphantly.

'Oh yes,' he said obligingly.

'Except I had no choice,' she murmured as he told her to start counting down.

2

Kay dreamed of death. She was walking on a sandy beach. Her feet were bare, her hair loose around her shoulders. She was quite alone and she was lost. There was a clear, clean light above her. It was dawn and the clouds were parting to show a bright beam of sun. She wanted her mother to be there with her. But there was no one. She wanted Ralph but he was miles away. Her footsteps left deep prints in the wet sand, and she prayed that someone would find her and show her the way. When she turned around there was a figure behind her. First of all in the distance, then coming closer and closer. A man in black, hooded, carrying a scythe.

When she woke it was Raymond King's face she saw bending over her. 'Kay, Kay, wake up!' He was gently but insistently slapping the back of her hand.

Her sleep had been dark and dense, spiked with dazzling lights, with urgent voices and shifting shadows. She forced herself to swim up to the surface of consciousness. This was not death, this was life. She was alive. Alive! She took in a deep breath. Her lungs filled with air. Energy seized her. Beneath her breastbone she felt a sturdy, regular beat.

'I have a new heart,' she told Mr King. Waves of wonder and joy rolled over her.

'Indeed you have.'

'Thank you,' she told him fervently.

'How are you feeling?'

'Marvellous! Fantastic!' It was only now that she could allow herself to realize just how ill she had felt for the past weeks. How she had sensed death running behind her, snapping at her heels.

He smiled — a knowing, professional smile.

'Does everyone feel like this?' she asked. 'Like a kid at the best birthday party ever?'

'A certain euphoria is quite normal,' he responded. 'To begin with.'

Kay ignored the implied warning of a need for caution. 'I feel so well!' she exclaimed. 'I feel I could do anything — run miles.'

'Hooked up to all these lines I think you'd find that difficult.'

She looked around her, noting the tubes that sprouted from her neck, from her limbs and her chest: all the paraphernalia of intensive care. And the bones in her chest ached from the assault they had suffered. She didn't care. She was back in the world, in the business of real living. The old, used up, useless heart had gone and the miraculous new heart was working away inside her, so strong, so sure.

She smiled up at her surgeon, reflecting that whilst he was a man of awesome skill and great experience, he could have no idea of the sensations surging within her; of the delight she felt in the renewal of her power and strength; of the curious and thrilling sense that a turbulence had been stirred up inside her and now the whole atmosphere around her was altered, like the feeling in the air after a violent thunderstorm.

'I'm a new woman,' she told him. surprised to hear herself sounding somewhat skittish, almost flirtatious. 'New heart, new woman!'

'Mmm.' He pursed his lips slightly.

'Just wait until I'm on my feet again,' she murmured, feeling herself succumbing to a renewed surge of drowsiness. 'I'll show you.'

King smiled and shook his head like a tolerant parent with an overexcited child.

When she woke it was to a sense of renewed exhilaration. In her half-sleeping state her mind had buzzed with the triumph of coming through the transplant procedure and being given a fresh chance to live. She saw herself in a new role as a pioneer, a daring combatant in the dangerous arena of medical progress. She was living on a new psychological plane, buoyed up with the success of the miraculous surgical intervention performed on her. Her spirit was fired with philanthropic zeal; she made a resolve to become an advocate for transplant surgery, helping others to come to terms with the issues involved. Spiritual and political commitment swept through her.

Ralph was sitting beside the bed as she returned to full awareness. 'Well,' he said, patting her hand tentatively, as though she might be damaged if he were too vigorous, 'well, well! You made it. Good girl.' His eyes scanned the tubes and monitors to which she was attached and Kay saw the anxiety which creased his face.

'It's all right,' she reassured him. 'I'm going to be fine. I just know it. I can feel it in my bones. And *here*.' She pressed her hand over the new heart, jubilance surging up yet again as she registered its firm, steady throb.

'You're not out of the wood yet,' Ralph said, brutal and grim.

'I know, I know. There's a risk of rejection, risk of infection. All kinds of risks.' She grinned, recklessly optimistic.

'I've been talking to your man King,' Ralph told her. He paused. She saw his hand slide to his pocket, feeling for the packet of Benson & Hedges, longing for the comfort within. 'I

31

gather from King that you can probably come out of here pretty soon,' he said.

'If there are no complications I'll be out in two weeks,' Kay said. She and Ralph had been through all this before; the various stages of her recovery period. It had not seemed to be a problem for him.

'Mmm.' He chewed hard on his lip. 'You're going to need quite a bit of looking after, you know.' He stared at her in dismay, a stranger wired up to machines.

'By the time Mr King says I'm ready to go home, I'll be just fine,' she said. 'You've no need to worry about me.'

'There's no question of your going home to that flat,' he said. 'You'll come and stay with me. I'll get on to one of those care agencies. Hire a nurse or whatever. You know I'm bloody useless at hands-on stuff.'

She turned to him, sensing through the clouds of waning euphoria and departing anaesthetic that the last twelve hours had taken their toll on Ralph.

'You know what you always say, don't cross bridges . . . ' she ventured.

'Yes, yes. Of course you're right.' Ralph looked at Kay's pale face. Her skin seemed as transparent as that of a fallen leaf and he cursed himself for blurting out his worries. Poor kid, didn't she have enough to deal with already? That consultant chap had spelled it out that she was by no means in the clear. All sorts of pitfalls lurking. God, he'd never forgive himself if he got her upset and the new heart couldn't take the strain. 'Forget I said anything about it. We'll manage. Of course we will.'

★ ★ ★

The next day Kay woke feeling hungry. She ate porridge and toast for breakfast and then the nursing staff washed her, unplugged all her lines, got her on her feet and had her walking a few steps.

Her legs were weak and unsteady, but beneath her breastbone, sawn in half and painfully sore, the new heart was still sturdily beating, stoutly pumping.

'You wait,' she whispered to it conspiratorially, 'you just wait until this poor, hacked-about body gets well again.' The rest of the morning was taken up with going down to X-ray, having her blood tested then being wheeled across to the gym where the physiotherapist put her through a gentle exercise programme: a few more steps walking on her own, then some arm swinging to keep her upper body mobile, her lungs functioning properly.

'Keep it steady, keep it slow,' the therapist warned.

'I want to do so much, start really living again,' Kay told her, taking in a long, exultant breath. 'Only a week ago I thought I was finished. The Grim Reaper was coming for me.' She swung her arms. 'Well he'll have to wait a while.'

'You're doing fine,' the therapist agreed, 'but you've got to remember not to expect too much of yourself to begin with. You've had major invasive surgery, it takes time to get back to full strength.'

At lunchtime Kay's renewed hunger prompted her to wolf down watery spaghetti bolognese, then polish off every scrap of a doughy sponge pudding drowned in a puddle of thick glistening custard.

She mopped her lips and then looked down at her chest, placing her hand over the spot where the transplanted organ beat. 'I have to get my strength back,' she told it softly. Talking to her new heart seemed a perfectly natural thing to do, as instinctive as a parent's crooning to a newborn baby. She felt a need to explain and reassure, as though the heart were a visitor arrived from a foreign country who needed to be shown the ropes and helped to settle in.

Her mind shied violently away from

thoughts of the previous owner of her heart and she began to create a shadowy story of how her new heart had been created in some unknown place and had been given to her like an exquisite and unexpected gift.

She knew that she was evading an issue that was too painful to contemplate, that at some point she would have to face up to thinking about the person who had died in order that she could live. But not now, not yet.

Ten days went by and Ralph was busy planning for her discharge from hospital.

'I've got people from the care agency on stand-by. You can sleep on the bed in the study downstairs if the steps are too much. Oh, and I picked up some chicken breasts and salad and that kind of stuff from Sainsburys. Healthy eating.'

Kay was touched. She knew Ralph never bothered to stock up the fridge. He ate out at local pubs or at the homes of widows who had designs on him. 'Home,' she said to him grinning widely. 'I'm coming home.'

★   ★   ★

Having unpacked her case in Ralph's plumply upholstered guest bedroom she set about trying to fit herself back into the mosaic of

35

normal life. The first thing was to persuade Ralph that he did not have to hang around in the house, following her about in a clumsy imitation of cheery unconcern and making her anxiety escalate.

'I'll make us another cup of tea,' he decided. 'How about that?'

'I'll make it myself. Go back to work,' she told him.

'No, no. Took the day off. Nothing much going on at the moment.'

'I don't believe you,' Kay said. 'You can't wait to jump in the car and see what a mess they're making of things in your absence.'

'Nonsense!'

'Not so.' Kay countered. 'You've always thrived on wheeling and dealing; it's what keeps you sharpened up. You get a kick from giving your staff some regular hassle and bullying. And you've always hated dossing about.'

Ralph looked startled, uncertain how to respond.

'I don't think staying around here brewing up endless tea will do either of us any good,' she concluded.

'No, you're probably right. And I'd rather have a stiff Scotch, I must admit.' He grinned, and she could see that he was relieved at the prospect of being able to get back to the normality of life in the office.

'I'll have one waiting for you. When you get back.'

Alone in the house Kay went straight to the bathroom and looked hard at herself in the mirror. She judged that she looked OK. Pulling down an eyelid she saw that her eyes were clear and not yellowed or bloodshot, her skin was pale but there were no tell-tale warning blemishes.

She opened up the box containing the electronic thermometer which the hospital had provided for her. Laying it against her skin she checked out the numbers on the green digital display. Normal. Neatly, methodically she recorded the temperature reading on the chart provided.

She then unbuttoned her shirt and forced herself to look at the scar which snaked down her chest, marking the line where her breastbone had been carved open. The sewn up skin was thick and rubbery, an ugly, bulbous rope.

King had warned that the scar would never fade into invisibility. If it worried her, then later on she might like to consider cosmetic surgery.

No, she thought, touching the tough, curiously nerveless skin. This is a part of me now. A part of the post-transplant Kay.

She looked once again at her mirror image. The overall impression was much as it had always been: a tall, blue-eyed, big-boned, big-breasted young woman with a mane of golden hair that as usual, needed cutting and reshaping. But the face was another matter. Kay examined the expression in the eyes. Sometimes it seemed to her that the Kay prior to the surgery was different to the Kay who stared back at her now; that the old Kay had slipped quietly away to live a separate life. She wondered if other transplant patients felt the same way.

Having rebuttoned her shirt she washed her face and brushed her hair. Suddenly she felt hungry. She went down to the kitchen and heated up one of the ready-prepared meals Ralph had stored in the fridge. After the first few forkfuls the low-fat chicken breast in a white sauce with creamed potatoes seemed unsatisfyingly bland. She found an ancient, nearly empty bottle of Worcester sauce at the back of a cupboard and shook the few sticky black drops remaining on to the pale meat.

After she'd eaten she felt the familiar post-surgery fatigue take hold of her. She knew better than to resist it and went straight up to the bedroom, slipped off her shoes and jeans and slid beneath the sheets.

This time her dream was of the sea. She was sinking down. Her legs were swollen and heavy, immovable like tree trunks. She looked up and saw a dark shadow pass through the water above. A black-clad figure was pursuing her, coming nearer, reaching out to her. His mask had no more than slits for the eyes, and the pupils glinted as they focused directly on to her own. She felt herself become paralysed with fear as she stared into his eyes and saw death. She was going down, plunging down, down, clutching at emptiness. There was a grinding in her head, a red flash and waves of blood. Then just stillness and a sense of ultimate peace.

She woke with a start, her heart lunging against her ribs. She glanced at her watch. She had been asleep for just thirty minutes. She lay back on the pillows, taking deep slow breaths, waiting for her heart to quieten down. Fragments of the dream jostled in her mind, filling her with unease. And yet it had not been a nightmarish dream, surely. The ending had been so gentle, so infinitely peaceful.

She slid out of bed and went to the window, staring down into the garden. The leaves on the rose trees were pink and curled like babies' fists and the blades of the lawn shone silvery green in the early evening sun.

She felt a sudden renewal of grief for the loss of her mother, a lurch of dark despair at the absence of anyone really close who would help unravel the hard, tight ball of feelings inside her.

It's simply a dream, she repeated to herself, drumming her fingers against the window-sill. It's nothing more than a string of fantasies from the unconscious. But this was not the first time. This particular dream kept on coming. It seemed like a message. It seemed prophetic.

3

Eight weeks following her operation Kay was once again in Raymond King's consulting room.

She watched him studying the latest X-ray pictures on the monitor. The heart showed up against the silvery background like a grey, grainy ghost.

'Is it all right?' she asked, staring at the shadow image of the organ, fascinated and held. And suddenly desperately unsure.

'It looks fine. No abnormal signs at all.' His fingers sketched a path over the shadowy outer areas surrounding the heart. 'And your lungs also are functioning well.'

She had no need to ask what abnormal signs he looked for on the X-ray films. He had explained to her right at the start the risks for the new heart: that her body might reject the new organ, that it might suddenly become enlarged, start to fail.

'Your recent blood sample is fine,' he said, glancing down at the notes on his desk. 'White cell count normal, no indications of liver problems.' He glanced up. 'I did warn you that the steroid treatment you're taking

41

to combat the risk of infection could have an effect on the liver?'

'Oh yes,' she said drily. 'You gave me all the bad news. In detail. Loud and clear.'

'I gave you no good news?'

'You gave me a new heart, a new chance.' She heard the reverence creep into her voice as she spoke the words. She tried to stop this, to sound matter of fact. But it never worked like that.

'I was just the technician, not God,' he said. 'The donor gave you the heart.' He took up his stethoscope and began to listen to her heart from a number of points on her back.

Kay's nerves shivered from the coldness of the rubber disc against her skin. 'I'm only too well aware of that,' she said defensively, interpreting his words as some sort of admonition. 'Don't get the idea I take the gift of the heart for granted. I think of the person who gave it to me every day.'

'Mmm.' He was concerned now with listening to her heart through the wall of her chest. At the same time his fingers rested on her neck, finding a pulse.

'You've become tense,' he said. 'Relax.'

She took some long deep breaths.

'That's better,' he said.

She began to frame further words in her mind. Questions about her donor that he would not be able to ignore.

He frowned, letting the stethoscope drop down on his chest, measuring her pulse against his watch. 'Don't try to talk.' Eventually he straightened up. 'Good, good. Everything is fine. You're doing really well, Kay.'

'Am I?'

He shot her a sharp glance. 'Do you doubt it?'

'No.'

He paused. 'Kay, what is the problem?'

She hesitated. His unyielding demeanour warned against any emotional revelations. She proceeded with caution. 'I feel uneasy about my donor. About that person having to die so I can live.'

There was a gritty silence. 'There is no need to feel uneasy about having another person's heart,' he told her.

'I have to think of it simply as a body part,' she suggested, echoing his own words of the past. 'A pump.'

'That's right. A biological pump. And at the moment it's working very well. So don't do anything to upset it. Remember . . . '

'Take every precaution against infection, monitor temperature regularly, any signs of fever or diarrhoea get in touch with the hospital or the local doctor immediately,' she recited. He had drilled her well.

'Right. And no alcohol at present unless you're after a fatal hangover. And certainly no smoking.' He walked around his desk and laid his stethoscope on its green leather top with a slow, careful movement. 'Sit down, Kay,' he said, gesturing to one of the two chairs placed in front of his desk.

Obediently, she sat. She felt that she had been issued a summons. She realized that he had tuned in to her mood, had sensed her conjecturings and the drone of anxiety within her. When she had first met him she would never have credited him with such sensitivity. She had thought him a brilliant technician, a man hardened against human frailty. A man who dealt with scalpels and blood and body tissues, not people. But in the months that she had known him she had come to believe that he was much more complex than she had at first believed. She looked steadily into his eyes. '*Well?*'

'It's not uncommon for transplant recipients to experience guilt about benefiting from the death of their donors.'

She gave a dry laugh. 'Is that supposed to make me feel better?'

'Perhaps not. But most patients are reassured to know that they're not alone in the various predicaments in which they find themselves.'

She leaned forward. 'Don't *you* experience guilt, Mr King? Doesn't it sometimes bother you to be playing the role of God? Taking out people's vital parts, putting them inside other people?'

There was a noticeable return to coldness in his voice as he said: 'That's a grossly sentimental and melodramatic way of putting it. And I've no intention of getting into the playing God debate.'

'You've been through it all before?'

'Enough to have become thoroughly sick of it. You see, Kay, the issues to me are perfectly clear both practically and morally. When one death has already happened why contribute to a second?'

She did not reply.

'It has always seemed to me,' he continued, 'that doing something instead of doing nothing is by far the worthier moral choice.' He looked at her with grey unsmiling eyes. 'A life has gone — and that is always a cause for grief. But in so doing another life can be saved.'

'You're saying why play a part in two deaths when one has already happened?'

'Exactly.'

'But *you* don't carry the dead person's gift inside you,' she reminded him.

'Does that really make any difference to the

45

essential moral issue?'

'Maybe not. But it makes a great deal of difference to how you feel. To how *I'm* feeling.'

He swivelled round in his chair and stared out of the window. Turning back to her he said tersely: 'Kay, I'm a doctor, and I believe in what I do. I haven't got time to waste on homespun philosophy. If you think it would help to talk to a counsellor or psychologist, I'll willingly refer you to one.'

She hesitated, and then gathered up her courage. 'I need to know about my donor,' she said.

'You mean *want* to know,' he countered, his voice chilly and uncompromising.

'All right then, want. Is it possible for me to find anything out?'

'There are appropriate channels you can go through. I'm sure you already know that there are co-ordinators of information for both recipients and donors. Sister Marshall will be able to give you the details.' He had now gone very cold on her. 'But I have to warn you that if the donor's family wish their relative to remain anonymous then you won't be given access to the information. If the donor's family don't want you to know, then it will not happen.'

For a moment she was crushed by his

unspoken reminder of the power of those in authority to withhold knowledge. 'Do you know the identity of my donor?' she flashed back at him.

'No. The heart comes through the co-ordination service. The surgeons on my team have details on its suitability in terms of blood group and size, but apart from that we get very limited information and that is the way we prefer to work, as I'm sure you will appreciate.'

'All right,' she said. 'I understand that you can't divulge confidential information.' She stared hard at him, at the same time silently sure that he would have the information, or at least would have no difficulty in gaining access to it. 'I'll go and talk to Sister Marshall.'

'Some recipients find it therapeutic to write to the family of their donors,' he offered. 'The co-ordinator would be happy to send on your letter.'

'Dear Grieving Family,' mused Kay, 'thank you very much for letting me have your beloved relative's heart. It's been a life-saver.'

King's face was grim. 'I think maybe I should go ahead and refer you to a specialist counsellor so you can talk through this whole issue.'

'Yes, maybe you should.' She looked

directly into his eyes. 'Was my donor murdered?' she shot at him, suddenly plunging in where before she had been merely tip toeing.

'Whatever makes you say that?' He was clearly very shocked by the question.

'I keep dreaming about it. I have this dream about murder. My heart is telling me about it. I know you'll think that's hysterical woman's talk. But I believe it.'

King lowered his head and touched his eyebrow with the tips of his fingers. Kay heard his resigned sigh. 'Your donor was not murdered,' he said. 'on that point, at least, I can assure you. The bodies of murder victims are required for autopsies. The appropriate procedures to be gone through can take days. There is no question of the organs being used for transplant purposes. You know very well that organs must be removed as soon after death as possible in order to be used in transplant surgery.'

Kay sat silent. She had not felt this degree of mulishness and impotence since she was in primary school.

'I can't help you with this, Kay,' he said. 'And I don't intend to spend any more time talking about it. As far as I am concerned you have received the healthy heart of a man or woman who died in an accident. Almost all organ donors are killed in that way. They receive a severe blow to the head with no associated trauma to the chest and abdomen areas. The significant majority are victims of everyday road traffic accidents.'

Kay bowed her head.

'Will you talk to a counsellor?' he asked. 'I know someone who I think could help.'

'Yes.' She looked up. 'But I won't stop trying to find out about my donor.'

'That's your decision. But I very strongly advise against it. It's only eight weeks since you had major surgery. You need to channel all your energies into warding off infections that could lead to the rejection of your heart. You need to focus on regaining your physical health. These fruitless imaginary speculations will do nothing except sap your energy.'

He stood up and walked to the door, holding it open for her. As she passed through he laid his hand on her shoulder and said gently: 'Think about getting yourself back into life Kay. Why waste time brooding about death?'

4

An appointment to see a counsellor arrived four days later. Kay could only assume that King had thought her to be in a bad way and in need of urgent help. And she was beginning to have an uneasy sense that he might be right.

She made no mention of it to Ralph when she joined him for one of their regular Sunday lunches at a local hotel. She could imagine his indignant response. What the devil do you want with one of those shrink johnnies? You're no candidate for the funny farm . . .

In addition she could tell as soon as they met that he was preoccupied with some concern of his own. He sat at the table across from her his brows pulled together, his eyes only half taking in the surroundings. At his side a waiter carved undulating slices from a huge joint of roast sirloin.

Ralph skewered beef and roast potato on to his fork and swilled them down with a gulp of burgundy.

'How are you getting on?' he asked eventually. 'You're looking a bit pale.'

'I've always been pale,' she said.

'Yes, that's true.' He watched her picking at her grilled salmon. 'You should have had the beef with me. Get a bit of good red meat inside you.' He stopped. Took a huge swig of wine and looked sheepish. 'Bad turn of phrase. Sorry.'

Kay smiled and patted her breastbone. 'This lump of good red meat is doing very nicely,' she teased.

Ralph grimaced.

'Don't worry,' she told him. 'Bad turns of phrase pop up all the time. A friend rang the other day to tell me she'd thrown up her job, had a sudden change of heart. It's just one of those association of language things, like talking about cemeteries having a skeleton staff.'

'So what have you been doing with yourself since you deserted me and moved back to the flat? I've been worried about you this past week, thinking of you stuck there on your own. You should have stayed longer with me. When will the doctor give you the OK to go back to work?'

'I don't mind being on my own. In fact I quite like it,' said Kay firmly, wondering if she was convincing him. 'And the summer vacation will soon be coming up so I won't be back at work for a couple of months whatever the doctor says.'

'You've always been far too independent, from when you were a little girl,' he told her, really meaning solitary. He was, of course, conveniently forgetting that he had been partly to blame, whisking her mother out to dinners and golf club bashes, leaving the small Kay in the care of a string of uninvolved babysitters.

Kay put her knife and fork together on the plate. Half of the food was left. She wished she could drink some wine and lull herself into a state of light-headed contentedness; forget her growing obsession with dreams of death.

'So what are you doing to while away the time?' Ralph enquired in accusing tones.

'I read. Listen to Radio Three. Experiment with baking bread. Go to see films in the middle of the day if I feel like it.' Sit and think a lot she added to herself. And talk to my new heart. She had to admit those last two would not have sounded good if she had voiced them.

Ralph looked alarmed anyway. 'You need to get out and about Kay. Get your social life going again.' He frowned. 'That bloody bounder Luke has got a lot to answer for clearing off just when you needed him.'

Kay shrugged 'I'm not sorry he's gone. I'd already been thinking it wouldn't work out in the long term.'

Ralph drained his glass. 'Huh.'

'I've started playing my cello again,' she said.

'Well that's positive at least. Your mother would have been glad to hear about that.'

Kay's mother had been a talented pianist and an opera enthusiast. Their shared musical interests and abilities had been a strong bond between them.

'What about that quartet you play in? Have you been getting together with them?'

'I've got plans for a supper party with them some time soon,' Kay told him. 'So you see, I'll soon be getting back into the swing of socializing.'

'Mmm.' Ralph forked up more beef, swigged down more wine. Kay could tell that in his view supper with a group of pale-faced, earnest musicians talking about the string music of Bartok and Beethoven was hardly the spice of life.

'Have you got any concerts coming up?' Ralph asked.

Kay shook her head. 'I've pulled out for the next few months. Public performing is pretty strenuous physically and mentally. Mr King thought it best to wait a while.' She decided not to tell Ralph that the quartet would have no choice but to find a stand-in cellist, that she had probably lost her place with the ensemble. Nor did she try to explain that in a curious way the thought did not upset her. Her need to spend time in her flat on her own, to have quiet and solitude and the time to reflect were currently far more important than giving concerts.

She most certainly did not tell him that after a meal out with Peter, the leader of the ensemble, whose marriage had recently broken up, he had walked her back to the flat, anxious to go over all his previous explanations of why he had to look for a replacement cello player. And that she had given him wine and coffee, and that they had sat and listened to Yo Yo Ma's recording of the Bach cello suites, and after that had somehow found themselves in her bed.

The sex was tentative and self-conscious. She could tell that Peter was put off by what he felt to be her invalid frailty, that he was in bed with her mainly because he was sorry for her.

The next day she had been a bit sorry for herself, had felt ill at ease and disoriented, as though the whole episode had been experienced by someone else. And Peter had not been back in touch, which was a source of relief and yet somehow unsatisfactory.

'Maybe you should have a holiday,' Ralph suggested. 'Go find some sun. God knows there's precious little here.' He looked out of the window where a low sky hung like a grey lid over the June afternoon.

She shook her head. 'No. I still feel the need to be within easy reach of the hospital.'

Ralph reached for his cigarettes, took one from the packet and tapped it briskly against the back of his hand. 'Sorry!' he exclaimed, glancing at Kay and swiftly cramming it back into the box. He summoned the waiter with a click of his fingers and pointed to the empty burgundy bottle.

'You've got something to tell me haven't you?' she said to him.

'Bloody clairvoyante,' he grumbled with a small rueful smile. 'Just like your mother, you could always read me like a book.'

'Go on then.'

'Don't know where to begin.' His smile intensified at the sight of the waiter's arrival with the new bottle.

'You look as guilty as a schoolboy,' said Kay. 'So it must be love or money.'

Ralph tasted the wine, gestured to the waiter to fill up the glass. 'More the former than the latter,' he admitted, 'although I wouldn't call it love yet.'

'You've got a girlfriend!'

He made a snorting sound. 'God, doesn't that sound ridiculous! A man of my age.'

'No.'

Relief showed on his face, closely followed by renewed anxiety. 'Do you mind Kay? Your mother's only been dead a year.'

'Tell me about this girlfriend,' said Kay, who thought she probably did mind, but preferred not to spoil things for him.

'Her name's Isobel. She's fifty-one, divorced, two grown-up children.'

'Let me guess,' Kay interposed speculatively. 'She and the ex have a big pricey house to get rid of and your firm's handling the sale.'

'Hole in one!' He curled his fingers around his glass. His eyes glazed over with private thoughts and a tiny smile of satisfaction curled his lips.

They're sleeping together, thought Kay. And having a pretty good time of it if Ralph's lechy smile is anything to go by. And poor Mum *has* only been dead a year and I doubt if she was having a pretty good time of it lately, sex-wise or otherwise. Ralph had more or less ignored her, out most nights at the golf club or his masonic lodge. Mum alone in the house reading novels and listening to her old LP opera recordings. They'd been just another example of a tired, decades-old marriage increasingly held together by little more than stubborn habit.

'What's she like?' Kay asked, genuinely curious. 'Isobel. What does she look like?'

'Brunette, slim, a good-looking woman,' Ralph said, a flush coming to his cheek. 'Glamorous is the way my father would have described her. I suppose that's an old hat word these days.'

Kay smiled. Then, on sudden impulse she said: 'Don't get hurt, Ralph.'

'I'll be very cautious, very sensible,' he told her with a wink.

He's thinking of marrying her, thought Kay.

'She's a nice woman, Kay,' he said. 'I've made her sound a bit racy I suppose. But she's very genuine. Heart in the right place.' He groaned as his last words sounded in his ears.

She laughed. 'Don't apologize.'

Ralph leaned forward. 'I'm taking her on holiday to Italy next month. A week in Rome, ten days on the coast.'

Kay felt her mouth go suddenly dry. Ralph was her chief mainstay, even if a rather flimsy and spasmodic one. The thought of his absence unnerved her.

'Do you mind?' he asked, his voice low and urgent.

'Of course not. You don't have to ask my permission to go on holiday. With or without your girlfriend,' she added raising an eyebrow in exaggerated mischief.

'You'll be all right?' he asked with the anxiety of one who has already plumped for his own pleasure.

'Of course I will. I'll be fine,' said Kay for what seemed like the thousandth time since her operation. 'Simply fine.'

*   *   *

The counsellor was not as Kay had imagined. She was female, for a start, and small and plump, wearing a nondescript shirt and skirt from which nothing very much could be deduced.

Kay had been expecting someone far more charismatic. A kind of psychologist version of Raymond King: lean, elegant and thin-lipped with penetrating eyes that pierced into one's subconscious.

The idea of sharing her troubling, insistent dream with Janet Plowright seemed unpromising.

Janet's room was small and boxlike with plain beige walls and a pale green carpet. The only furniture was a black plastic-topped table and three battered armchairs. There was no phone, no computer, no apparent link of any kind to the outside world. A monk's cell without the mystique of religion.

Kay sat in one of the chairs with Janet sitting opposite her.

'Do you object to my taping our conversation?' Janet enquired, gesturing to a small tape recorder on the table top.

'No,' said Kay, although she felt doubtful.

'And is it all right for me to call you Kay?'

'Yes.'

There was a silence.

Janet smiled and opened her hands.

'You want me to start?' Kay asked. She suddenly felt very nervous, as though this was the first day at a new school.

'This is *your* time, Kay,' said Janet, quiet but firm. 'It's for you to decide what you want to talk about. You can say whatever you want in this room.'

'I'm not sure how to begin.' Kay heard the tremor in her voice. She had a sudden memory of the first interview with Dr Gregory at the beginning of her illness, the ragged beat of her heart as the drama of the consultation unfolded. Her palms began to prickle with sweat just as they had done on that appalling, astonishing day.

'Why don't you begin by telling me very simply why you're here?' Janet suggested. 'Mr King sent me a brief referral letter. But I need your version of what has motivated you to come and talk to me. Once you've spoken about that then you can move on in any directions you like.'

'All right then.' She took a deep calming breath. 'Two months ago I had a heart transplant. I thought I was going to die. I would have died if a suitable organ hadn't been found for me.'

Janet nodded. She offered no comment.

'After the operation I was in a really high mood. Ecstatic to be alive again. Mr King didn't seem surprised,' she elaborated, recalling his tolerant smile. 'Apparently it's quite usual for transplant patients to feel that way.'

Another nod. No comment.

'Anyway the euphoria didn't last all that long. I soon came down from the high. And then I started to feel guilty.' She stopped. There was a silence.

'You felt guilty because someone had to die so you could live.' Janet spoke the words as a statement, not a question. Her voice was warm, but impartial.

'Yes.'

Long pause.

'This sense of guilt — is it still with you?'

'No. Well I'm not sure. No, not in the same way.' Ask me something, thought Kay. Don't make me do all the work. Ask me what's really bothering me now.

'Go on,' said Janet.

'I think about the new heart all the time. I wonder who it belonged to, what that person was like. I mean simple, basic things like whether the person was a man or a woman. Sometimes I feel really desperate to know.' She linked her hands together, clenching her fingers, stretching the skin tight over the knuckles. 'At first I was worried that the heart might not like me.'

'And now?'

'I've got over that.'

'You think it does like you?'

'I told myself it was a silly question to be asking. A heart is just a biological pump. It doesn't have a brain.'

'Are those your own thoughts? Your own words?'

'It's hard to be sure. I suppose I've got quite a bit of medical jargon from the various doctors and nurses I've talked to over the last few months.'

'Let's get back to your own thoughts. Do you think of your heart as a biological pump?'

'I never thought of my old heart at all until it started failing,' Kay confessed. She felt prickles run across her scalp. When she was a small child they had often been a precursor to an outburst of sobbing.

'And what about your new heart?'

'That's different.' Her face stilled. 'It's special. It's like a separate creature that has been placed inside me for safe-keeping. It needs caring for, looking after. It's so precious.' She sighed. The relief of saying all this out loud was considerable. But would Janet understand? Or would she simply note Kay down as a highly disturbed patient?

'Go on.'

'You'll think I'm crazy,' said Kay.

'No. In here you say what you like and you don't get labelled crazy.'

'I love this new heart. But I get worried thinking that it could be a bad-luck heart. That the first person who owned it died.' She bit into her lip. 'Died young — and that I'll die too.'

The doom-laden words echoed through the long silence that followed.

'A fear of death must be very common for people like you who have experienced such a serious illness.'

'I suppose so,' Kay agreed. 'And my mother died not very long ago, so maybe I've got dying on my mind.' But it's not just that, she thought wildly. It's far more than that. What's in my head is bizarre, surreal. Terrifying.

'Were you and your mother close?' Janet asked.

'Oh yes. She was a lovely mother.' Kay had a sudden recall of the agony of loss after her mother died, the guilt she had felt in recalling all those times when she had not appreciated her enough, when she had been dismissive and critical because her mother was so unfailingly tolerant, so utterly sweet. 'We used to play duets together. She was a pianist.'

'And you?'

'I play the cello. Well, not very much at the moment.' She considered. 'In fact I don't do very much full stop at the moment. I just brood. I'm becoming reclusive and self-centred and weird. And I'm beginning not to like myself very much any more.'

'Tell me about your father. Is he still alive?' Janet asked.

'Yes. Oh, well not my real father, he died when I was very small. I don't remember him. My stepfather's alive. He's been really good to me since I got ill.'

'You sound as though that surprised you.'

'It did a bit. He was pretty cavalier with my mother. Not cruel, just detached, more interested in his work and his masonic lodge pals. He took her for granted.'

'But he's been supportive to you whilst you were ill.'

'Mmm.' She gave a brief, brittle laugh. 'But now he's got a girlfriend. Well, she's fifty-odd but all her parts are still in good working order apparently.'

'You sound angry about it.'

'It's difficult for me. It all seems too soon.'

'Are you married Kay?'

'No. I was living with a man when I got ill. We split up.'

Janet gave one of her slow inscrutable nods. Kay imagined her playing back the tape after the interview was over. what would she make of it? What was Janet really thinking about her, Kay?

'Do you know what medication you are currently on?' Janet asked.

Kay recited the cocktail of drugs she took every day.

'And have you been told of the possible side-effects these may have?'

'Oh yes. The cyclosporin is the worst — that's the drug to prevent rejection of the transplant. It makes you grow gorilla hair on your arms. And it can have possible psychological effects so they tell me. Although no one has said quite what those might be.'

'Do you think the feelings you've been telling me about and those 'possible psychological effects' might be linked?'

'Perhaps.' Kay thought about it. 'No, I

don't think so. I think the feelings come from *me*. Deep within.' Automatically she pressed a hand over her breastbone. She glanced at Janet, who had noted the gesture and continued to look calm and unperturbed, something Kay found oddly unnerving. 'You must think I'm terribly melodramatic.'

'I think you are doing your best to put into words the shock you've endured after an enormous upheaval in your life.'

'So maybe I'm sane and normal after all?' Kay queried with a degree of sarcasm.

Janet smiled. 'When people have suffered major shock and loss they have to struggle for a time to come to terms with it all.'

'I'm different from how I was before,' Kay said bluntly. 'I've changed since the operation. As soon as I woke up I felt there was something different about me.'

'What was different?'

'An atmosphere, a sensation within my whole being. As though the new heart was seeping into me.' Oh God, she said silently, this sounds so crazy.

'Many patients who have undergone major, life-threatening surgery describe feelings of disorientation,' Janet told her in even tones. Kay was beginning to find her calm insistence on normality infuriating.

'My feelings are different,' Kay insisted stubbornly.

'Of course they are. Every person's feelings are unique,' Janet said gently.

'I've had my old heart taken away and a new heart put inside me,' Kay cried, hearing her voice shrill and harsh. 'That's not the same as having your appendix removed.'

'I'm not denying the seriousness of what has happened to you, Kay.'

'Oh Jesus!' Kay's head drooped. Suddenly she began to cry. She was angry with herself, but she couldn't stop. Tears rolled down her cheeks, her nose started to run.

Janet handed her a tissue. 'There's nothing wrong with crying in this room. Cry all you want to. It's not a sign of weakness, or abnormality.'

Kay took the tissue and blew her nose. 'I'm sorry, I'm sorry.'

Janet said: 'Kay, you've had a terrifying illness. You've undergone a medical procedure that defies imagination. You're temporarily without your job and your music activities that normally sustain you. You feel unable to share your present life with your friends. In addition, your personal history has been coloured with significant episodes of loss. Your father died when you were very young and you are still grieving for your mother.

And now your only close relative is taking up a new life. There is no need to be ashamed of weeping.'

Kay raised her arm and brushed it over her face in the gesture of a despairing child. 'I've been having bad dreams,' she said.

'Yes?' Janet spoke encouragingly.

The silence seemed to go on and on.

Kay found she could not speak. She had an overwhelming need to get out of the room; to go outside and take huge breaths of air. 'I think I've had enough for today,' she muttered, springing up and stumbling to the door.

Janet stood up and followed her. Before the counsellor could utter any more soothing words Kay found herself rounding on her, shouting into Janet's face.

'I keep dreaming of murder!' she yelled in fury. 'It's a dream about my donor. The dream is telling me my donor was murdered. I got my heart because someone was murdered. It's the heart that's telling me. And I can't just sit around any more doing nothing about it.'

5

That night, as though to endorse Kay's protests against Janet Plowright's tranquil reassurances, her unconscious mind reeled once again through the ill-omened dream, drawing her back into a fantasy world which was now as real and familiar as anything in her waking life. She felt herself once more immobilized by terror as the eyes of her pursuer glittered into hers, holding her with their magnetism, silently foretelling her death. So insistent and vivid was the image that Kay woke sweating, her pulses drumming with a sickening sense of menace and evil.

She got out of bed, unnerved and disoriented, understanding that a milestone had been reached; that the time had come for action to replace reflection.

Having completed her morning routine of temperature checks and pill swallowing Kay prepared herself scrambled eggs which she drenched with HP Sauce. Afterwards she sat for a time drinking tea, trying to persuade herself that the dream was nothing more than a common-or-garden nightmare, probably brought on by the spicy snacks she indulged in before going to bed. That it was most certainly nothing at all to do with her dead donor.

The persuasions did not work. Pushing the breakfast things to one side she got out a writing pad and started to draft a letter to the family of her donor using the Parker 51 pen that had once belonged to her mother.

After several attempts she arrived at a short, simple version which satisfied her. She wrote of her sympathy for the family's loss, told them of her gratefulness for their permission to allow the heart of their loved one to be given to someone else, and finally expressed a wish that they would write back to her as she would very much like to meet them and thank them again in person.

No matter how she shaped the phrases and sentences they seemed unsatisfactory; either over-effusive or cold and detached. In the end she realized that the only thing that mattered was to convey her feelings as simply and clearly as she could.

She sealed the letter into a plain envelope and posted it to the co-ordinator, who acted on behalf of recipients of transplants, with a request that it be forwarded to her donor's family.

Three days later the co-ordinator phoned her. Her letter had been returned with a note of thanks and a request that no further contact was made.

Kay's disappointment was acute, the sense of rejection hitting her like a blow in the stomach. 'Are you sure it got to the right place? The right people?' she demanded.

'Oh yes.'

'Had the letter been read?' Maybe the family couldn't bring themselves to look at it. Maybe the co-ordinator could send it on again, reassuring them there was no threat in the message. Kay found it impossible to accept that the letter had just fallen into a void.

'It had certainly been taken out of the envelope, so I would presume it had been read.' The co-ordinator's tone was firm, reasonable and kind. It was the same soothing, head-patting voice that seemed to be adopted by all the professionals Kay was encountering.

Where next? Kay wondered. What to say, what to ask, what to do? She squashed the instinct to muster all her powers of persuasion and make an emotional appeal to the co-ordinator to simply reveal her donor's name. Through the course of her illness she had come to understand that medical confidentiality was sacrosanct, an article of faith for all the staff concerned.

'I know this is disappointing news for you, Kay,' the co-ordinator said gently, 'but I'm sure your letter was very much appreciated. At least you can have the satisfaction of thinking about that.'

'They sent it back,' Kay protested. 'And so quickly.'

'Some families find it extremely painful to think about the relative they have lost. Think of it from their point of view, how hard the loss must be. Especially when that person has had organs removed from their body.'

'Yes, yes. I do understand that.'

'And you have to remember that for them you are a stranger,' the co-ordinator reminded her kindly, 'someone outside the family group.'

'Yes.'

'You're obviously upset about this Kay. Perhaps you'd like to think about talking the situation through with a specialist counsellor?'

Kay gave a short laugh. 'Perhaps not,' she said, putting the phone down.

★　★　★

There was laughter around the table. The sound of people in their vigorous youth enjoying themselves.

Mindful of her recent hermit-like existence and Ralph's exhortations for a return to some kind of social life, Kay had invited members of the quartet and their partners to supper. Peter had regretfully declined the offer, citing parental illness as his excuse. He had made some vague undertaking to phone her later in the week, and Kay, recalling their mistake in ending up in bed together had felt nothing but relief.

She had been to the supermarket early in the morning and filled her fridge with huge red tomatoes, bulbs of garlic, fresh chillies and a big chicken. Four bottles of good Chilean red with their corks drawn stood breathing near the stove.

It was a day on which she was feeling up rather than down. She had people to cook for, an entertaining evening to look forward to and a number of plans for the future simmering in her head.

Fiona and Duncan — second violin and viola — had appeared early, each with their partner. Duncan came with Ursula, an amateur flautist who earned her living as a tutor with a national association concerned to help dyslexics. Fiona was with Hugo, a new boyfriend Kay had not met before.

'Hugo is one of the newly spawned breed of information technology wizards,' Fiona said by way of introducing him. 'So please take that as an explanation for any deviation from normal human behaviour that he might exhibit during the rest of the evening.'

Raven-haired and vibrant, Fiona was exotically swathed in a slinky aubergine dress slit up to the thigh. She gave Kay a huge hug then followed her into the kitchen, leaning up against the oven as Kay poured wine.

'Are you all right, sweetheart? Why have you been avoiding me? Leaving those stand-offish messages on the answering machine?'

Kay took out some glasses and began to pour the wine. 'I've been avoiding everybody.'

'At least that means I wasn't the only one getting the cold shoulder.'

'It wasn't like that!'

'Just teasing.' Fiona accepted a glass of wine and twirled the stem between her fingers. 'How long have we known each other?' she demanded.

Kay thought about it. She and Fiona had shared a rented flat in her last year at university. 'About a quarter of our lives I suppose.'

'Yes.' She moved close to Kay and put her arms around her. 'And I don't want to lose you now.'

Kay sighed. 'Sorry. I haven't been avoiding

you. I needed to be on my own for a time. And anyway I was rotten company.'

'I forgive you,' said Fiona. 'But don't you dare go on being so brave and lonely when you know I'm here for you.' Her intelligent brown eyes stared into Kay's for a moment, then she picked up the tray of glasses and went off to distribute them.

As the four musicians caught up on gossip from the world of amateur performing, Hugo wandered around Kay's sitting-room, staring at the paintings on her walls, hoicking books from her shelves and riffling through the pages. He paused beside her cello and plucked at the strings in a very unmusician-like way. 'This is one handsome brute of an instrument,' he remarked, twirling the cello on its spike as though it were a child's toy.

Kay nodded in agreement.

'Are you any good at playing it?' he wondered.

'Moderately.' Kay sat down beside Fiona who looked at Hugo and then raised her eyebrows heavenwards.

'He's still just on trial,' Fiona said. 'First time I've been out with a man who's tone deaf.'

Duncan laughed. 'Maybe a smart move! Less risk of criticism.'

'I bet you get plenty of dirty jokes about

having a cello between your legs,' Hugo commented to Kay.

'I've had my fair share.' Kay smiled. She had the feeling Hugo was the sort of man who was never silent for long and was likely to provide some good entertainment through the evening. It also struck her that as a computer expert he might be able to provide her with some tricks-of-the-trade information which could prove useful. 'Do you know the most famous and probably the rudest cello joke?' she asked. 'The Thomas Beecham one?'

'Not a chance,' said Fiona. 'Hugo's a clean slate as far as music goes.'

'Tell me!' Hugo commanded.

Kay sipped at her mineral water, creating a dramatic pause. 'There was a flamboyant cellist who got hauled over the coals by Beecham for her playing technique. 'Madam,' he said, 'you hold between your legs an instrument that could give pleasure to thousands, and all you do is sit there and scratch it.''

Hugo roared approval. 'I'll remember that.'

They moved to sit at the table. Hugo glanced around the company. 'Am I the only non music man present?'

Ursula smiled at him. 'I think you are.'

'Why is it that musicians always stick

together?' Hugo enquired.

'So they always have someone to play with,' the others chorused.

As they progressed through Kay's highly spiced Mexican chicken and swilled down the Chilean red, the noise around the table steadily increased.

Hugo grasped the wine bottle and began topping everyone up. When he got to Kay she shook her head and placed her hand over her glass.

'You don't drink?' he asked.

'I do normally. I'm a real wino. But I can't at present.'

'Ah, yes.' Hugo looked suddenly uneasy. 'Fiona mentioned . . . you've had some major, er, surgery.'

'Transplant,' Kay said. 'I had a heart transplant ten weeks ago. It's one of those embarrassing things like body odour and death that everyone would rather not mention. So there! Now I've mentioned it! Taboo time over.'

Everyone was quiet for a moment. Kay burst out laughing. 'Oh for God's sake. Someone crack a joke. One of the worst things about illness is being deprived of humour. Your own and everyone else's.'

There were smiles of relief.

Duncan poured water into his glass and

drained it in one go. 'This was good stuff, Kay, but pretty hot,' he commented, gesturing to his empty plate.

'I think I must have let my hand slip a bit with the chillies,' Kay said, recalling being rather more liberal than usual. 'I've noticed since the operation that quite a lot of food seems rather bland.'

'You mean your taste has changed?' Ursula asked.

'Yes, I suppose it has.' Kay reflected on her new liking for Worcestershire Sauce and curried mayonnaise, flavours she had never particularly enjoyed previously. 'Maybe my surgeon did some experimentation on my taste buds when he had a few moments to spare,' she joked. 'Or perhaps a big op stirs up all your insides, gets your hormones jumping about. Don't pregnant women get cravings to eat all kinds of weird things?' This is the sort of therapy I need, Kay thought. Being able to joke again with friends. Stop taking myself and my situation so deadly seriously.

'But it's interesting you say your food preferences have changed,' said Fiona slowly. 'I read an article in one of the tabloids last week about a boy who had had a kidney transplant. He started getting a craving for shellfish, which he'd always hated before. And then it turned out the donor was a top chef whose speciality was seafood.'

'Creepy,' said Hugo. 'But maybe a load of tosh. Has anyone done any impartial research into it?' He looked questioningly at Kay.

'I wouldn't know,' she admitted, thinking it was time she found out. 'Most people I've talked to at the transplant centre seem to want to steer clear of the whole business of taking on someone else's personal qualities just because there happens to be a lump of their flesh inside you.'

'I wonder why that should be?' Fiona mused.

'My surgeon takes the view that there's no special mystique about having someone else's heart put inside you. For him a heart is simply a biological pump, a piece of body equipment. He thinks you're just going to stir up trouble for yourself if you get into any psychological or spiritual stuff.'

'And what do you think, Kay?' demanded Hugo.

'I'm keeping an open mind,' she said cautiously.

'Do you know who your donor was?' Hugo persisted.

'No.'

'Wouldn't you like to find out?'

'Oh, for Christ's sake Hugo!' Fiona protested.

'No, it's OK. And, yes, I would like to find out. But it's not that easy. If the donor's family don't want the identity revealed then there would be a problem in discovering it.'

'Presumably the information will be stored on a database somewhere,' said Hugo. 'Even the creaking National Health service has got round to that, surely!'

'Yes,' Kay agreed, 'but that's not particularly helpful as far as I'm concerned. I know hardly anything about computers and information technology.'

'No. But I do,' smiled Hugo.

'Oh for God's sake, you've been watching too many films about IT whizz kids hacking into secret and impregnable databases,' Fiona protested.

'Yes. And most of them are way off target,' said Hugo waving a dismissive hand. 'I'm a highly knowledgeable and reliable whizz kid.'

'What about the moral issue?' asked Kay. 'The rights and wrongs of digging around to procure confidential information?'

Hugo gave another of his grins. 'What about it?'

'Some people would be outraged to think of someone simply ignoring ethical codes. They'd say I should respect the donor's family's wish for privacy.'

Hugo shrugged, unimpressed. 'Fair enough.'

At the end of the evening, as he and Fiona were leaving, Hugo leaned over to Kay and said: 'Don't forget, if you ever want help in getting 'information', all you have to do is give me a call.'

'I might just do that,' she told him with a casual smile.

'Of course,' he added grinning, 'if it all blows up in my face, Kay, I'll say I never laid eyes on you.'

6

Ralph telephoned from Italy. 'Weather's marvellous!' he boomed. 'The sea's as smooth as a duck pond. Air like wine. You should be here. It'd do you a power of good.'

He was at his most gung-ho, a sure sign that he was enjoying himself to the full and feeling as guilty as hell.

'How are you and the girlfriend getting on?' Kay asked.

'Astonishingly well, considering I'm a self-centred old bore.'

'You've never been boring,' said Kay. 'Not one of your faults!'

'Hah! And what are you doing with yourself?'

'Oh, all those things Mr King told me. Plenty of gentle exercise, plenty of rest. Keep taking the pills . . . '

'Hmm!'

'And a bit of socializing too. You'd approve.'

'Good. Splendid. Well then, don't overdo things.'

Staring out of the window a little later, drinking tea and nibbling on a chicken tikka sandwich, Kay reflected on the dismal failure of her recent efforts to further the search for her donor. She had been in contact with various professional and voluntary organizations engaged in advising patients who had received organs from donors. There was just one message coming through loud and clear. The one King had already told her: if the donor's family didn't want anyone to know, then it didn't happen.

The spirit of honesty and integrity in which she had begun her enquiries soon began to seem like gross naïvety. She realized that she was going to get very little further information unless she drew some weapons from the armoury of lies and deception.

Scraping up the crumbs of bread from her plate she pushed it to one side and, without giving herself time for further misgivings, swiftly redialled one of the voluntary agencies she had contacted earlier. She was relieved to have her call taken by a different volunteer to the one she had spoken to previously, it made it easier to introduce herself by her mother's maiden name and announce herself as a therapist currently working with a young woman who was showing signs of marked emotional disturbance following a heart transplant.

The dissembling words fell out with an

oiled elegance that amazed her. And the response was immediate and decisive.

'I'll put you through to one of our advisers,' she was told. 'Please hold.'

The man who took her call had a low sympathetic voice which communicated totally genuine sympathy. 'None of the support workers here are trained therapists,' he told her. 'We're here simply because we're the relatives of recipients or organ donors. My wife was a heart and lung recipient. She survived twelve and a half years. She died six months ago.'

Sweat broke out on Kay's forehead. Oh, Christ! Could she go on with this?

'We all receive a brief training from a professional counsellor on how to talk recipients through problems,' he added reassuringly into Kay's stunned silence.

Kay jerked herself from her doubts and stabs of conscience. She knew she must either put the phone down or press on.

She said: 'My client is a young woman just out of her teens. She received her new heart around ten weeks ago and since then she's been experiencing a recurring dream about her donor.'

A sympathetic murmur came down the phone.

Kay grimaced. She wanted to grind the

deception in the dust and blurt out the truth. But then she would simply be back to square one in her search for insider knowledge. She steadied herself for the next speech, trying to remember Janet Plowright's professional style of speaking, fragments of Janet's therapy jargon.

'The dream has been very disturbing for my client. She seems to have become entirely preoccupied with thoughts of her new heart and its previous owner.'

'That's very common,' the man interposed quietly.

Kay wondered if she heard conjecture in his tone. She was convinced that her voice must be shot through with a self advertising confession of guilt. Had he seen through her? Was she completely unconvincing in her therapist role? Her heart began to pound.

'I should tell you,' she said steadily, 'that I'm not experienced regarding transplant patients. The reason this particular client has come to me is because I've seen her and helped her in the past.' She paused. 'I know her history.'

'Ah, so she had personal and emotional problems prior to her surgery?' he said, unknowingly offering credible detail to embellish Kay's fabricated story.

'Yes.' Of course! thought Kay, trying to

form a picture of her fictitious client. 'Over a number of years in fact. So it may be that her reactions are not necessarily typical of other recipients. Although, of course, each person is unique in their feelings and reactions.'

'Oh, indeed.'

'My problem is that whilst I feel able to work with my client on her feelings of isolation and disorientation, I am concerned that, because of my lack of experience with transplant patients, I might not be offering her appropriate guidance with regard to her tormenting thoughts about her donor.'

'Yes, yes, naturally. I do understand.'

Kay heard the depth of human sympathy in the voice, pushed it to one side and ploughed on. 'She has recently become very insistent that she should discover the identity of her donor. It has become a compulsion for her, an obsession.' Sweat was now erupting beneath her shirt, trickling down her breastbone. Don't stop, she told herself. Go on, go on! 'I'm aware of the medical ethics and confidentiality in these cases and clearly my task is not to help her find the identity of her donor, even though she is begging me to do this.'

'No, this is a delicate situation. Not at all simple. Mmm.' He paused, obviously wondering how to advise.

'I think,' said Kay, keeping her voice low and unhurried, 'that what I need is to have a clear understanding of the procedures involved for people who want to find the identity of their donors. I can then explain the full difficulties to her. I think she has come to believe that I'm blocking her from getting information, that someone like me should be able to winkle it out very easily if I just try hard enough.' Her heart was beating so frantically now she clasped her hand over her chest as though that could steady it.

'I understand. She sees you as part of the establishment, someone who has automatic power to gain access to confidential information.'

'That's it. And I do believe that until we have got this issue of the donor's identity dealt with I won't be able to help her to come to terms with the terrifying experiences of the past few months.'

'Right. I think I can help here. As a first step your client should get in touch with the transplant co-ordinator who should be able to tell her all she needs to know about the procedures for contacting donor families. She will be able to reassure her that no one is trying to block her right to information. And of course to confirm that people in your profession have no short cuts to finding the identity of donors.' He gave Kay a swift and very clear résumé of the procedures she already knew inside out.

She thanked him. There was a sudden sense of disappointment. She had felt she was beginning to get somewhere. But now she could think of nothing further to ask. She supposed that was it.

'If you have details of the hospital at which the transplant took place I could give you some contact numbers which might be useful,' he said. 'Do you have pen and paper?'

Kay quoted the name of a major transplant centre in the north, and carefully wrote down the information he volunteered: names of co-ordinators and their secretaries, contact numbers of social work departments. All the things she already knew.

'That's very much appreciated,' said Kay, knowing she had made very little progress at all. She prepared to close the conversation. 'You've really been most helpful — '

'Just one moment,' he said. 'I'm trying to find the name of someone in the social work section.' Kay could hear the crackle of paper, imagine him rapidly riffling through a notebook. 'I seem to remember that she had a case rather similar to yours, a young heart recipient. There was some concern because this young man managed to discover the identity of his donor even though the family were very strongly against it. He went to visit them and caused some problems. I think there might even have been a court case about it.'

Kay waited, feeling wretched in the face of this man's unhesitating kindness.

'Yes, here we are. Paula Jennings. Here's her contact number. It might be useful to talk to her. You never know. Every little helps.'

Kay rather doubted that Paula Jennings would be able or willing to offer her a blueprint for unearthing protected information. But she expressed thanks nevertheless.

After she put the phone down she stood very still, breathing deeply. She then went to the bathroom and checked her pulse, temperature and blood pressure. The latter was slightly raised, but not significantly so.

She made fresh tea, took two shortbread biscuits from the jar and settled down on the sofa, swinging her legs up on to the cushions.

That was the first and last time she would act the role of therapist.

The stress of making the call and all its attendant deceptions had taken their toll. Her body felt as though it had endured a bout of intense activity. Fatigue overwhelmed her and she fell into a deep sleep.

The dream came again. The gimlet eyes

bored in to her. But this time the pursuer spoke, demanding the prize of the beating heart which he had been cheated of before. Assuring her he would have it.

She woke in terror, clutching her chest, every nerve in her body screaming out for help. Her head seemed to be filled with a loud, drumming ache. Coming up from sleep she felt as though she had sunk down so many levels from everyday consciousness that trying to wake was like being drawn from the bottom of a fathomless well.

Sitting up and rubbing her hands up and down her upper arms she eventually realized that the drumming was not in her head but a rhythmic banging on her door.

She stumbled from the sofa, pulled open the door and saw Fiona standing there with a bottle of wine and a bag of warm food that smelled enticingly spicy and exotic. There was a tentative, quizzical look on her face. 'OK to come in?'

Kay made a raw sound in her throat. 'Oh God, I'm so pleased to see you, Fi.'

Fiona wrapped her arms around Kay's swaying figure and propelled her back to the sofa. 'Have you eaten at all today?' she asked.

'Just toast and sandwiches.'

'Hmm.'

'Not enough. I know, I know! I'm not

taking proper care of myself.'

'I'll put some plates to warm and get this served out. Don't move a muscle.' She brandished the bottle. 'Is it all right if I open this? I'm gasping.'

'Yes, but I'll have orange juice, more's the pity. It's in the fridge.'

She heard Fi moving about in the kitchen; the comforting clatter of plates and clink of glasses. Friendly, warm, companionable sounds. God, I didn't realize how lonely I've been getting, Kay thought.

'I told them to throw in plenty of chillies,' Fiona said bringing through plates of pilau rice heaped with a fiery-looking sauce. 'And there's extra dry lime pickle to blow our heads off.'

'Where's Hugo?' Kay asked, forking up volcanic prawns and pickle and closing her eyes in pleasure.

'Watching international footie on TV. We still have our own social lives,' said Fiona sardonically. 'Not quite joined at the hip yet. Although we did stay in bed nearly all last weekend.'

Kay glanced up from her plate. 'Are you really keen on him?'

Fiona rolled her eyes. 'Let's put it this way. If anyone had told me I'd be stupid enough to fall madly in love with a bloke who is deaf to music, is football-crazy and has allowed his grey matter to be infiltrated by the internet, I'd have told them to get their head seen to.'

'Madly in love! So that's how it is?'

'Sadly for me, yes.'

'Not sad, Fi. Happy. I'd like to be in love again,' Kay said.

'You will be,' Fiona said. 'And then you'll wish you weren't!'

Kay had always envied Fiona's love life. She seemed to have the knack of being free without the downside of sluttishness. And she had always been quite happy to talk about what actually went on in bed with her various lovers. It used to have the effect of making Kay feel woefully inadequate. There had only been Luke for her. And she did not think their sex life had in any way matched up to Fiona's accounts.

'Do you still miss Luke?' Fiona asked, as though tuning in to her thoughts.

'No, not at all.' Kay paused. 'In many ways I'm glad to be on my own again. I must be growing into a hard woman.' She frowned. 'Do you think I've changed since the operation?' she demanded of Fiona. 'Become more self-centred? A touch hard-bitten?'

Fiona looked at her. 'I think you have changed. But I wouldn't say hard-bitten.'

'What then?'

'You're more single-minded, more determined. Kind of steely.'

'I had to be like that to pull myself through the idea that I might die, that I might simply cease to exist,' said Kay. 'And that the world would be a sadder place without me,' she added with a wry aim at humour.

'It would have been,' said Fiona.

Kay felt sudden tears spring up in her eyes. She brushed a hand over her cheekbone.

Fiona watched her. 'This is all about finding who your donor was, isn't it?'

Kay stared down at her plate. 'I don't think I can go ahead with it.'

'Why not?'

'Too risky, too selfish.' She laid down her fork. 'Too bloody difficult.'

'I think you should do it,' Fiona said unexpectedly.

Kay was astonished. 'You're the first person to say that! Apart from Hugo.'

'Oh, his interest is simply a symptom of his desire to flex his hacking-into-database muscles. But seriously, I think you've reached the point when you've got to take this particular bull by the horns.'

'I can't believe you're saying this!'

'I've known you a few years,' Fiona said, 'And I can see there's something that has really got to you around this issue of the

92

donor. I'm not sure what it is and I'm not going to poke and pry. But for what it's worth I think you could be heading for some kind of breakdown if you don't take some action and put your mind at rest.'

'You should go into therapy work,' said Kay.

Fiona leaned towards her. 'Surely it's not that difficult to find out about the donor? And I'm not talking about performing surgery on computers.'

'I honestly don't know,' Kay admitted. 'I don't seem to be able to think it through calmly and logically.'

'OK, let's think together.' Fiona cleared the used plates to one side, seized the notepad that lay beside the phone and sketched a circle into which she placed a capital letter K. 'Right, here you are waiting for a heart. Someone dies who has an organ that fits the bill and clearance is given that it can be taken from the body and used for transplant. What next?'

Kay gave a quick description of the role of the co-ordination services.

'OK. So the procuring service send the harvesting team off to collect the heart. Now, I'm presuming all this co-ordinating takes place by phone?'

'Yes.'

'So someone somewhere will have recorded

the location of the donor's body — a hospital, most likely.'

'Yes.'

'The first person to take the message, a receptionist or secretary, will probably be told the location and given a few basic details because if not they won't get put through to one of the professional big guns. Right?'

'Right. And I suppose they'd be likely to jot it on a pad.'

'Exactly.'

'Receptionist's notepads get used up and thrown away.'

'True. But it's more than likely that the actual co-ordinator will also make jottings. Hospitals may be fully computerized but I'll bet staff still use brown cardboard files and make handwritten case notes.'

'Yes, they do. But they keep them in locked filing cabinets in locked offices.'

'Not when they're in use.'

Kay laughed. She imagined herself at a follow-up appointment with Mr King, trying to flick through his case notes when his back was turned. Or craning over the co-ordinator's secretary's shoulder in the administrative office. Unthinkable, undoable, even if the information was there.

'No,' she said. 'I'm no sleuth. I can't snoop.'

'How desperate are you for this information?' Fiona asked.

There was a beating pause. It occurred to Kay that she would not be able to rest, that she would have no happiness or peace of mind until she had walked through the landscape of her dream and reached the terrifying truth that lay at its core. And that there was only one key to unlock the dream's secret.

'Very.'

'I thought so. Well?'

'I haven't the nerve.'

'Oh yes you have.'

7

The taxi was hung about with cuddly toy dogs and had seats as furry as an unclipped poodle.

Kay settled herself in the back, hoping the driver did not want to engage in jokey conversation during the time it would take to drive to the hospital: over an hour judging by the traffic.

After a few minutes of silence he asked if she would object to his listening to the radio. 'I'll just have it on quiet,' he reassured her.

Kay murmured her lack of objection. She anticipated Radio 2 and sentimental tunes, but what came through was *Woman's Hour* and a talk on the handling of the problems thrown up by disruptive adolescents in school.

'I wouldn't be a teacher for love nor money,' the driver said at the close of the item.

Kay made more assenting murmurs and stared fixedly out of the window. Her mind skittered over the problems that lay ahead and her vow to herself that she would not return home without having achieved something positive, something that would bring her nearer to her donor.

The voices from the radio drifted around her. There was a man talking about organic farming and then a novelist discussing her research methods.

The traffic ground almost to a standstill as they neared the hospital. Cars glinted in the brilliant sunshine. Summer had finally arrived and it was going to be a hot, humid day.

The driver came to a halt at traffic lights. He opened the window and leaned his elbow on the sill.

The woman had just about come to the end of her ten minute slot. 'I've very rarely found anyone reluctant to talk to me,' she said. 'People love to talk about themselves, their work, their hobbies, their love lives. In fact it's quite amazing what secrets people will let you in to if you tell them you're writing a novel.'

'Doesn't surprise me,' commented the driver. 'When you've been doing this job long enough, nothing people do surprises you.'

Kay went first to Mr King's administrative office. His secretary, Pamela, looked up from her paper strewn desk and gave a welcoming smile. 'Hello, Kay! How are you?' The smile modified into a look of faint concern. 'You didn't think you had an appointment today did you? Mr King's not here; he's at a conference in Madrid.'

'Lucky him,' smiled Kay. 'No, I wasn't expecting to see him today.'

Pamela blew out a puff of relief. 'Thank goodness. Just for a moment I thought I might have sent out a batch of wrongly dated appointments.'

'A bit of a headache.'

'A nightmare.' Pamela tilted her head, observing Kay with a questioning look. 'So what can I do for you?'

'I wondered if you could look something up in my file.' Kay felt the familiar prickle of cold anxiety, sweat breaking out against her ribs.

Pamela's eyes became tinged with faint alarm. Or so it seemed, Kay realized she could be imagining it. 'It's just a detail connected with my claim for sickness benefit.'

Pamela got up from her chair. 'I'll get your notes out.'

Kay thought she could hear the other woman's mind silently wondering why such simple information couldn't be gained by a phone call.

Pamela unlocked her desk drawer and took out a small bunch of keys. She opened a low, metal cupboard that ran along the back wall of the room. As the door slid back Kay saw rows of brown cardboard holders hanging from a runner like clothes in a wardrobe. Each was labelled with a name and Pamela soon located Kay's. She reached into the holder and drew out a simple buff folder.

'Now then,' she said, laying the file on her desk, 'what do you want to know?'

'Well . . . it's mainly the exact dates of my appointments before the operation. And when the actual recommendation was made for a transplant.' Her voice felt muffled and strangled in her throat. Surely Pamela would see through this amateurish attempt to throw up a smokescreen and would order her off the premises without delay.

'You needn't have come all this way for that,' Pamela said with a note of maternal chiding. 'In fact the secretary at your GP practice could probably have told you enough for the benefits people.'

'Yes. I was in the area anyway, I'm seeing a friend for lunch.' Anxiety surged up.

'Never mind,' Pamela soothed, 'it's really nice to see you again anyway. You're looking really well.' She opened the file and identified the date of the first appointment.

As she took up a pen to jot it down for Kay, a teenage boy appeared in the doorway. His long thin face wore a hunted and pleading expression. He looked from Kay to Pamela. 'I'm trying to find the histology department,' he said.

'You're in the wrong block,' Pamela told him. 'Histology is on the ground floor across the central courtyard.'

'I've been there,' he said. 'I've been all over.' He swayed against the door.

Pamela laid the pen down. 'You need to take the lift and go down to the ground floor. Then follow the signs for H wing. When you get across the courtyard go through the red doors. Then go down the corridor right to the end and you'll find histology reception just on the right.'

The boy gave a huge sigh. His eyes were swimming with tears.

'I'll take you,' said Pamela. 'Kay, would you keep an eye on things here. I'll only be a couple of minutes. There's a kettle and coffee in the kitchen next door.'

She took the boy's arm and marched him off. Kay heard the doors of the lift open and close.

She stood transfixed for a moment. Then she bent over the desk and riffled rapidly through the pages of the file, her eyes searching for the date of her transplant. The file was partly word-processed, but mainly filled with Mr King's scrawls which for the most part were either indecipherable or incomprehensible.

On the day of the transplant there were some brief notes timed at 4.30pm. 'Possible organ ident., blood gp match, weight OK. Procuring team alerted. Patient notified.'

Kay scanned further. There were references to the start time of surgery, some technical jargon that she was not familiar with, and what looked like an indication of the success of the surgical procedures. After that the date moved on to the next day.

Kay rubbed her hand over her forehead. Flicking through the remaining notes yielded nothing but brief accounts of her follow up appointments. Her eye was caught by one of the last entries: 'Clinical signs all good. Kay showing indications of post-op. anxiety. Refer for psych. counselling.'

Hmm.

Realizing that this particular search had drawn a resounding blank Kay turned the file back to the page Pamela had been consulting before she left. She went through into the kitchen next door and filled the kettle. As Pamela's heels echoed down the corridor Kay poured the boiling water on to the granules and carried the steaming mugs through into the office.

'Bless you,' said Pamela. 'Sorry to run out on you like that. The poor boy was in a bit of a state.' She took a long sip of coffee, wedged her mug into a vacant space on the desk top and returned to an inspection of the file. 'Now, where were we?'

* * *

Once again the effort involved in lies and deception took its toll on energy levels. From Pamela's office Kay went down to the café in the reception area and ordered a milk shake and a tuna sandwich. She sat down on one of the café's cheerily coloured banquettes and reviewed her options. Her original plan had been to visit the transport co-ordinator's office as the next possible source of information. Recalling that there was quite a walk to get to it, as the room was in a separate section of the transplant centre complex, she decided she needed half an hour's rest to recoup the mental and physical stamina she would need for another bout of duplicity.

She settled herself back against the mock-leather padding of the banquette and closed her eyes. At home she would instantly have slept, but caught in the flow of human traffic moving through the café she was unable to relax and shut her mind off from the here-and-now.

She waited for precisely thirty minutes then

gathered her things together and set off for the wing housing Sister Marshall's office.

Walking through endless corridors and domed, plastic-covered bridges reminiscent of something from a fun park, she noticed the office of the hospital's social work department. Her memory sprang into action, throwing up the name of the social worker given to her by the kindly widower volunteer worker. Kay had toyed with the idea of making contact with Paula Jennings but had decided against it. She had run through the likely progress of the conversation in her imagination, anticipating all the pitfalls. Her mother used to have a friend who was a social worker. Contrary to all the TV stereotypes, she had been a woman of ferocious energy and intelligence who combined a frightening range of general knowledge with a razor-sharp sensitivity regarding human motivation. There would be no chance of bamboozling her with a half-baked attempt at some phoney impersonation.

As Kay approached Sister Marshall's office, she saw the transplant co-ordinator come through the door, juggle with her clipboard and bag as she locked it behind her, then come striding down the corridor.

'Why, Kay!' Sister Marshall exclaimed, swivelling to a halt. 'How good to see you.'

Her eyes swept over Kay with swift professional appraisal. 'You're looking marvellous. A wonderful advert for our section!'

Kay's mind speedily emptied itself of all the spurious reasons she had previously contrived to explain the reason for her visit.

'It's always good to see former patients, especially our success stories,' Sister Marshall continued. 'It's usually only the ones with difficulties and complaints who bother to come back and see us.'

'Yes,' Kay agreed feebly.

'Look, I'm just off to a management team meeting. I'd really like to stay and talk, but . . . '

Kay opened her hands in a gesture of understanding. 'It's all right, I was around in the hospital anyway. I just thought I'd drop by.'

'That's so sweet of you. Next time you come you must give me a call and we'll have a nice chat.'

Kay recalled all the reassurance and support the co-ordinator had offered from the time a transplant was first suggested. She had a sudden understanding that there would never have been any question of deceiving Sylvia Marshall, even if the circumstances had been more propitious. It would have been like stabbing a friend in the back.

She watched Marshall walk energetically

away, then trailed back to the main building and ordered another coffee.

It seemed to her that a turning point had been reached. She must either give up her search, go home and start rebuilding her life, or she must draw together all her resources of courage and initiative — then seize the moment.

* * *

Standing in one of the plastic bubbles housing the public phones provided by the hospital, Kay waited to be put through to Paula Jenning's office.

'Hello?' The voice was crisp, light, young.

'My name is Kay Fox. I'm a novelist. I wondered if you could spare a few moments to talk to me. I'm researching a book on a young man who has had a heart transplant.' Kay heard her voice rushing. Her cheeks were burning.

'Really!' There was a terrifying pause. Then: 'Oh, how interesting.'

'I hope it will be. I got your name from one of the volunteer support services for transplant patients. I wondered if you could help me with some information on the issue of donor identity. I gather you had a rather special case . . . '

'Yes, I did.' There was now a faintly guarded note creeping in.

'Naturally I don't want to ask any intrusive questions about individual cases, but . . . ' She swallowed hard.

Paula Jennings filled the gap. 'Maybe it would be a good idea if you gave me a quick idea of the story,' she suggested, sounding enthusiastic, 'and then the questions would make more sense to me.'

'Right.' Kay sketched out the scenario: a young woman heart recipient who begins to have dreams about the death of her donor; who thinks the donor was murdered; who needs to find out who the donor was and bring the murderer to justice.

'Gosh!' said Paula. 'What imagination. I'm much too pragmatic to come up with anything like that. So you want to know how a patient might be able to find a donor if the identity is being withheld at the family's request?'

'Yes.'

Paula took her through the familiar territory of information storage computerized and handwritten. 'Getting knowledge of identity from written information is probably quite difficult. Transplant co-ordinators discourage the casual noting down of names. Donor details are not normally on file at the hospital where the transplant takes place. And, in any case, the identity of the donor is not really of great interest to the procuring and surgical teams. In fact many staff prefer to know as little as possible about the actual person.'

'I see.' Kay's fingers trembled against the receiver. 'So, how would my heroine make a start at finding out?'

'One way would be to think in terms of hacking into the national database at the UK Transplant Support Services. That kind of thing goes down well in novels doesn't it?'

'Yes,' said Kay who had read enough thrillers whilst she was ill to recognize the truth in that. 'But it's an angle that has been rather overdone in recent books.'

'You want something a bit different,' Paula said, laughing. 'Actually the easiest ways of finding out are the simplest, most obvious ones. My particular client got hold of the information with very little trouble at all.' She stopped. 'I'm a bit worried about telling you the exact details of what happened. If it came out in your book just like it was, there could be repercussions.'

'Of course,' said Kay, disappointment sinking like a weight into her stomach.

'Let's put it this way,' said Paula. 'Sometimes non-medical staff pick up little bits of information simply by being around at the time. For example porters or cleaners could overhear the harvesting team talking about going to a hospital or clinic in a certain town, discussing how long it would take them to get there and back, et cetera. There's a lot of excitement when a suitable organ is identified as you can imagine.'

'Yes.' Kay's mind began to reel through possibilities.

'Knowing the location of the donor can be a useful starting point. There could be reports in the local press of the death, and that an organ was used for transplant. It wouldn't be too difficult to follow things up from there.'

* * *

Kay returned to the café and forced herself to eat a lunch of omelette and french fries. She went to the ladies' cloakroom and swallowed the cocktail of pills that were keeping her heart secured in her body. Then she made her way to the wing where patients were prepared for transplant surgery.

She sat down in the empty corridor and picked up one of the magazines stacked up on a side-table for visitors' use.

People came and went. Nursing staff, physiotherapists, members of the public who were lost and searching for other units.

An hour passed. Two hours.

The rumble of trolley wheels had her heart bumping. She turned, hoping against hope to see the porter who had brought her to and from her surgery. Or any familiar face. But the trolley was loaded with tea and soft drinks and was pushed by a woman she did not recognize.

You're making a fool of yourself, an inner voice said. You're blundering about in areas you know nothing about. You're chasing shadows, stirring up trouble for yourself. All because of a dream. Stop it. Give it up. Get yourself a life.

'No,' she said softly. 'I'm going on.'

The dialogue continued, going nowhere, resolving nothing.

When it got to four o'clock she decided that she had had all the luck she was going to get for the day. She went back into the reception area and telephoned for a taxi to take her home.

8

Kay woke the next morning feeling the need for some practical activity, something to keep her hands and body occupied. Maybe if she was physically *doing* things then her mind might break out of the circular ruts it had become grounded in and find solutions that had previously remained elusive.

She got out the brass scales and weights that had belonged to her grandmother and started to spoon out strong white flour. The yeast, as soft as a child's modelling clay, was softening in warm water, sending little jewelled bubbles to the surface. She ground sea salt into the flour, then added sesame seeds, oil and unrefined sugar the colour of honey. The yeast went in last in a beerily fragrant puddle.

She used her hands to mix, relishing the thick, warm stickiness as the mixture bound itself into an elastic lump. In the expectant interval while the mixture swelled and blossomed she got out her sheet music and began to leaf through the baroque section.

The sudden buzz of the entry phone surprised her. She was not expecting anyone and she had dropped the habit of encouraging casual callers.

She was even more surprised when the caller announced himself as Hugo. 'Just passing by,' he said. 'Thought I'd say hello.'

Kay considered the obvious retort of, Then say hello and go away, and considered it churlish. He was, after all, Fiona's self-confessed love object. 'Come in,' she told him, pressing the button to release the main front door.

He entered all smiles, rubbing his hands in a worryingly anticipatory manner. 'Super smell!' he exclaimed. 'What are you up to?'

'Baking bread.'

'Wow. I thought it was a dying art.'

'I've only recently revived it.' She cleared away the scattered sheets of music from the sofa and gestured to him to sit.

He sat. But only for a moment. He was soon on his feet, prowling the room, peering and poking, just as he had on the evening of Kay's supper party.

Kay felt unease. 'Coffee?' she enquired.

He followed her into the kitchen, still roaming and restless. He seemed to be just behind her whichever way she moved.

She spooned granules into mugs and gestured to the kettle. 'Would you carry on with this?' she demanded briskly, noting that her dough needed attention and determined not to lose the critical moment. She divided the risen lump into two large patties and threw them on to the floured counter. She began to work on them, kneading and mashing, leaning hard on the heels of her hands, stretching and folding. Lovely, satisfying work. Except Hugo was there creating tension in what could have been a perfect moment.

'Milk?' queried Hugo, opening the fridge as though he were a regular visitor.

'Bottom shelf, in a chipped china jug.' She tried to balance friendly politeness with anything that might possibly smack of flirtation.

She cut the dough and rolled it, pushed it down into four oiled tins.

'I've never seen anyone do this,' Hugo said, looming behind her.

Kay arranged the tins in an orderly row. She could think of no suitable retort.

'What happens now?' he asked.

'A five minute pause.' Her voice was stripped of any nuance of feeling, designed to keep him well at arm's length. 'We drink our coffee.'

He drank leaning up against the counter. He was big and loose-boned, his features crooked and chunky, his eyes illuminated with what Ralph would call a come-hither look. She felt a strong undercurrent of sexuality flowing from him like a dark river.

He picked up a recent biography of Jacqueline du Pré which was lying open next to the bread tins. Ralph had bought it for her before he left for Italy. Hugo flicked through the pages of print until he came to the photographs. 'Good-looking girl,' he said. 'Sexy.'

'Yes. She was a remarkable cellist as well,' Kay said, regretting the pinched tartness of her voice.

'You're quite like her,' Hugo said, looking from the book to Kay, his eyes flicking from her hair to her feet. 'Hasn't anyone ever mentioned it before?'

'Yes. But then, I'm blonde, I'm a cellist; it's hardly surprising.' She turned her attention to the loaves which were now ballooning over the edge of the tins. Hugo's eyes fixed themselves on her hands as she stroked salty water over the domed tops of the loaves and sprinkled them with sesame seeds. Hot air rushed out of the oven as she opened it and slid the tins inside.

A smell of hot yeastiness filled the kitchen. Kay had a nasty feeling that Hugo found this rather sexy as well. She wished she had begun the morning by cleaning the

113

resin from her cello strings.

'Have you done anything towards finding your donor?' he asked.

Kay blinked. She hesitated, throwing away the moment when she could have made a lie sound convincing.

Hugo smiled. 'So what have you come up with?'

'Nothing.'

'Bad luck.'

'More likely bad management.' She thought about her clumsy attempts to play the detective and gave a rueful smile.

'Well, you know I'll do anything I can to help if you run up against a brick wall. You've just to say the word.' He refused to be put off by her coolness, her determination to stay detached. Kay suspected that he had not even noticed.

'Thanks, Hugo,' she said. 'I think this is something I need to do on my own.'

'Sure. Fair enough.' He put his coffee cup in the sink and then stood, looking down at her.

Go away, Kay told him silently. You belong to Fi.

'How about joining me for a drink one night?' Hugo said.

'You, me and Fi?' she queried, her voice stiff with disapproval.

He shook his head, quite unabashed. 'Nope. Just you and me.'

'Does Fi know about this?'

'No. I only just thought about it.' He grinned. His eyes openly told her he was lying.

Kay could not quite believe in this barefaced come-on.

'People don't keep their partners on a ball and chain any more,' he said. 'Just a quick drink. What's the harm?'

'No thanks, Hugo,' Kay said firmly.

'You're worried about what Fi might think?'

'Of course.'

'Well . . . ' He shrugged, his meaning clear: why bother Fi with things which did not concern her.

Kay suddenly saw the humour of this situation. She burst out laughing. 'Hugo, will you just please go now?'

'OK.' He was not at all offended.

At the door, he said, 'But the offer stands, remember. Both offers.'

★   ★   ★

Kay waited a few days and then went back to the hospital. She walked through the endless corridors of the transplant wing and eventually located one of the porters. She described the porter who had wheeled her to and from surgery some three months previously and wondered if there was any chance of seeing him.

The man looked startled, then suspicious.

'It's nothing serious,' Kay reassured him. 'There's just something I'd like to ask him. I'm not out to cause any trouble.'

'Sorry,' the man said, 'we get all sorts of things going on here. We have to watch our backs you know.'

'Yes. I'm harmless, I promise.' She gave him a faintly teasing look at which he softened.

'His name's John,' he told her. 'He's been on leave the past two weeks. He'll be back on the evening shift starting Monday.'

Kay's heart gave a small bound. She was getting nearer.

★　★　★

Ralph was sitting on the terrace drinking gin and tonic with his cigarettes and an ashtray to hand. Enticing fragrances were wafting from the kitchen.

'Hello there. This is an unexpected surprise,' he said, getting up and kissing her a little awkwardly. 'Drink? Or are you still teetotal?'

'Afraid so.' She accepted a glass of mineral water. 'Is this a bad time to call? I've been at the hospital. I didn't like to pass the end of the road without coming to say hello.'

His face creased with guilt. 'I've been neglecting you haven't I?' He lit a cigarette and drew on it as though it had life-saving qualities.

'No, no. I just felt like being a bit spontaneous!' She realized that she had made a bad mistake, had a sense of being a gatecrasher. She reminded herself that Ralph had his own life. She should respect that. She sniffed the scents of cooking wafting from the kitchen. 'Something smells very appetizing.'

'Yes. Isobel's coming round in half an hour or so.' Ralph shifted uneasily in his chair. 'And one or two friends from the golf club.'

'You're having a grand dinner party,' said Kay gaily, annoyed to find herself prickling with hurt at being left out.

'Why don't you stay?' he offered, but a little too hastily.

'Because I've got a hot date,' she said with deliberate mystery.

'Really?'

'Mmm.' She forced a teasing smile. He could make of it what he wanted. 'Who's creating the mouthwatering smells?' she asked.

'Bon Appetit Catering.' Ralph took a swallow of gin and grinned. 'A couple of poofters. But they're rather good actually.'

Kay thought of her mother; harrassed and pink-faced in the kitchen, preparing and serving gourmet dinners single-handed whilst Ralph guffawed with the guests in the drawing-room. But when she left she kissed him anyway. And meant it.

★   ★   ★

'Now then, my duck, it's good to see you again. And looking in the pink!' John the porter leaned on the rails of his trolley looking pleased to be given a brief diversion from his conveyancing duties.

Kay had seen him straight away as she walked into the transplant unit. There had been no time to calm herself, to prepare the role she was to play. She found her mouth drying as she struggled to frame her next words.

'New heart going all right is it?' he wondered.

'Yes. Brilliantly.'

'I remember you well, love — and you're a changed girl from the one who came in that night for your operation. You looked like a ghost.'

'I thought I might soon be one,' said Kay.

'It's amazing what these doctors can do.'

'Yes.'

She noticed the look of mild speculation on his face beginning to intensify. 'Did you come all this way just to see me? I've heard you were looking for me.'

'Yes.'

'Well, well!'

It came again: the familiar feeling of wanting to give in, to give up. Not to get herself in somewhere deep and find herself unable to get out. She pushed the fears back. 'I've been trying to contact the family of my donor.'

'Oh yes?'

'It's difficult. I haven't got very far . . . ' she forced her eyes to make a contact with his. She willed him to understand what she was after.

There was a long pause. 'You've got the idea I might know something about your donor? Is that it?'

'Yes. And have you?'

'Well, it's a tricky one,' he said slowly. The chummy smile was now decidedly unsettling. But she knew without a doubt that he had relevant information.

'I expect it is,' she said.

He stared at her as though he could not

believe what she was suggesting. 'This is well out of order, love. I could get into big trouble.' He raised his eyebrows. He was playing her like a fish on a line.

'I suppose you could.' She wanted to take control of the interchange, to stop appearing so needy, so dependent on his good will. But that was dangerous. She could lose all she had so far gained. But it was the only option she could think of. She adjusted the strap of her bag and glanced down at her watch. 'Look, I'm sorry I've bothered you. Will you just forget about it please? I'm not back to my normal self yet. Still a bit wobbly.'

'No! Steady on. Wait, love.' There was a new urgency in his tone. She turned back and saw that he was looking around to see if there was anyone listening in.

She stared straight into his face.

'I do know something that will help you.' He paused, took another glance around. 'But it'll cost you, I could be putting my job on the line . . . '

Her instinct was simply to ask how much he wanted. She knew that would put her straight back into a defensive position. 'What do you know?'

'The place the harvesting team went to get the heart.' He raised his eyebrows. 'Worth having, eh?'

'OK, how much?'

He did not respond immediately. 'I'll need to think about that.'

Kay was sickened by the way things had gone, the look of rockhard calculation in the burly, amiable John's eyes. 'All right,' she said. 'Shall I come back tomorrow?'

'No! Give me your number. I'll call you at home.'

She hesitated, automatically resisting, somehow afraid. But what was the point in withholding her number. He wouldn't have any problem getting it from Pamela's files if he was determined and careful enough.

She took out a notebook.

'Don't waste paper, love,' he said, holding out his hand. 'Just pop it on there.'

She had to grasp his palm to hold it steady as she wrote. His flesh was warm and damp. Before she left the hospital she went to the public cloakroom and washed her hands in hot, soapy water.

★   ★   ★

The phone rang out eight times, nine, ten. 'Come on! Come on!' Kay banged her palm down against the table.

'Hello?'

'Fi?'

121

'Yes. Are you all right, sweetheart?'

'Yes. No. I needed to talk. Have I disturbed you?'

'You could put it that way.' Fiona gave a throaty laugh.

'Oh, God, I'm sorry.' Kay imagined Fi and Hugo grappling together stickily. She grimaced. 'Listen, Fi, I think I'm getting somewhere in finding something out about my donor.'

'Yes. So what's the catch?'

'The person with the information wants money.'

'Huh! How much?'

'Ten thousand.'

'Jesus! That's appalling, outrageous.'

'I suppose Ralph might call it making the most of a business opportunity.'

'You haven't told Ralph about this have you?'

'Good heavens, no!'

'God, this is awful. What are you going to do?'

'I'm not sure.'

'Who is this person from hell?'

Kay gave a thumb-nail sketch of the outwardly affable, easygoing John. She was still stunned from the brief telephone conversation with him only minutes before. He was adamant about the figure of £10,000.

'If it ever came out what I'd done, I'd lose my job. Simple as that, love. This is security money for me. Insurance.' He made it sound very reasonable, a simple, friendly transaction.

'Can you afford to pay?' Fi asked. 'Don't answer that if you don't want to,' she added hastily. 'Most people would rather discuss the most sordid details of their adulterous affairs than tell you anything about their finances.'

'I could actually afford to pay him. My grandmother left me money and so did Mum.'

'Hah! Woman of substance!'

'Don't let it put you off me,' Kay said, laughing. Already Fi's refusal to be dragged down into despondency was lightening her own mood. 'Fi, I'm worried about giving into him. I've got this feeling that if I shell out then somehow he'll have a hold on me. Want more. Oh, I don't know!'

'You mean some sort of blood sucking? But surely it's you that could blackmail him, rather than the other way round?'

'I suppose you're right. But there's worse. He's bothered to find out quite a bit about me. He made a real meal about my having a rich daddy, suggesting that he'd be only too willing to stump up the money.' Kay recalled the porter's softly manipulating voice and winced.

'Jesus!' Fi exclaimed. 'That's grim.'

'Just what I thought. On the other hand if the information he has is genuine it could really move me on.'

'Yes.' Fi paused, reflecting. 'There are rather a lot of 'ifs' though, aren't there?'

'Do I hear a voice of caution?'

'Oh, I wouldn't go so far as that.'

★ ★ ★

Once again Kay sat in the transplant wing and watched patiently as people passed by. Porter John had said he would meet her in the car park when he arrived for his shift. They could talk there without attracting attention.

She had arrived an hour earlier than the appointed time. This was deliberate and calculated. She judged that if she gave herself time to absorb the hospital atmosphere and to recapture the feelings she had experienced before the life-saving transplant took place, then in some way she would be enabled to finalize her decision. She had her cheque book with her. She had moved funds into her current account. But she still had not made up her mind.

A plump, middle-aged woman wearing green overalls came past pushing a trolley loaded with vast teapots, empty crockery and glasses. She looked at Kay and pulled a face. 'Oh, my poor legs!' Balancing on one of them, she eased off a shoe and wriggled her toes.

Kay smiled in sympathy.

The woman glanced behind her. The corridor was more or less empty. 'I'm going to have a quick sit down,' she said, parking herself on the chair next to Kay, taking off her other shoe and massaging her foot. 'Ooh, I could kill for a cigarette.'

'When do you finish your shift?' Kay asked.

'Six-thirty. Another two hours. Still, the time soon passes if you don't think about it too much.'

'I suppose it does,' Kay agreed.

The woman was peering at Kay, wrinkling her forehead as though trying to recall the whereabouts of a lost object. 'Don't I remember you?'

'I don't really know. I was a patient here a few months ago.'

'That's it. You had a new heart didn't you?'

'Yes.'

'What you must have been through.' She sighed to think of it. 'How are you going on?'

'I'm doing well.' Kay turned to look at her

companion. 'I'm sorry, but I don't remember you.'

'No, you wouldn't. I was just coming off my shift when you arrived. Next day I was transferred to the main hospital. Mother and baby unit. They have plenty of excitement there too.'

Kay came on the alert. She kept her voice steady and neutral. 'As much excitement as the transplant unit?'

'Maybe not quite as much. It's more routine I suppose. After all, people have been having babies for thousands of years haven't they?'

Kay could only agree.

'I especially remember the night you came in. There was a real panic on in the unit wondering if they could get the heart brought over in time.'

'I knew nothing about that,' said Kay. 'And quite honestly, I'm glad I didn't. Had it to come a long way — the heart?'

'Oh, yes.' The woman became suddenly still and focused. 'Yes. Now where did they fetch it from? Somewhere seasidey. Oh, my memory!' She screwed her face into a ferocious frown as though to squeeze the place name along the tube of her recollections. 'Well, never mind. They had to get a helicopter to fly it over. It was real high drama!'

Kay stared at her. Her heart had begun its urgent, heavy beat.

'We were all keeping our fingers crossed. But they got it here in plenty of time.' She smiled at Kay. 'And here you are to prove it.'

'Yes, here I am.'

She patted Kay's hand. Maternal, kindly. 'So you just take care, won't you?'

'I will.'

She replaced her shoes and stood up. 'Right then. Better get going, don't want the powers that be to catch me here gossiping.' She positioned herself behind her trolley, leaned hard on it and began to push. She stopped. 'Torquay!' she exclaimed. 'That's the place. Torquay! I once went there when I was a kiddie.' She tapped her head and grinned. 'See, the old brain's still in good working order.'

As the wheels rumbled away Kay sat quite still. The woman's words sang and buzzed in her head.

In the car park she told porter John that she could not afford the £10,000. That she had discussed the issue of finding her donor with her father and been warned about going any further; been warned very firmly against handing out money.

John's disappointment and deflation were obvious. She even felt a little sorry for him.

127

9

Kay had been ready and waiting for a quarter of an hour when Fiona's car slowed and then halted in the road outside her flat.

It was just gone 6 a.m. Already the sun was beaming down from an azure sky and the streets glimmered with golden light. 'Make the best of it,' the weather forecaster had warned after the eight o'clock news. 'It'll be dull and raining by the afternoon.'

'Off on our great adventure to glorious Devon,' Fiona said, pulling out into the road without checking thoroughly and stamping on her brakes to avoid an alarmed-looking cyclist who shook his fist at her.

'God, I'm a terrible driver,' said Fiona cheerfully. 'Hugo goes to the most ridiculous lengths to avoid being my passenger. Except when he wants me sober at dinner parties so he can drink himself into a stupor and get chauffeured home.'

'Should I be clenching my knuckles into alpine peaks?' Kay wondered, preferring not to think too much about Hugo.

'Not yet. Wait until we get on the motorway. Here, take the map. I'm hopeless at navigating as well.'

Despite these warnings Fiona guided the car safely through the alarming stop-go antics on the M25, one hand lightly grasping the wheel the other tapping out a jaunty rhythm.

'Did I tell you Peter had found a new cellist for the group?' she asked.

'No. Who is it?'

'A doll named Harriet. Another leggy blonde like you, Kay sweetheart. Only this one's around seventeen. All wide blue eyes and juicy red lips. A real babe.'

Kay gave a groan. 'Can she play?'

'She's learning.'

'How did Peter find her?'

'Very willing I should think.'

Kay smiled, internally wincing.

'Steer well clear of married men who've got uncoupled,' said Fiona drily.

Kay glanced at her, wondering if Fiona knew anything of her one night stand with Peter. She decided she did not, and to leave it at that.

'We did our first concert last night,' Fiona announced abruptly. Kay could tell she was uneasy, wanting to get this piece of news over with as quickly as possible. 'A really posh wedding bash.'

Kay was silent for a moment. 'What did you play?'

'We played Schubert.' Fiona paused. 'Schubert lost.'

Kay laughed. 'As bad as that?'

'We hadn't rehearsed enough. It was all a bit ragged. We need you back in the group as soon as possible, Kay.'

'Yes.' Kay knew that her days with Peter's quartet were over and suspected that Fiona knew too. Harriet was in, she was out. And maybe in a strange way she was relieved. But she was grateful to Fiona for not pursuing the issue.

Staring through the window Kay watched London gradually fall back into the distance; watched the peripheral suburban sprawl dwindle away and eventually surrender to the dominance of the countryside.

They turned off the motorway and stopped for lunch at a pub in a Wiltshire village where the local people seemed to be speaking a foreign language.

'They're all oohs and aars,' Fiona whispered.

'I suppose they think Londoners are all ays and oys,' said Kay.

Moving on they saw the huge columns of Stonehenge, awesome against a now darkening sky.

'This is a really good girls' day out,' said Fiona grinning. 'I'll bet you're glad you didn't opt for your first choice of a lonely ride on the train.' She glanced sideways at Kay. 'Are you nervous? About what you might find out?'

'Yes.' Kay replied. I'm teetering along a ledge between existences, she thought to herself. The old life has gone and the new one hasn't yet shown itself. But there was a powerful sense that it soon would.

They reached Torquay in the early afternoon and went straight to the reference section of the central library. Kay had telephoned the day before and made arrangements to look at the local newspapers for the week of her transplant.

Because it was less than six months from their publication the newspapers were still stored in their original printed format. The librarian handed them over, dog-eared and creased, and they took them to one of the long tables at the far end of the reading room.

'Bit homespun all this,' said Fiona looking at the grubby newsprint. 'I thought we'd be scrolling through microfiche in a secret darkened room.'

They identified the newspapers they would look through first: those printed on the day the organ was taken from the donor's body and those for the next few days following.

They had both somehow prepared them-selves for a long search, imagined tedious

131

hours poring over tiny print. Breaks for coffee and sandwiches. Hopefully a final moment of success.

In the event it took just ten minutes before Fiona found a quarter-page spread describing the death of a young woman whose sports car had toppled from high cliffs into Babbacombe bay just a few miles from the town. There was a picture of the car which had been horribly crushed by its fall on to jagged boulders at the base of the cliff. The driver, on holiday in the area, had been taken to the general hospital. The woman was not named for personal reasons, but it had been confirmed by the consultant caring for her that permission had been given for her organs to be removed and used for transplant.

Kay felt a singing in her ears. Heat tingled through her body like a fever breaking. 'That's it! That's her!'

'Steady,' warned Fiona. 'It is a possibility, but we can't be sure yet.' She ran a finger over the lines of print, swiftly rereading. 'It doesn't say the organs were actually used. There's no mention of the heart being used for a transplant.'

'No, no. It must be her,' Kay insisted. 'I know it. I can feel it. Oh, the poor thing!' She found her breathing coming in harsh gasps. Sorrow and pity for the dead young woman who had bequeathed the gift of her heart overwhelmed her. 'Oh God, what do we do now?'

Fiona placed a warning hand on her arm. 'Kay, calm down. Listen to me. You've got to get more information before you start doing anything at all. There's no point getting excited about the wrong woman and charging around like a bull in a china shop.'

'You're right. Sorry.' Kay stared down at the picture, imagining the woman's injuries, her pain, her fear. It was only then that she realized the mismatch between her dream and the reality of the woman's death. Her dream was of drowning. She had always taken that for granted. The donor had been killed in a drowning accident. Her mind began a frantic search for an explanation. Nothing presented itself, but it would in time. She had no doubt. Her pulse was racing. 'I know it's her. I just know. I've found her. Oh, God, Fiona, I've found her.'

People at nearby tables looked up, startled to hear such emotional intensity in the soothing and detached ambience of the library.

'Kay, steady down! Get a grip,' Fiona said.

'Sorry, sorry.' Kay got out a handkerchief and blew her nose. She placed a tender hand over her frantically bucking heart. 'It's all right,' she whispered to it.

'Think about it,' Fi cautioned. 'Even if this is your donor — and I grant you it looks likely, we know hardly anything at all yet. We don't know who this woman is or where she lives.'

For Kay these words of cool reason were unbearably harsh. 'Fair enough. But we will. We'll find out. I haven't got this far just to chuck in the towel.'

She took a closer look at the photograph of the wrecked car. 'You can see the number plate. Look, Fi!'

'Yes.' Fi was as patient as a mother with an overexcited child. 'But you can't make out any letters or numbers.'

'We could get the picture blown up.'

'I doubt if you'd see anything even then. The police probably had them taped up for security reasons.'

Kay carefully straightened and folded the newspapers, stacked them into a neat pile on the table top and stood up. 'Come on, let's get out of this hallowed atmosphere. We'll walk along the front by the sea and get something to eat.'

Pushing their way some time later through the crowds thronging the wide promenade they found a vacant seat where they could stare across the huge bay and polish off the fresh-baked scones, raspberry jam and thick yellow clotted cream which Kay had bought at a local baker's.

Behind them the streets climbing the hillside were faithful to the bright, sun-drenched photographs in the shops which could well be depicting similarly ascending streets on the south coast of France.

'The newspaper office should be able to show us the original photograph of the car,' Kay said. 'We might be able to make out some of the letters or numbers. Something to work on at least.' She glanced at her friend who had left her cream-smothered scone untouched and was staring out at the boats in the bay. 'Are you getting fed up with all this, Fi?'

'What?'

'This quest of mine. Am I becoming not only self-centred and obsessive but boring as well?'

Fiona smiled. 'I was doing some self-centred brooding of my own as a matter of fact.'

'Oh God, Fi, what's the matter?'

'Just the usual. Given that I'm a single, fit and fertile young female.'

'You're pregnant!'

'I did the fiddling about thing with tubes of pee this morning. Result resoundingly positive. Same as when I did it last week.'

This should be wonderful news, thought Kay. A new vigorous life just beginning. But Fiona had a bewildered, hunted look about her which meant this could be tragic news.

'So what now?' Kay asked. 'Does Hugo know?' She closed her eyes. Oh Jesus, Hugo!

'No.'

'Are you going to tell him?'

'I don't know yet.'

'You're not thinking of an abortion are you?' She found herself hollow with dismay at the prospect. And yet before she had always taken a low-key, pragmatic stance on the issue.

'It's an option.'

'Don't, Fi. Don't do it.'

'Kay!'

'Sorry. This is the post-transplant Kay talking. I would never have been so dogmatic before. I would never have been so *sure*.'

'Sure that it's wrong to crush a life?'

'Sure that the baby inside you will be a wonderful human being,' she burst out impulsively. 'You can't kill it, Fi. You can't. It's a miraculous, tiny speck of new existence.'

'Hugo is its father,' Fiona pointed out with a wicked glint.

Kay recalled the interchange in her kitchen: a scene of seduction played out over rising

136

bread dough. She felt a sinking in her stomach. 'And you're crazy about him,' she insisted. 'You love him.'

' 'Crazy about' and 'love'! Not necessarily one and the same thing.'

'Oh, Fi!'

'You might be amazed to hear this but I don't want a baby without a marriage, without a forever-and-a-day father.'

'Will that be a problem?'

'I honestly have no idea how Hugo will react. Shocking isn't it?'

'Just tell him. And then just ask.' As she spoke she could see Hugo's lazy come-on smile.

'Simple!'

'Simple.' Kay finished the last scone and crushed the bag firmly between her fingers.

'I love you, you obsessional, mad woman, Kay,' smiled Fiona, rising to her feet. 'Let's get this visit to the newspaper office over with and then push off back to the smoke. I'm not used to all this fresh sea air.'

★   ★   ★

'How are you going to play this?,' Fiona wondered, looking up at the offices of the town's main local newspaper.

'Emotionally,' said Kay.

137

'Oh!'

'From the heart,' Kay elaborated in dry tones. 'Because that's the way I'm feeling.'

Putting on a distraught expression Kay told the helpfully smiling girl in the glass-fronted reception office of the newspaper that she needed to see the original print of the newspaper's photograph of a woman who had been killed in a car accident on the Torbay cliffs.

She gave the date of the edition in which the photograph had appeared and then, pressing her hand over her breastbone, put on such a convincing display of emotional dramatics that Fiona had to remove herself from the scene and go and wait outside.

Pressing her clenched knuckles against her teeth, Kay spoke in a trembling voice which hinted at feelings too harrowing to try to explain. 'I really need to see that photo. Please! I can't tell you the reason. I think the car might have belonged to a friend of mine. We lost touch years ago, but . . . '

Alarmed, the girl swiftly assured her that there was no restriction on seeing prints of photographs that had appeared in their paper. No problem at all.

'I'll ring the photography section. They'll bring the folder along in just one minute. Perhaps you'd like to sit down.' She indicated chubby little sofas framing a visitors' waiting area. 'There's a coffee machine just round the corner.'

Kay obediently sat. She did, in fact, feel genuinely stirred up now, hovering on the brink of knowledge she had been stumbling towards for what seemed like an eternity.

A young man came to sit down beside her. His face was gentle and sensitive. He had a livid meat-coloured bruise on one cheekbone. Kay found herself staring at it, and swiftly looked away.

'You're the person wanting to see some prints of a crashed car?' he asked.

She nodded. Her body had become heavy and yet at the same time hollow.

He drew three shiny black and white photographs from a large brown envelope and spread them slowly on the table in front of Kay. 'You think this car belonged to a friend?'

Kay's stomach twisted with sensation as she looked at the shattered car displayed from a variety of angles. She nodded. 'I lost touch years ago. And then . . . ' she felt suddenly overcome with dizziness. She swallowed the saliva that had gushed into her mouth. For a moment she feared she would vomit.

'Are you all right?' he asked.

'Give me a minute.' Her voice was a croaky whisper. She took some steadying breaths and forced herself to look once again at the photographs. To be confronted with the violence of her donor's death, the image of a helpless woman's body smashed against rocks, sent a tumult of horror and pity shuddering through her body.

'It wasn't a friend,' she whispered. 'It was the donor of my heart. I'm trying to find her.'

She saw disbelief flicker in his eyes. He said nothing.

'I've told a lot of lies,' she said quietly. 'But what I've told you just now is the truth.' She looked once more at the pictures, realizing that she was unlikely to find anything more in them than she already knew. Two of the shots showed the sides of the car which gave no clues as to its registration. The other picture was the shot that had appeared in the newspaper, showing the car from the front. The bonnet was tilted up, wedged against a large piece of rock, but the number plate was entirely obscured by the rock's shadow and she saw now that there was no indication of any lettering or numerals that it would be possible to work with.

'I took these shots on the understanding that the number plates would not be identifiable,' the photographer told her. He was watching her, assessing, thoughtful. 'I have to be very careful,' he continued. He touched the angry mark on his cheekbone. 'I got this from the hit man of a drug dealer who was not at all pleased to be captured on film.' He raised an eyebrow. 'You understand my position . . .'

'Yes. I see.' She sagged with disappointment.

'You had a heart transplant?' he asked.

'Yes. Ten weeks ago.'

He pushed the photographs into a neat pile and slotted them back into the envelope. He looked around and then reached for one of the magazines stacked on the table. In the white margin at the top of the back page, he made some speedy jottings with a thick, bluntish pencil. As he got to his feet, he pushed the magazine towards Kay.

And then, without looking back, he walked away. She watched him step into a lift at the end of the lobby, watched his body shrink to a thin line and then disappear as the doors rolled together.

She looked at what he had written. There was a full registration number and details on the make of a car. The letters became dizzy and shimmering as she looked at them. This was the car her donor had been killed in. Within that car the heart which was now beating inside her had beat inside another woman.

She recalled the days before the transplant; the terrible, breathless waiting. She had lain on the sofa, listless but unable to sleep in the long spring afternoons. She had felt her strength draining away like the last grains of sand slipping rapidly towards the neck of an hour-glass. And through that time, a healthy, fully alive woman was holidaying in the south of England, driving her sports car along the high cliffs, living life to the full, never giving a thought to her mortality, the grains of sand trickling finally away.

She was still staring at the pencil marks on the paper when. Fiona came to find her.

'Well?' Fiona sat down beside her.

Kay gestured to the message the photographer had left.

'Ah,' said Fiona. 'So what now?'

'I'm not sure.'

'Are you absolutely sure you want to go on with this?' Fi asked quietly. 'You still don't know for certain you've got the right person.'

'Oh, I'm going on. I'm so nearly there.' She stopped. 'Aren't I?'

Fiona said nothing.

Kay's mind hummed, leaping through a succession of fragmented possibilities. 'Can you find a dead person from a set of numbers and letters?' she asked Fiona quietly. Only minutes ago she had felt such elation. Now

142

she was uncertain, filled with misgivings. Maybe she was destined never to find her donor. And maybe that was right.

Fiona took her hand, stroking and straightening the clenched fingers. 'I've really no idea. Maybe nerdy net-head Hugo will. Can we go home now, sweetheart? I think I'm beginning to miss him.'

10

'I need some advice.' Ralph's voice held a trace of uncharacteristic diffidence.

Kay was cooking supper for him. He had arrived from work looking exhausted, clutching a bottle of red wine and a half bottle of single malt. He had poured himself a glass of the whisky straight away then leaned up against the kitchen door frame taking long swallows and looking grimly reflective.

Kay was padding around the kitchen putting the finishing touches on a traditional English supper. A steak and kidney pudding was steaming on the hob, mashed potatoes heavily laced with garlic were browning under the grill.

She poured herself a glass of mineral water and steered Ralph through into the sitting-room.

'I'm not sure how good I am at handing out advice,' she told him. 'But I'm listening.'

'I'm sixty-nine,' he said with heavy regret.

'Yes?' Kay tilted her head. She waited.

'I ought to know what's what by now, wouldn't you think?'

'This sounds like woman trouble,' Kay offered.

'Absolutely right.'

'Isobel?'

'Yep.'

'Well at least you're not turning into a Don Juan, a new woman every week!' Kay smiled. Usually he rather enjoyed being teased.

'Huh!'

'Are you thinking of marrying her?'

Ralph's head jerked up. 'Good Lord, you're getting devilishly blunt these days. Straight to the point and no messing.' He stared down into his empty glass.

'I thought you needed a little help,' Kay poured him more whisky, 'to get to the point.'

'It's not easy,' he agreed.

'So what's the problem? Have you told her what's on your mind?'

'Oh, yes.'

'And?'

'She seemed to like the idea.'

'Well then?' Kay smiled encouragingly.

'It's a big step, marriage.'

'Agreed. So what made you ask?'

'Loneliness, I suppose,' he said. 'Fear of being left on my own. Fear of dying on my own. Besides which she's a nice woman.'

Kay was shocked. It struck her that this was the first time she had heard Ralph

145

confess to such naked feelings of vulnerability.

'But quite frankly,' he said, 'I'd rather we just lived together. You know, like you young people do. Partnership, not marriage.'

'Would Isobel object to that?'

'I haven't broached the issue with her. And I don't intend to. I belong to another age, Kay. Men like me don't ask women like her to shack up with them.'

'Let me get this sorted out. You want to live with Isobel. But you feel you can't live with her unless you ask her to marry you. But you don't want to get married.'

'It sounds cock-eyed, I know.'

For Kay, it simply sounded out of character. Ralph had never been a man to dither over moral dilemmas; to dither over much at all.

They sat down to eat. She poured wine for Ralph who drank eagerly. 'Basically it all boils down to the business of money and wills,' he said.

He told her that he had recently drawn up a new will making her the main beneficiary, leaving her his house and a major control of both his businesses. 'There'll be a little wodge of capital too,' he said as she topped up the wine in his glass. 'But I'll have to leave a bit to my two nephews; my dear sister would never forgive me.'

'Ralph,' exclaimed Kay, 'I never expected you to leave me all that. I never even thought about it . . . ' She suddenly felt desperately uncomfortable.

'No, I know that.'

'You should share everything between the three of us. After all, your nephews are blood relatives, I'm just your stepdaughter.'

He made an irritable gesture with his hands, waving her protests away. 'Oh, for God's sake I've always thought of you as my own daughter. You shouldn't need me to tell you that.' He took another gulp of wine. He was putting away the drink even faster than usual.

'No,' she agreed, chastened. 'I'm sorry.'

'The money would have come to you at some time anyway. In my previous will I'd left everything to your mother.' More wine disappeared. 'Listen to me, Kay, there could come a time when you're going to need all the funds you can get.'

A horrible silence fell. Kay suddenly caught his drift; she felt his pity and sympathy reaching out to her: poor, ill-fated, damaged Kay.

Her face tightened with cold resolve. 'Ralph, let's get things in perspective. I'm not an invalid. I'm not a broken doll. I'm going to be all right. Whatever happens I'll deal with it. And as for money, I shall manage fine. I've got a good job and there are the investments Mum left me — '

He stopped her. 'You don't know yet that you'll be able to go back to work.'

'Of course I will. It's only twelve weeks since the operation and I'm feeling almost a hundred per cent back to my old self.'

'You don't look it,' he said. 'You've lost weight. Your face is all bones and hollows and you're as white as my grandmother's sheets.'

She dropped her cutlery on to her plate with a clatter. 'Bloody hell, Ralph!'

He held up a warning finger. 'Just hear me out. You have to face facts, if you got ill again, how would you manage? And don't tell me the state will look after you.'

'They did a brilliant job looking after me before.'

'Granted. Our great National Health Service is still pretty good at swashbuckling surgery. I'm talking about more mundane things.' He stared at her, his eyes glittering with wine and the determination to make her see things his way. See sense.

Rage skittered through her brain. 'You're thinking of me as a broken vine. A poor wretch in a wheelchair not able to look after myself.'

He gave her a long hard look. 'It has to be faced.'

'God!' She felt mutinous and completely lost for words of retaliation.

He tried appealing to her. 'Kay, my lovely sweet Kay. How could I die in peace wondering if you'd be able to afford to get yourself properly looked after? What do you think I'd feel at the prospect of you being stuck in some dire long-stay place for no hopers. Or tethered somewhere in a poky flat with half a dozen different 'carers' turning up each day to do whatever they have to do for you.'

'There's nothing like being optimistic for the future,' she said with icy sarcasm. Within, she was horrified, seeing into a bleak and terrifying future she had not allowed herself to conjure up before. She gathered together the used plates, took them through into the kitchen and banged them into the sink. Her hands shook as she reached into the fridge for a cream sponge cake she had made earlier in the day, happy in the thought that it was one of Ralph's favourites.

'I'm not talking through the top of my head here,' he continued as she returned, placing the cake on the table and hacking into it with a serrated knife. 'Isobel knows quite a bit about what goes on in this area. She has an ancient penniless aunt who's currently going through the mill. She had 'care in the community' until she was half dead and now she's banged up in some residential place that reeks of wee and last week's cold dinners.'

'You've been talking me over with Isobel?' The words came out in a thin croak. She placed a forkful of cake into her mouth. It felt like grit as she chewed it and forced it down.

'Yes.' Her outraged expression seemed to surprise him. 'We talk about you a great deal. I worry about you.'

Kay reached for the wine bottle, poured herself half a glass and drank it at one go.

'Steady!' Ralph said.

Beads of sweat broke out on her forehead. Nausea welled up. She ran to the bathroom and was instantly sick. After that she steadied down.

Ralph was looking concerned when she rejoined him.

'It's OK,' she told him. 'I'm all right.'

'I didn't mean to upset you,' he said lamely. 'I simply want to make sure you're provided for.'

'Yes. I know.'

'If I marry Isobel I'll have to cut her into

my will. That means there'll be less all round — '

'Ralph, I don't want to hear any more of this,' she said with quiet warning. 'And I certainly don't want to be a factor in your decision as to whether you make an honest woman of Isobel. If you want to marry her, go ahead. If not, then don't. But don't lay the responsibility on me.'

Ralph reached into his jacket for his cigarette case, then let it drop back into his pocket.

'Go ahead,' said Kay, wanting to make peace. 'I'll open the window.' She willed him to shut up now, but he was beyond heeding the usual caution signs.

'You see,' he said, lighting up and taking a long, comforting pull on his cigarette, 'I wouldn't worry so much if you were married. If there was some good man and true to take care of you.'

Kay stiffened and then flared. 'God, Ralph, you have the sensitivity of a rhinoceros. Do you really think it helps to keep reminding me what a failure I am? A martyr to ill health, a poor wretch destined for life's great dustbin, a pathetic and pasty specimen who's too feeble even to pull a bloke.'

The evening was more or less over after that.

The next morning Kay slept in after an initially restless night. She took a long shower and then went through the morning ritual of checking and recording vital signs (all reassuringly normal) and swallowed her various prescribed medications.

She ran scalding water into the kitchen sink, squeezed in detergent then submerged all the soiled paraphernalia left over from the previous evening.

She worked slowly and methodically, gaining pleasure from the careful wiping over and rinsing of each plate, each item of cutlery. To do a simple task well somehow calmed the agitation which kept resurfacing as Ralph's predictions of infirmity and dependence replayed in her head.

11

Kay gave Fiona an hour or so to have finished her supper with Hugo, then telephoned her.

Hugo answered. 'Kay! Hey, great to hear from you? How's things?'

'I'm fine.' She realized she was not sounding too friendly. 'Fit as a fiddle,' she said cheerily.

'What have you been up to?'

'Pathetically little.'

'So, when are we going to see you?' We! He sounded very married. The bastard! Kay wondered if he knew of his current status as a potential father.

'Well . . . '

'Did you want to speak to Fi on her own? Girl talk?'

Kay raised her eyes heavenwards. Such a show of sensitivity! 'Yes please. But let's all meet up soon.' She made it sound chummy yet neutral, the kind of sociable suggestion she might have made before he revealed himself as a lady-killer. The rat wasn't going to run away with the idea he'd got to her.

'Great. There's a fantastic new Chinese place opened up just across the road from here. Or perhaps you'd prefer something more spicy?'

Damn you, thought Kay. But she was smiling as she waited for Fiona's voice.

'I was just wondering how you were, if there have been any . . . developments,' Kay told her.

'Everything as before, sweetheart.'

'I see. Good.' She paused. 'Is this a we-can't-really-talk-about-it-now situation?'

'It is.'

'But you are all right?'

'Yeah, I'm basically OK. And you? Any developments?'

'Absolutely nothing.'

'It looks like we've both been good, sensible, non-assertive girls. Must be the calm before the storm.'

*   *   *

Kay arrived at the restaurant a few minutes early, ordered mineral water and began a perusal of the lengthy menu.

Fiona's peppery perfume was the first indication of her presence. She swooped over Kay, kissing her cheek.

'You girls sit together,' Hugo decreed, positioning himself facing them in what Kay considered a somewhat proprietorial manner.

Kay thought Fiona looked drawn and tired, but maybe it was simply her imagination. She found herself frustrated at not being able to talk to her friend on her own. There was a sense of being excluded from Fiona's confidence, as though she and the rakish Hugo were already an established couple with secrets that transcended mere friendship. That's the power of sex, she thought, and felt a momentary stab of envy and self-pity.

'So, how's the search going?' Hugo asked, looking up from his fried seaweed and catching Kay's eye.

She shrugged. 'Nothing yet.'

'Fi said you got a registration number.'

Kay bridled internally. So he knew all about the outcome of the trip to Torquay. But then had she really expected that Fi would keep it secret? Stop being so super-sensitive, she instructed herself. She looked Hugo straight in the eye, adopted a light tone. 'I thought I was home and dry. I had this naïve notion that if you got registration details it was fairly plain sailing to find out the last owner of the car and their address.'

He gave a knowing smile.

'I meant through fair means, not foul,' Kay said. She glanced at Fi who was looking thoughtful. Kay noticed the way she was fiddling with her chopsticks, pushing food around the plate rather than capturing it.

'What fair means have you tried so far?' Hugo asked.

Kay realized she would either have to shut up about the whole business now, or share it without reserve. She reached for the soy sauce, shook a generous amount over her bowl of rice, then said: 'I telephoned the DVLC. Their customer enquiry unit. They were very friendly, not at all official.'

'So what did they say?' Fi asked.

'Well, first of all, what did *you* say?' Hugo interrupted, leaning forward.

'I quoted the number and asked if I could have information on name and address of last owner and so on.'

'And so they asked why you wanted it?'

'Yes.'

'And you told them the truth?'

'Yes.'

'And they said — let's have a request in writing.'

'If you know all the answers, why ask the questions?' Fi said acidly, giving Hugo a beadily warning eye.

He spread his hands in a gesture of surrender and apology. He leaned back in his chair.

There was an uneasy pause.

'So did you?' Fiona asked. 'Write to them?'

156

'Yes. I got a very polite letter back telling me they were not able to give the information I had asked for. My reasons for asking didn't fit any of their criteria for responding. I hadn't been involved in a road accident. I didn't need the information so as to bring any criminals to justice, et cetera, et cetera. They suggested I get in touch with the transplant co-ordinators' service.'

'Back to square one,' Hugo said.

'So what would you have done?' Kay asked him, struggling to suppress her feelings of annoyance. 'I'm assuming that you'd consider the truth a rather weak weapon.'

'In this case, yes.'

'Well?'

'I probably wouldn't have approached the DVLC at this stage. If this car is a write-off then it will most likely have gone to a scrapper's yard somewhere. I'd be inclined to find out which yard and go along and do a bit of digging around, a spot of wheeling and dealing.' He popped a wedge of fried pork into his mouth. 'Or should I say wheedling and dealing!'

'The scrapyard people would have information about owners?' Kay asked, surprised.

'Oh yes. They buy the vehicle, whatever is left of it. Technically they're the new owner. The police will pass over the logbook to them if it's readily available. That means they don't have the bother of having to notify the DVLC that the car is a write-off. The scrapper has to do it instead.'

'How do you know all this, Hugo?' Fi asked. She was shaking her head, smiling at him in disbelief. An indulgent smile made up of equal portions of irritation and admiration.

'Through living in the real world!' he grinned. 'Before I got into computers and got rich, I used to drive old bangers and haunt scrappers for spare parts. When you hang around places you find things out.'

Kay imagined herself turning up in a scrap-yard with her middle-class accent and her polished looks. She thought of the tough hardened men who worked there, with their knowing salacious eyes. 'I don't think I could do that,' she said. 'Winkle out secrets eyeball to eyeball.'

Hugo's eyes flickered appreciatively over her. 'I doubt if you'd have any problems,' he said, his meaning clear.

'What other methods would you try?' she asked, ignoring the innuendo. 'Besides visiting the scrappers, or hacking into some national database.'

'You wouldn't need to hack,' he said. 'Think about it, there are hundreds of staff working at an organization like the DVLC.

There's bound to be someone with access to the database who could be persuaded to get the information you're wanting. It's not as though you're trying to do something criminal, it's mainly an ethical question, as you yourself pointed out, Kay.'

Persuaded. He meant bribed. Kay thought of John the porter's greedy eyes and felt revulsion.

'Another road in would be through the police,' Hugo continued, forking up the last grains of rice in his bowl and leaning over to take some of Fiona's. 'There was an item in the news only a day or two ago about an ex-police inspector turned private detective who got done for getting protected information from a former colleague who has ready access to the Police National Computer. They both got done of course. But there will be plenty doing it who don't get caught.'

'But surely there are all kinds of safeguards,' protested Kay. 'I can't believe officers in the police can get hold of any information they like willy-nilly.'

'Listen,' Hugo said patiently, 'an officer has to log in the purpose of any enquiry he makes to the PNC, but he can always give a convincing sounding reason such as needing to gain crime intelligence, or information about a hit and run crash for instance. These requests are made in their thousands every day. They only get subjected to random checks. The risk of getting found out if you put one in that looks dodgy is pretty small.'

Fiona and Kay stared at him, finding it hard not to be impressed.

'I'm asking no more questions about how he knows all this,' Fiona said. Shooting an assessing glance at her lover she moved her rice bowl so as to prevent his plundering it further.

'And then there are insurance companies and their investigators,' Hugo went on, engrossed in his theme. 'They carry full information on car owners.' He raised an eyebrow. 'Surely, Kay, you must know someone who knows someone?'

She thought of Ralph. Of his friends at the golf club and at his masonic lodge. Police and bankers. Powerful men with networks of useful connections.

She felt her heart begin to bob against her ribcage. She stood up, her legs a little unsteady. She hated the way she was so easily upset these days. 'I'll be back in a minute,' she said, looking around for the sign to the cloakrooms.

She leaned against the small, pink basin, taking in deep breaths. She splashed cold water on her flushed cheeks and anxiously inspected her face in the mirror. The eyes looked back, sunken and hunted. She realized that this search for her donor was taking its toll. If she didn't take proper care of herself she could be in real trouble.

Fiona slid through the door. The space in the washroom was cramped and breathless. Standing beside the basin they were almost pressed up against each other.

'Sorry, sorry,' Fiona said, confronting Kay's mirror image. 'All I can say is that I think his motives are pure. Or at least based on the unlikely emotions of kindness and a simple desire to help. At least they'd better be.'

'I'm losing my nerve,' Kay told her. 'I'm no good at poking about and pretending to be what I'm not. I can't bring myself to tell any more lies. I think I'll just drop the whole thing.' But I won't, she thought. I can't.

In the past week the dream had been coming most nights. It had stamped itself on her inner eye and torn into her emotions. She was now convinced that her donor had died as a result of some evil action, of violence perpetrated by the aggressor who dominated her dream. And yet she recognized that this belief was quite contrary to what she had discovered regarding the circumstances of her donor's death. She found herself caught between the pressure to go forward in her investigations and the fear that if she did so she could put herself at serious risk.

She recalled Raymond King once telling her that mental and physical health fed from each other. If you kept yourself steady and calm and rational then you gave the chemistry, and physiology of your body the chance to heal itself after the assault of surgery. Allowing herself to be driven on in this obsessive investigation could be an act of madness, a way to destroying herself. If she got herself to a low point of exhaustion and stress, what then? She could get an infection; her heart could be at risk of rejection. And would King be able to save her a second time? Would another compatible heart obligingly present itself? She had heard stories of patients who had waited for the heart that never came. She had had her chance. It would be wicked to throw it away.

But then she recalled once again that a young woman had died so she could live. She felt the warmth and strength of the heart inside her. She replayed the images from the dream and knew that she could not push them back into the darkness from which they had sprung.

Fiona turned Kay to face her and wrapped her arms firmly around her. 'Poor love,' she said.

'What about you?' Kay asked. 'Have you told him?'

'No.'

Kay moved out of Fiona's hug and straightened up. She rubbed the tips of her fingers over her moist cheeks. 'Why not?'

'Same problem as yours in a way. I can't bring myself to do it. Every time I get to the point of opening my mouth, it somehow shuts.'

'You haven't done anything about having an abortion?' Kay asked urgently.

Fi shook her head slowly. 'I haven't done anything much at all. Simply carried on living my life.'

'Maybe that's the only thing worth worrying about,' said Kay, feeling too weary to think of any other reply.

* * *

Ralph telephoned the next morning.

'Oh, hello!' She felt suddenly awkward, recalling the final scene of their last meeting.

'Call a truce?' He was gruff and rueful.

'There wasn't really a war. You just said what you needed to.'

'I was bloody out of order. I'm sorry. It's just that I worry about you.'

'I know. I love you for it.'

There was a silence. She imagined his face,

lit with sudden pleasure and cringing with embarrassment.

Maybe this was the perfect opportunity to appeal to Ralph for help. She could come clean with him about her preoccupations of the past weeks; ask him about those masonic friends of his who might know someone who knew someone who could ferret out sensitive information.

'Now listen,' he commanded, 'I want you to come over and meet Isobel. Soon as possible. I'll get her to look in her diary and I'll book the two cooking poofters. Don't want either of you two women complaining about being slaves in the kitchen.' He was back to his normal self, booming and buoyant.

The moment had passed. The tentative questions framing themselves in her head quickly dissolved. And when she heard the connection click off after his goodbye she felt huge relief.

★   ★   ★

She took her cello from its case, polished it, tuned it and embarked on some serious practising. At first she was ragged and fumbling, horribly rusty. She started off with Handel's G minor sonata, a piece she had learned soon after she started playing the cello. Hugging the warm wood of the instrument against her she gradually shed her self-consciousness and became lost in the playing, in the effort of shaping and colouring the phrases. She played for three hours; straight through with no break. Then she ate tuna sandwiches laced with chilli sauce followed by an energy-giving banana. After an hour's sleep she began again. Bach's C minor Suite this time. She grew demonic, her arms and her back sore with the rewarding ache of doing something she loved and had almost abandoned. Doing something worthwhile.

It was dropping dark when the phone rang.

'Damn!' She drew her bow once more across the strings.

The answering machine picked up. 'It's Fi.' An uncharacteristic hesitation. 'Kay, if you're in, will you phone back right away?'

Kay sat rigid, her bow raised. God, something awful had happened. She could hear it in Fi's voice. The baby? A bust up with Hugo. An abortion?

She punched out Fi's number.

'Hello, Kay?'

'Fi! Are you all right? The baby?'

'Yeah, yeah. The baby's still anchored in there, all's well with the world. Well, more or less . . . '

165

'Fi, what is it? Tell me!'

'Look, Hugo . . . he . . . '

'Oh God!'

'Kay, he went plunging in where angels fear to tread. He's got the name and address of your donor.' She allowed time for the news to sink in. 'Don't ask me how. He hasn't told me and I'd rather not know.'

Kay could not speak.

'Are you angry?' Fi asked.

'Yes. I don't know. No.'

'Well I can't decide whether to love him or leave him.'

'It was you wasn't it?' Kay said softly. 'He couldn't have done it unless you told him the number to chase.'

'True.'

'You memorized it with that in mind?'

'Not at the time. I just have that kind of photographic memory. Lots of us musicians do.'

It doesn't matter, thought Kay, knowing that in whatever way Fi had set things up she had meant it as an act of friendship.

'They say that knowledge is power,' observed Fi. 'And power can be used or not, as you decide.'

The next leap forward is huge, thought Kay. An act of terrifying choice.

Part Two

12

Majid Nazar, a criminal lawyer who had recently taken silk, was preparing to celebrate his thirty-ninth birthday by escorting his mistress to the opera, then taking her to dine in the West End.

When Majid arrived at Jennifer's town house in St John's Wood she was not quite ready for him and had given instructions to her son Freddie to look after him.

Freddie was twelve years old. He was at home on vacation from Eton. He knew exactly how a guest should be cared for and, having enquired what Nazar would prefer to drink, brought him a single measure of whisky with just the right amount of cold water added.

'Becoming a QC is one of the options I'm considering for my future career,' Freddie told Majid, hovering politely beside the door as though ready to melt away if the guest showed signs of wanting to be left alone. 'Would you mind if I asked you a few questions?'

'Please do.' Majid smiled invitingly and patted the vacant cushions of the fat sofa on which Freddie had installed him. One of the options I'm considering, Majid repeated to himself with gentle amusement. Such breathtaking confidence. Some would say arrogance. Majid reflected that he himself had been forced to swim through a thick, oily sea of prejudice and scepticism simply to reach the lowest rung of the legal ladder up which he had now climbed quite a good way. His parents had been uneducated and poor, firmly planted among the labouring classes, and worst of all one of the first immigrant families from the Gujarat to Bradford in Yorkshire in the 1950s. Swimming through an oily sea, with one's legs tied together and carrying a ball and chain was more like it! 'Ask away,' he told Freddie.

The next ten minutes went pleasantly by with Freddie posing the kind of questions which served mainly to demonstrate his conviction that he would have no difficulty in making an entrée into the profession if his final choice lay in that direction.

Majid knew there were some who would have been irritated at Freddie's gentle presumption, would have envied all the advantages enjoyed by those who had impressive genealogy, substantial wealth and excellent connections on their side. He harboured none of those feelings, believing that a hard fought victory always yields the greatest satisfaction. And beside the pleasure he took in his own achievement was the huge pride he felt for his dead father, who had given Majid the confidence to believe he could battle against all odds, and triumph.

His father, a man of little education but sharp intelligence, had now been dead for ten years. He had been a cultural pioneer, ferociously ambitious to succeed in the climate of Macmillan's 'you've never had it so good' post-war Britain. During the early years after the family's arrival in Bradford he had worked a night shift in a clattering weaving shed and used the daytime hours to build a business grinding and packaging Asian spices. By the 1970s his company was exporting around the world and the family were rich. They had moved to a detached house in the suburbs and there had been no financial hardships for Majid when he went up to Cambridge to gain a first in English literature before studying law.

Whilst rooted in the Muslim culture and firmly embracing the discipline of the Koran, Majid's father had been something of a visonary who had been troubled by the tacit agreement of his fellow Asians to the unofficial apartheid that had developed in Bradford's inner city, more or less unnoticed by the outside world. The mill in which he worked had been almost exclusively staffed by Asians. They could afford housing only in the poorer areas of the city from which the white population gradually moved out. They shopped at their own shops, worshipped at the newly erected mosque, worked in factories where English was rarely heard. Children coming into the city were placed in immigrant centres to be taught English. Yet even in the late 1960s it was not unusual for children born in the city to have virtually no working knowledge of English by the time they started school at five years old.

Majid's father had understood the futility of walling himself and his family into a ghetto. It may have rendered a difficult situation tolerable, but he wanted something much better than that.

Whilst quietly supporting the passive acceptance stitched into the fabric of Muslim life — Allah must be obeyed, fathers must be obeyed, wives must obey husbands, girls must obey everyone — as a man of natural intelligence and thoughtfulness he understood that life was about change, and that each individual must strive to bring it about and improve his situation.

Majid recalled his father expounding his philosophy in the evenings whilst the women prepared the meal.

'The prophet Allah himself had been moved to transform the world,' his father would remind Majid, setting their discussions within the reassuring framework of Muslim discipline.

'We have come to this country to escape the poverty in our own. We must take all the opportunities that are here for us.' His father's penetrating brown eyes had rested on Majid, his eldest child, his only son and his greatest hope for the future.

Majid, who regarded his father with the same reverence he had been taught to render Allah, could still recall his boyish excitement at the prospects which must surely be waiting to unfurl before him.

His father had maintained that as immigrants they were uniquely placed to draw from both the Asian and the British cultures.

'We must take whatever is of worth and put it to good use to build a new and different life. We must keep our Muslim values but draw on British imagination, we must maintain our Muslim discipline but teach ourselves the value of British freedom of thought, make every use of the chances offered through the British education system.'

These were dangerous and unpopular

views amongst many of his fellow country-men. Majid's mother was quietly sceptical, concerned for her two daughters. How would she arrange good marriages for them if they started to behave like English girls, showing their legs and prostituting themselves with boys. But his father's brother, Majid's uncle, spoke out violently against even the smallest concession to the values of the local English community, seeing it as a fracture in the cultural wall which was their own people's sole protection. The wall would gradually crumble until they were all submerged in a filthy swamp of godlessness, greed and misery.

Majid's father, however, having noted his son's huge thirst for knowledge and his appetite for hard work had understood that he would only achieve his potential through becoming a part of the English way of life.

Majid had absorbed and internalized his father's words and through his adolescence in the seventies had made it his business to be aware of the trends evolving at the cutting edge of British culture: raised political awareness; new deals for the workers; growing ambition amongst sections of the population who had once been taught to expect little; and the rolling tide of feminism — perhaps the one aspect of British culture that his father had chosen to ignore.

And now, thirty years later, chatting to Freddie in Jennifer's brocaded, antique-strewn drawing-room Majid felt himself to be completely at ease with the British middle class. Cambridge had done that for him. Cambridge and literature. Rowing and cricket. The opera and travel. But most of all his expertise in British law.

After some discussion of the most prestigious universities in which to study law, of the chambers which were most highly regarded, of the opportunities for pupillage with top flight barristers, Freddie mentioned to Majid that his great uncle had taken him to look around court one at the Old Bailey when he was small.

'I thought it was rather like a church,' he observed with a mischievous smile. 'It was the little canopy over the witness box I particularly took to. I thought a bishop would be stepping up any minute and delivering a sermon.'

For Majid, his first sight of Court Number One at the Bailey during his first months as a pupil had seemed an almost religious experience. The dignity of the panelled, richly carved chamber had been imbued with all that he associated with English history and tradition. Its hushed calm carried a sense of perpetuity, an intimation of order and nobility and rightness. It amused him to note that Freddie's memories were of a childish delight in a theatrical witness box.

'It is the kind of place that gives rein to the imagination,' Majid agreed. He knew that Freddie's unnamed great uncle had been a judge of national repute. It was one of the snippets of information about her family which Jennifer occasionally let drop. 'Did you go up into the public gallery?' he asked. 'You get a good view of the whole court from there?'

'No,' said Freddie apologetically. 'But my uncle took me to sit on the bench.'

Of course, thought Majid. 'You should try sitting in the gallery some time,' he told Freddie. 'Or in the dock.'

'Terrifying,' said Freddie.

'Exactly. Those are the places where you can begin to understand the extremes of human terror and hope.' An approximation of these words had been said to him in the first weeks of his pupillage by the very clever and manipulative female counsel to whom he had been assigned. She had scared him out of his wits at first, given him a hard time, and forced him to learn fast to keep up. She was as dominant and wilful as any Pakistani matriarch. But she had technical knowledge and a power base on a world stage which few Pakistani women could aspire to. Majid had often wondered if it had been a deliberate plan to place him under the wing of such a woman, a challenge to his upbringing in a culture which revered female docility.

He noticed that Freddie was watching him, his expression reflective. Majid guessed that the boy was glimpsing avenues of thought down which he had not travelled before.

'Do you prefer prosecuting or defending?' Freddie asked earnestly.

'Ah, now that's a very interesting question.' Majid sketched out a teasingly open-ended answer that invited further comment and more questions. He listened to Freddie's views with close attention and answered each point with honesty and consideration.

By the time Jennifer swept in, majestic and perfumed, he and Freddie were conversing like old friends.

'Get me G and T darling,' Jennifer instructed her son. 'One ice cube, tiny strip of lemon.'

On Freddie's departure she offered Majid each cheek in turn for a kiss, then moved away, her silk dress rustling. 'Have to keep things a bit low-key,' she told him, turning her eyes in the direction Freddie had gone. 'Has he been interrogating you?'

'Only on the practice of law.'

Jennifer grimaced. 'He can be a bit persistent.'

'He's charming,' Majid reassured her.

'I'm afraid the pal he was going to stay with tonight has gone down with flu. Freddie'll have to come along with us. *Ménage à trois*. I've managed to wangle an extra ticket for the opera.'

Majid gave a wry smile. Jennifer could wangle more or less anything from anybody. It was a quality bred into her pedigree and nurtured from babyhood.

'Do you mind awfully?' she asked.

'No,' said Majid. 'Will Freddie?'

'Oh, he loves being with adults. Always has done. He's one of those children who'll be far happier when he's left childhood.'

'He likes opera?'

Jennifer shrugged. '*Carmen* is pretty jolly isn't it. And we trained him up from an early age to sit still.'

★   ★   ★

'That was super,' was Freddie's verdict on *Carmen* as they settled themselves in one of Jennifer's favourite restaurants overlooking the shiny snake of the Thames. 'Absolutely splendid stuff.'

Jennifer shot a sly glance at Majid. *Told you so.*

Majid ordered champagne which Jennifer would expect and Freddie would be able to drink without getting legless. He himself would drink very little. A taste for alcohol was a part of the English culture he had not adopted. He liked to be clear-headed, in control. But he knew better than to make himself conspicuous by refusing wine and had learned the knack of making a glass of claret last the whole evening without anyone noticing. He looked through the vast picture window at the procession of river traffic ferrying tourists through the late July evening and thought of King George making his similar watery journey nearly 300 years ago serenaded by Handel's music. The thought gave him a glow of pleasure.

He looked back at Jennifer and Freddie and reflected how much he was enjoying being here with them; the easy warmth of their company, the sense of family. He was well aware that any notion of being included in their family circle was quite spurious. He was no more than one of the satellites revolving round their sun. He knew that Jennifer's infidelity was mainly a result of her boredom and loneliness when her diplomat husband was out of the country and that she was firmly committed to her marriage. He also knew that adultery, carried out discreetly, was not viewed within her social group as a sin and that he, Majid, was probably little more than an exotic plaything in Jennifer's eyes.

He looked at her across the table and smiled at the thought. His regard for Jennifer was warm and genuine, but hardly any more noble than hers for him. She suited him at this stage in his life, just as he suited her. She was sexy and amusing, level-headed and invariably cheerful. She was an ambassador of well-to-do female Englishness. A woman who was well educated, well travelled, cultured and unfailingly gracious. She was a decorative escort and an enthusiastic bed-mate. She was also pleasingly low-key emotionally. If he told her they were to split up this evening, she would be sorry. But not devastated, and quite prepared to be civilized about it. And if she were to break things off with him. Well, it would be more or less the same.

The waiter brought fragrant fish soup, then placed grated cheese and a dome of *croûtons* in the middle of the table. Freddie most politely offered these first to his mother and then Majid before helping himself.

Jennifer permitted Freddie a second glass of champagne. The two of them wished Majid a happy birthday and drank a toast to his health and happiness.

'Do you go home to visit your own country regularly?' Freddie asked.

Majid paused just a second too long. Jennifer stiffened.

'This is my country,' Majid said smiling, gesturing to the river and the city beyond. 'Britain. I was born here.'

Freddie blinked but did not falter. 'Were your parents born here?'

'No. They were born in Gujarat. In a tiny rural village.'

'I've never been to Pakistan,' said Freddie. 'I've been to India,' he added half apologetically.

'I've only been a dozen times myself,' Majid told him. 'My parents didn't want to return at first. They needed to settle in Yorkshire, get used to the terrible weather!' There was no question of his father's getting together the air fare, but he did not want to embarrass Jennifer and Freddie with that. 'It's a good place, my parents' village. You'd like it, Freddie. It's very quiet during the day once the sun becomes strong. People stay in their houses in the shade. But at night everything comes to life. The heat from the daytime is still in the air and there's a hum and bustle of people wandering around in the markets and shops. And the sky is a wonderful deep indigo.'

Freddie looked impressed.

'Tell me,' Majid mused as they waited for the restaurant's next offering. 'Do you think the racial tension in Britain has increased in the past few years?' He cited two recent murders of black teenagers to illustrate his query.

Freddie considered for a moment and produced an informed and eloquent response which offered a balanced case for the belief that on the whole racial prejudice was less widespread than it had been at the time of Enoch Powell's rivers of blood speech, but that there did seem to be a core of violent feeling amongst a small minority of extremists.

Majid smiled. He reflected on the vast school fees Jennifer and her husband were shelling out and thought they were probably getting value for money. 'Do racist jokes still flourish in schools?' he asked Freddie. 'In your school?'

For a brief moment Freddie appeared disconcerted. Jennifer raised her eyebrows, poured herself more champagne and left her son to fight his own battles.

'Yes,' said Freddie. 'I'm afraid they do.'

Majid liked his directness. He remembered

the stream of 'Paki' jokes at his schools in Bradford. Frighteningly vicious and obscene. Told with relish only a decade or so after the world's shocked reaction to the horror of the holocaust.

Majid decided to risk developing this theme. 'I'll tell you one someone told me when I was a student at Cambridge. It was about a well-to-do Englishman who was startled when his new Asian neighbour greeted him each morning with the words, 'I am better than you, sir.'' Majid enjoyed putting on a parody of an Asian accent, teasing his audience with the spinning out of the story to its eventual punchline. ''I am better than you sir, because I do not live next door to a Pakistani.' ' He leaned back, smiling to himself.

Freddie and Jennifer laughed, perhaps more with relief than anything else.

At the end of the evening Majid put them both in a taxi then walked along the river to his flat on the South Bank. Standing at the window in his sitting-room he admired the expanse of shimmering water and the glinting floodlit splendour of Tower Bridge. He regretted the lack of a satisfying bout of sex with Jennifer to round off the evening. It was quite a few weeks now since they had had the opportunity to be alone together. But there would be other times.

The sternly correct voice on the anwering service informed him he had three messages. The first was no more than a series of sighs and scuffles. The second was an earnest request from his current junior, Theo, for advice on some points regarding their preparation for the defence in a murder case. The call was timed at 6.45 p.m. A perfectly acceptable time to telephone. But perhaps he should suggest to Theo that calls at home should be confined to emergencies. Thoughts of Theo made him think of Freddie and the ways in which they were alike. Both of them born with a silver spoon in their mouths, intelligent, good-looking, expensively educated, imbued with a quiet unshakeable confidence.

He snapped into sudden alertness. The third message was from his cousin Balbinder. Message timed at 9.30 p.m. 'Majid. I'm sorry . . . something awful. Could you ring back? Could you come . . . ?'

He stood, his pulses drumming. This was the third time in as many months that he had been called to a crisis in Bradford.

'Repeat?' the answerphone voice asked him.

'No!' He was alarmed to find himself shouting. He went to stand again at the window. It had rained almost all day and the river was full and fast flowing, the whirls on its surface whipped into agitation, the crests spiked with horns of silver. He wanted to stand here, just to stand and gaze at the restless, timeless flow of the great capital's river.

He moved back to the phone and dialled a Bradford number. His fingers tightened on the handset as the rhythmic purrs began. And went on . . .

13

Fifteen hours before Majid received the phone message which prompted him to get into his car and drive in a northerly direction towards the start of the M1, Kay had taken the train from King's Cross bound for Leeds. From there she changed to a local service which took her into Bradford via one of the steepest descents into a station she had ever experienced. She hoped the train had good brakes.

She could not remember visiting a Yorkshire city before. Her mother had friends in Scarborough on the east coast with whom they had occasionally spent a weekend, and at Ralph's instigation there had been many holidays in the highlands of Scotland. But that, she was ashamed to realize, was the limit of her knowledge of the north of the country.

'Bradford!' Fiona had exclaimed. 'Where the hell is that? I don't think I know anywhere that's off the northern edge of the tube map.'

'It's a bit further up than Cockfosters,' Kay agreed.

She had booked herself into the city's

largest, and thus she reasoned, most anonymous hotel. It had a slick, international feel about it; the kind of newly appointed luxury hotel that could have been anywhere in the world.

By the time she had unpacked her minimal amount of luggage and carried out her routine checks of vital signs it was around one o'clock. Although her stomach was tight with expectation and anxiety she knew she must eat something. The basement dining-room was airy and hushed, its rows of chrome-framed tables mainly empty, its gleaming, polished wood floor and spotlights making a self-conscious effort to be trendy. She ordered chicken tikka sandwiches with lime pickle and forced them down through sheer will power and a stern determination to keep chewing.

It was hard to believe she was here in this strange unknown city. So close to the family of the donor whose imagined personality had tantalized and obsessed her for all the long weeks since her transplant. It was even harder to believe that very soon she was going to leave the hotel and, armed with her street guide, find and board a bus that would take her to the very house where her donor had once lived.

The centre of the city surprised her with its

meticulously laid out gardens, its domed Alhambra theatre and its magnificently restored Wool Exchange. Running off the wide main roads was the occasional thread-needle street that was almost Dickensian.

The bus laboured up a steep ascent from the city centre and made its way through dusty, tired-looking streets and boarded-up shops. Further on there were signs of energy and life, shops with brown sacks of vegetables stacked on the pavements outside, beans and chillies and sweet potatoes, set amidst peeling plaster and crumbling brick as though arranged for an artist to capture on canvas.

She got off the bus and reopened her street map, trying to orient herself. The people around her were mostly Asian, many of the women in saris topped with hand-knitted cardigans, or silky pyjamas. Some of the men wore tunics and loose trousers. On the skyline a mosque raised its head. Several of the shops she passed were piled high with rolls of vividly coloured fabrics, some of them heavily embroidered and glittering. A beautiful Asian woman swathed in a green and yellow sari smiled at her encouragingly as she paused to look more closely.

Kay had lived in London all her life, was used to meeting people of all races and colours on its streets. Yet here the atmosphere hummed with foreignness; she felt as though she had stepped into another continent, a part of the exotic east.

Eventually she found the street she was looking for. It was narrow and cramped, lined with old, stone, terraced houses. The doors and a scattering of stones were painted in assertive shades of purples and scarlets and limes. Some of the houses had been sandblasted and glowed golden yellow against their soot-blackened neighbours.

There were no cars about and small children played quietly on the pavements. Neat, delicate women with glossy black hair and perfect make-up carried shopping bags into their houses. Walking along, Kay noticed a number of lace curtains twitching. She felt out of place, acutely conscious of her height, her pale skin and her blondeness.

She identified the house she had come to visit and stopped a few yards before she reached it. She had prepared meticulously for this moment; had rehearsed her speech over and over. She forced her legs to propel her up the short, narrow path to the house. Her tongue dried and her throat seemed to have a fist jammed into it.

★ ★ ★

189

Keeping a hawklike eye out for police cars and speed cameras Majid maintained a cruising speed of a hundred as he drove up the motorway. He arrived in Bradford around 3 a.m. and as he drove to his aunt's house was already calculating how long it would take him to get back to London if he managed to steady down the inevitable hysteria that awaited him and set off back by six.

His silver BMW was too big to park in the street without blocking the way for other vehicles. He left it on the main road, listening to the farewell buzz of the alarm as he pressed the key to set it.

The short walk up the street reactivated memories of childhood. Visits to his father's brother's house, the fragrant spicy meals his first wife used to cook, the strong sense of religion and family. He recalled his father's contrasting restlessness, his drive to take the initiative, to work and acquire wealth so that he could spread his wings. Moving to a part of Bradford where brown faces had never been seen before had not made life any easier, but it had taken the family away for ever from the stranglehold of the old, stubborn ways set up centuries before as a consolation for poverty.

Majid rapped on the door with his

knuckles. His mind threw up a vivid image of his uncle Javed who had lived in this tiny house for all his years in England. Javed had wanted to live his life as though he were not in Britain at all, holding on tight to the old Asian prejudices and judgements. He would have lived like that if he'd gone to the moon Majid thought. He remembered the rule of tyranny and terror Javed had subjected his daughters to, his rigid insistence on a total adherence to Muslim values. He must himself have been terrified by the notion of change.

'Majid!' exclaimed his cousin Balbinder, opening the door and pulling him inside. 'Oh, thank goodness you're here.'

He followed her into the front room. The gas fire was burning even though it was July. He looked at the heavy red flock paper covering the walls and had the impression the room had grown smaller since the last time he saw it.

The television was on, showing an Asian video. A dark-eyed beauty was remonstrating with an eagle-faced hero. Balbinder hurriedly switched the set off. 'It's one of Mother's. I'm sorry. I had to do something to pass the time until you arrived.'

Majid had a sense of being smothered. He did not know how Balbinder could bear to stay on here, looking after her volatile mother and her ignorant, arrogant brother. 'So what has happened,' he demanded.

'Mother cut her wrists with one of the kitchen knives,' Balbinder said wearily. 'I called the ambulance. She's in hospital.'

Majid pressed the tips of his fingers to his temples and sighed.

'The doctor I spoke to said she is going to be all right.' Balbinder spoke calmly but her fingers trembled as she fiddled with a long gold earring.

'Was it a suicide attempt?' Majid tried not to make his voice sound too hard, too lawyerlike. 'Did she really mean to take her life?'

Balbinder dipped her head and began to cry.

'I'm sorry. Those were bad words to choose.' Majid cursed himself. A Queen's Counsel should surely be able to do better.

'I'm not sure what she meant to do. She was beside herself. Sobbing and screaming. Well, you know . . . '

Majid nodded.

'She went to the bathroom and got the tablets the psychiatrist had given her for anxiety and threatened to take them all. I took them from her.'

Majid imagined the cat fight that had ensued. The spitting and snarling and clawing. His aunt could be a tigress when she wasn't bowed down with a long face and endless woes.

'I thought she'd calmed down.' said Balbinder. 'And then I found her in the kitchen. There was blood all over the chairs and table.'

Majid drew in a breath. 'Poor Balbinder! And where was Mudassar?'

'He'd gone to bed. He's got exams on at the moment. He said he needed to sleep.'

'He takes all the privileges of the man of the family and none of the responsibilities.' Majid observed with icy fury.

'He's only sixteen,' Balbinder said mildly.

Majid walked to the window, pushed aside the curtains and looked out into the darkness. The street had a greasy sheen underneath the orange lamps. He felt empty of words of comfort to offer Balbinder. Her life had so often been perched on the edge of frustration and suffering, but the last few months must have been almost unbearable. He ached to be away. To get into his car and leave all this behind. Family anguish. He had witnessed enough of it in his childhood to last him for ever.

As though from a distance he heard Balbinder speaking to him once more. 'I haven't told you what brought all this on.'

He turned back into the room. He had assumed his aunt's dramatic actions had merely been a continuation of a long-established see-sawing of violent moods. He sat down beside Balbinder. 'Well?' He spoke in the irresistibly gentle voice he used to coax revelations from scared witnesses.

'I can hardly believe what happened. It was such a shock.' Balbinder pulled at her earring until it seemed she would tear her ear lobe in two. 'This woman we've never seen before arrived on the doorstep. She said she was the person who had got Parvinder's heart.'

Majid froze.

'She wanted to come in and talk to us. To thank us for letting Parvinder donate her heart.'

Majid groaned. He recalled the desperate scenes in the hospital on that terrible day, heard his aunt's primeval screams, felt her hand gripping his shoulder like a desperate claw.

'Are you sure she wasn't an impostor?' he demanded. 'Someone getting a thrill from playing a terrible joke?' He had done everything he could to stop any leak to the press of an Asian family's startling decision to allow one of their members to donate an organ. He thought he had been successful, but it was never possible to identify and seal every possible chink. And there was no shortage of people who would find it entertaining to do a little Paki baiting on an issue as tender as this.

'She was genuine,' Balbinder said. 'I'm quite sure of it. I could feel it somehow.'

There was a silence. Majid's anger and disbelief boiled within him. 'How could this unknown woman do such a stupid, insensitive thing? Is she ill? I mean psychiatrically ill?'

'No, she seemed very reasonable. Very steady.'

'How dare she? How dare she?' Majid brought his hand down with a crash on the spindly gilt table in front of the sofa. His nostrils flared with fury.

'It was a stupid thing to do,' Balbinder agreed. 'But — I felt sorry for her.'

Majid shook his head. 'You've always been far too accommodating to everyone else's feelings. Who can blame you? What other options were you given?'

Balbinder glanced sharply at him. She said nothing.

'Tell me exactly what happened,' Majid demanded. 'How long did this woman stay in the house? What exactly did she say?'

'She didn't get the chance to say much. Once Mother realized who she was she started screaming and shouting at her in

Gujarati. She looked completely wild and mad. I think the woman was frightened Mother would attack her.' Balbinder gave another tug at her earring. 'I still can't believe it. That this woman should come here.'

'So what happened after your mother had finished her screaming?' Majid asked.

'Oh, the woman had gone long before Mother calmed down. As soon as Mother started yelling she looked terribly anxious and said how sorry she was for coming. She kept apologizing and saying how sorry she was over and over again. She almost ran out of the house.'

'How long was she here do you think?'

'No more than a few minutes. Six or seven maybe. No, perhaps not as much as that. It was all really quick.'

'Do you think she will come back?'

Balbinder's face crumpled with fresh anxiety. 'Oh! I hope not. No, I don't think she will. She was really shaken by what happened. I hope she is all right.'

'I don't think it's our job to worry about her. There's enough to think about here, in this household,' Majid said rather formally.

Balbinder nodded.

'How soon will your mother come home?' Majid asked.

'They didn't say. But I don't think it will be very long.'

'Will you be able to manage? Perhaps I should contact Social Services.'

'I'll manage,' said Balbinder. 'She just needs time. To get over all this sadness. Father dying like he did and then Parvinder so soon after.' Again her eyes brimmed with tears.

'She had enough to deal with before this wretched woman came along,' fumed Majid, thinking that this impulsive stupid act had pulled the family right back to the shocking day of Parvinder's death. All the hard work of recuperating from the searing grief would have to be gone through all over again. Reluctantly he realized there was no question of returning immediately to London. He would contact Theo and instruct him to carry on with his preparations on his own. It would do him no harm.

'Will you stay here tonight?' Balbinder asked hesitantly, following the thread of his thoughts.

'I'll go to the hospital,' he said tersely. 'And then I'll book in at a hotel.' He felt wretched saying this, leaving Balbinder in no doubt that he could not bear to sleep for even one night in the crowded, primitive house of his relatives.

Balbinder gave a sad smile. 'It's all right, Majid,' she said quietly.

He got to his feet and leaned down to kiss Balbinder on her cheek. At the door he suddenly thought to ask, 'What was this woman like? Was she Asian?'

'No. Very English. She had long, blond hair and blue eyes. She was a good person, Majid. I don't think she had meant to do any harm.'

Majid did not want to hear this.

'I wish Mother had listened to what she came to say. I wish she could have stayed,' Balbinder said. 'When she told us who she was I got this strange shivering feeling. I felt as if Parvinder had come back. That she was here in the room.'

Majid most certainly did not want to hear this. 'Please spare me that kind of notion.'

'But think Majid, this woman has Parvinder's heart inside her,' Balbinder persisted.

'Yes. But she is not Parvinder. She is herself.'

'You are always so logical and so practical,' said Balbinder. 'Some people would say you're cold.'

He flinched. 'I'm sorry.'

'Sometimes I miss Parvinder so much I don't think I can bear it,' Balbinder said.

Majid groaned. He grasped his car keys so that they cut into his flesh.

'You loved her too,' Balbinder reminded him gently. 'She broke all our hearts.'

14

Majid drove through the wide, empty roads. To the south of him the flank of the city on the other side of the valley spread itself in a myriad of shimmering orange lights.

The sprawl of hospital buildings was mainly in darkness outlined in a crossword puzzle of lighted windows. He followed the signs to the Women's Ward where he found the nursing station, staffed by a sole student nurse who was filling in a notes sheet.

Majid gave the name of his aunt and asked to see one of the doctors who had information on her progress.

The girl looked up, about to protest that it might take some time to locate a doctor. Seeing Majid's expression she instantly picked up the telephone.

A houseman eventually appeared. He was able to reassure Majid that Mrs Nazar was comfortable, that she had sustained mainly superficial injuries and that she was in no danger. She would probably be discharged later on the next day.

'Will you require a psychiatrist's report before that can happen?' Majid asked.

'It is usual in these circumstances.' The doctor sounded hesitant as though expecting a negative reaction.

'Quite. Our family would welcome it. And I would be grateful for the opportunity to talk with the consultant at some time after his, or her, conclusions.'

He was assured that would be perfectly in order.

'May I see Mrs Nazar?'

'She's sleeping now. We gave her a mild sedative.'

'I would like to see her anyway.'

Majid walked down the corridor and into the four-bedroomed ward. He stood for a few moments looking down at the figure in the bed. She was lying on her back, her iron-grey hair loose, covering the pillow, her arms stretched out over the sheet, their lower sections bound in a swathe of bandage. Her eyelids jerked and fluttered with some nervous pulse but she was oblivious of her surroundings and his presence, temporarily drugged into some semblance of contentment.

Mrs Kulvinder Nazar, said the label clipped to the bedhead. Majid recalled the day his uncle Javed had brought her from Pakistan to Britain; a bewildered young woman torn from her family in a tiny village in northern Gujarat. A second wife for a grieving man.

The first wife, Majid's aunt Sadeema had been sunny, docile and beautiful, everything Javed wanted in a wife. Except she had never been able to give birth to a live baby. And during her seventh labour she had suffered a sudden cardiac arrest and died.

Javed had returned to Pakistan to seek a new mate. But he was no longer young, and he had accumulated no wealth. The young women available represented the leftovers from the prime pickings in the marriage market. Kulvinder had not commanded a huge dowry, she had been sold cheap. A girl disfigured by a birth mark which covered half of her face. A make-do second wife for a sad, disappointed man.

Within two years Kulvinder had given birth to two beautiful and unscarred daughters and Javed had been pleased with her. But he had had to wait another seven years before she gave birth to the son every family breathlessly waited for. And it was well known in the neighbourhood that Javed had given her a very hard time during that long wait, responding to her depressions and her tantrums with coldness and violence. The girls had suffered similarly.

Mudassar, once safely delivered, had been

worshipped like a god. He had been given everything of the best; the most expensive clothes and the most extravagant toys; the most fervent prayers at the mosque. From babyhood the girls had to defer to him, to be his servants.

The girls. Beautiful, rebellious Parvinder. Steady, loyal Balbinder. Majid's mind ran on a little. He stopped it in its painful tracks.

He touched Kulvinder's bandages with light fingers. He noted how small her fingers were, poking from the dressings, childishly vulnerable. And yet her face was set in lines of bitterness and cynicism. She looked hawkish and old. She was only forty-eight but she was already used up.

*　*　*

Kay turned and fidgeted in her frilled bed listening to the soft rushing of the hotel's air conditioning. Her head ached and her skin prickled. She had slept very little and through the night she had experienced the first moments of real fear about her chances of survival.

Following the disastrous visit to her donor's family her blood pressure had rocketed and she had been terrified that her heart would never resume a normal rhythm.

It had beat in great heaving bursts, sending pain ricocheting through her chest and into her throat.

On returning to the hotel she had lain flat on the bed for a while placing her hands lightly against her ribs and concentrating on steadying her breathing. Eventually this had calmed her enough to make a reasonably sane-sounding phone call to Fiona.

'Success?' Fiona had enquired.

'I found them.'

Fiona was silent for a moment. 'Was it difficult?'

'It was appalling. Horrific!' Kay closed her eyes at the shame of it, of what she had done. She saw herself walking in through the door of the little house, smelled again the spicy, perfumed aroma hovering in the dark narrow passageway. The overlay of garlic; fat ripe garlic. And then those animal howls of shock and grief from that poor demented-looking woman. 'Oh, Fi!'

'Look, sweetheart, get on the next train and come home. Come and stay with us.'

'I can't face another long journey,' Kay told her. 'I'll stay here tonight. I'll be all right.'

'Will you? Are you sure?'

'Sure.'

There was a beating pause.

'You're not thinking of going back to see

203

them again are you?' Fiona said sharply.

Kay heard herself make a tiny choked noise in her throat.

'Kay!' cried Fiona in disbelief, 'don't go back there. Leave it. Get back to London and give yourself time to think things through.'

* * *

In the hotel dining-room there was a soft, morning-expectant buzz of conversation and the appetizing smell of freshly brewing coffee. Kay sat down at her small individual table with its welcome of budding pink tiger lilies and ordered a full English breakfast accompanied by croissants, pamplemousse juice and coffee.

Her heartbeat had now settled to a steady rate and her blood pressure had registered within the normal range when she ran through the morning test. She sent up a grateful prayer to whatever deity was listening for the reassurance of the chance to live some more of her life.

Glancing around the other residents she saw mainly business or professional people looking forward to a day at conferences or seminars. Some guests were already wearing plastic-covered identification labels. One or two were furtively making arrangements on their mobile phones.

A few tables away there was an Asian man on his own, sipping orange juice and sitting very still. He had a handsome warrior face and a grim expression. His skin glowed dark bronze against his white shirt. He glanced up and caught her interested gaze.

Having eaten as much as she was able Kay went to stand at the hotel's entrance, sniffing the air. It was misty and very warm; an almost tropical atmosphere. The moist air was full of city smells: diesel fumes, factory smoke and freshly baked supermarket bread. Returning inside she sat down on one of the foyer's striped sofas and consulted her train timetable.

She was aware of a figure sitting down beside her. She looked up and saw the Asian man who had caught her attention in the dining-room.

'Please forgive me,' he said courteously, 'but I wondered if I could speak with you for a moment?'

'Yes.' She was instantly on edge, wary.

He handed her his professional card. She looked at the name, noted the string of academic qualifications and the initials QC. A slow realization crept through her.

'I wondered if the name might be familiar to you?' he prompted.

Nazar. The same family name as that of Parvinder, the woman who had donated Kay her heart. Since discovering the name the week previously Kay had whispered it to herself whilst she stood in the shower, rehearsed it in her head as she waited in the queue at the supermarket till. Parvinder Nazar.

She nodded. Mr Nazar was exceptionally striking with his black hair, his dark eyes and his sculpted facial bones. It was a face she could imagine chiselled into the rock of a maharaja's palace. Splendid and intimidatingly grim.

'My late father's brother was called Javed,' he told her formally. 'His widow is Mrs Kulvinder Nazar. I think you might have visited her yesterday.'

Kay stared at him, pinned and immobilized by his gaze.

'Forgive me if I'm mistaken,' he said, his tone indicating that he was now satisfied that he was right. He opened his hands a little, inviting her reply.

'Yes, I did visit. It was Mrs Nazar's daughter I spoke to mainly.'

'Balbinder,' he told her. 'My cousin.'

Kay stared at him, hungry and desperate for some shreds of knowledge about the donor who had been a mystery for so long.

206

But looking at the man's eagle face she doubted if she was going to get any. 'Balbinder was very kind. I think she would have been happy to talk to me.'

'Possibly. She is a very level-headed and tolerant person,' he observed.

Kay interpreted the remark as a crushing rebuke.

'Mrs Nazar is in hospital,' he said.

Kay heard the icy accusation underlying the statement. She ran her hand through her hair, miserable to be implicated in another's suffering. 'I thought very hard before making that visit,' she told Nazar, irritation building at his air of judgement, his refusal to relax his grave, disdainful expression. 'I tried to get in contact by writing some time ago, but my letter was simply sent back.'

'It was I who returned it.'

His calm sureness of the rightness of his action sparked her anger. 'You were wrong to do that. It was cold and cruel, did you ever think of that?'

'I thought about my aunt and my cousins and how contact with you could disturb them by reawakening the shock and grief they suffered after Parvinder died. I did what I judged was best for them.'

He was not easy to argue with, Kay

thought. His explanations and reasoning were faultlessly logical.

'I had to think of what was necessary for me,' she said, keeping her voice low and steady.

'I can appreciate that you must have had a very difficult time, through your illness and the transplant,' he offered in clinical tones.

'Yes, I did,' replied Kay sharply. 'Do I deserve more of the same simply because I wanted to express my thanks to the family of the woman who made it possible for me to continue with my life?'

'Mrs Nazar cut her wrists,' he said. 'Some time after you left the house.'

Kay sagged. 'Oh, no,' she groaned. She looked once more into Nazar's censuring face. Guilty, guilty, guilty. she cried inwardly. 'Is she . . . will she be all right?'

'I've been told she's in no danger. And that she's comfortable.'

'Oh God! I'm so sorry. I'm so very, very sorry. What can I do?' She found herself sniffling like an upset child.

'There is nothing you can do.'

She closed her eyes. 'You must hate me!'

'I don't know you,' he said carefully.

That really hurt. 'I'll go away. I'll go home and leave you in peace.'

'I have to be honest with you,' he said. 'I

think you were ill-advised to visit my family. But there is no need for you to shoulder the full burden of blame for what has happened. You were a trigger, not the root cause.'

She absorbed these perfectly enunciated formal phrases then glanced at him, curious to read his expression. He looked calmly back.

'When were you planning to return home?' he asked.

'Today sometime. I'm not sure.' She shrugged, deflated with gloom and a sense of failure.

'And where is your home?'

'North London.'

'Ah, yes.'

He got to his feet, but instead of leaving he stood looking down at her. 'I shall be visiting the hospital again this morning to talk with Mrs Nazar's doctors,' he told her. 'After that I shall have lunch. If you're not in a great hurry to return to London, perhaps you would like to join me.'

15

Majid drove the car out of the city centre and within fifteen minutes they were passing through open countryside. The humidity of the early morning had been burned off by the sun and the fields and valleys spread themselves beneath a heat haze of shimmering light. Cows and sheep grazed in lush emerald green meadows creating an idyllic rural portrait.

'Yorkshire is very beautiful,' Majid remarked, briefly tilting his head in the direction of Kay who sat on her own in the back of the car. 'When it isn't raining and cold.' He raised a hand, indicating the Yorkshire moors to the east, the massive humps of the dales to the west.

Kay tried to focus her attention on the splendour of the distant, blue-tinted hills, but found her concentration entirely taken up by the presence of Balbinder who was sitting in the front passenger seat maintaining a calm, frozen silence which unnerved Kay far more than Kulvinder Nazar's histrionics of the day before.

Majid had given no indication of his

intention of including any other members of the family in his lunchtime meeting with Kay. He had left the hotel a short time after their post-breakfast talk, giving Kay a brief salute of farewell as he walked through the foyer. He arrived back three hours later bringing Balbinder with him.

It was clear that the two had discussed the condition of Kulvinder prior to this, and also, Kay guessed, the awkward problem of her own continued presence in Bradford.

Balbinder had looked tired and anxious, but had greeted Kay with perfect politeness. There was a resignation about her, a docility which at first made Kay wonder if she had been prescribed tranquilizers. Later on she had the sense that perhaps Balbinder's passivity had more to do with the presence of Majid than anything else.

Throughout the drive he was quiet and guarded, offering little information beyond saying that Kulvinder would be discharged from hospital care the next day. Yet Kay sensed his capacity to intimidate without offering any kind of overt challenge.

He stopped at a sixteenth-century deanery and led the way through to a shabbily stylish restaurant which provided the quality of a top London hotel at rather less vertiginous prices. The staff seemed to know him and offered a window table straight away.

'I don't drink,' Kay told him when he offered her the inspection of the wine list.

He tilted his head in a gesture of faint surprise, tinged with approval.

'Well, it's rather that I can't drink at the moment. It would interfere with all the post-surgery medication I have to take. According to my surgeon a glass of wine could result in a fatal hangover.'

Both Balbinder and Majid looked shocked.

'I'm sorry,' she said quickly. 'I've become so used to what's happened to me that I can even joke about it.' She saw that her companions regarded her medical condition as a grave matter and would also expect due respect to be shown to the memory of the previous day's close shave with tragedy. She had the sense of having made a clumsy blunder, like turning up at a funeral wearing a riskily short skirt.

'What do you do?' Majid asked her formally, stroking his fingers up and down his glass of mineral water and looking steadily into her eyes. 'For a living?'

'I'm a cellist. And a university teacher.' She usually put it the other way around. She recognized a need to make herself sound more artistic, more exotic.

'A cellist,' said Balbinder, looking up with

212

sudden interest. 'I admire anyone who can play a musical instrument. It's so difficult to do it well.' She stopped tinkering with her food and laid down her fork. She shot a swift glance at Majid. 'Parvinder used to want to learn the piano. Do you remember?'

Parvinder! Kay's heart jumped with excitement at the sound of the name. 'Couldn't that be arranged?' she asked Balbinder.

'I suppose so. But my father wouldn't pay for private lessons. And the state schools could no longer afford to offer free individual tuition.' Balbinder laid her hands on the table and stared down at them. The nails were a deep red, reminding Kay of the fat little pot called carmine in the poster-paint sets her mother used to buy her at Christmas when she was a child.

Balbinder seemed on the point of saying something further, but instead picked up her fork and returned to a contemplation of the contents of her plate.

Kay glanced at Majid who remained impassive, quietly inhibiting.

'Do you have a profession, Balbinder?' she enquired, feeling there was no alternative but to manufacture small talk.

'I work in a shop.' Balbinder gave a faint smile, revealing shining white teeth. 'It's a job, not a profession.'

Kay wished she had asked the question differently. 'Do you enjoy it?'

'Yes, I do. I sell fabrics and jewellery. They're both things I like very much myself.'

She touched the slender gold bracelets on her arms which tinkled softly as she moved. She was wearing a deep pink and gold tunic in a silky gleaming fabric with matching full trousers drawn in at the ankles. Her strappy, eastern-style sandals were one of the first things Kay had noticed about her when Majid brought her into the hotel. That and her smooth-skinned feet, the toe-nails tinted to match those of her fingertips.

The meal progressed in an atmosphere of courteous formality which Kay found both ludicrous and inappropriate, and yet could do nothing to alter. Majid directed the proceedings as surely as if he had the two women dancing on a string.

It flashed through Kay's mind that maybe this was how Asian men were used to treating their women, how they controlled them. She expunged the thought instantly, horrified to have caught herself out in the worst kind of racial stereotyping.

Eventually the food was finished and the plates removed. Majid glanced at his watch and leaned towards Balbinder, murmuring into her ear. She inclined her head to his.

Kay watched them, finding herself magnetized and fascinated. I carry something of their genealogy inside me, she thought. The cells and blood vessels of my heart were created from the same genetic pool as theirs. The notion was incredible.

She had little doubt that Majid Nazar was a cold, arrogant and controlling man. And yet there was something splendid about him; aristocratic and eaglelike. And Balbinder was so beautiful, so dignified and free from malice.

Kay felt a powerful surge of pride and excitement to be with them. To be seen to be connected to them as though she were a bride coming into the family. A flush of feeling washed through her.

Majid stood up. 'I shall go and ask for the bill, and then I think we should return to Bradford.'

He walked away and Kay looked uncertainly at Balbinder. 'I can't tell you how sorry I am about your mother,' she began, cringing at the inadequacy of the words.

Balbinder gave a sad, resigned smile. 'Ah, well . . . '

'It was all my fault,' cried Kay. 'I shouldn't have come to see you. I was a fool. If there's any way I can help you, please tell me.'

'Mother has often threatened to do this

kind of thing before,' Balbinder said quietly. 'She has been on tablets to calm her down for many years.' She stopped, nibbling at her lip. 'And since Parvinder died she has been in some dreadful moods. So black and despairing.' She looked up, locking with Kay's gaze, dark pain in her eyes.

'Do you and your mother live together on your own?' Kay asked.

'No, there is Mudassar, my brother, also.'

'What does Mudassar do?' Kay asked.

'He attends the local high school and makes the teachers' lives very difficult,' said Balbinder, a glint showing in her soft, dark eyes.

'Oh!'

Balbinder gave a faint smile. 'Some Asian boys are very arrogant,' she said. 'But he is still only young, he may change.'

'You have had to cope with all these problems on your own?' Kay asked.

'No, we have been lucky to have Majid to rely on. He has been so good, always coming to help when we needed him.' Her eyes were warm with affection.

'I so wanted to meet you!' Kay exclaimed with feeling, unable to remain calm and detached. 'To say thank you for letting Parvinder's heart be . . . donated.' Her imagination threw a picture into her mind, hitting her with the horror of the scene: the family gathered around the dying girl's bedside, the doctor groping for words to frame the request. She had a sudden new thought. 'Isn't organ donation against the Muslim faith?' she asked.

Balbinder nodded. 'Yes. But you see Parvinder had rejected our religion. She had rejected our whole way of life.' Balbinder gave a long, sad sigh.

'I'm sorry,' muttered Kay, more uneasy by the moment.

'That was not your fault, Kay,' Balbinder said gently. 'The bad things that have happened in our family are not your fault.'

Tears sprang in Kay's eyes. One rolled down her cheek and she did nothing to brush it away.

Balbinder reached out and placed her hand over Kay's, pressing it in sympathy. 'I have some pictures of Parvinder,' she said. 'Perhaps you would like me to get copies and send them to you?'

Kay stared at her for a long moment. 'Yes. Oh, yes.'

Balbinder lifted her hand and without warning placed it against Kay's chest, laying the palm against her breastbone. Her fingers found the thick ropy scar and traced a path down it. Kay sat, astonished and frozen.

'Parvinder's heart is there,' Balbinder said softly. 'My sister's heart. She saved you.'

Kay hardly dared breathe. 'Yes.'

'I'm glad for that,' Balbinder said. 'It makes her dying seem not so terrible. She didn't die for nothing. A part of her lives on.'

Kay felt herself dragged into some deep undertow of feeling, a current pulling her into the emotional tide of Balbinder's family. For a moment joy and huge relief surged inside her.

And then Majid was in the doorway, beckoning to them, and Balbinder withdrew her hand and retreated into her former demeanour of dignified passivity.

In the car Majid made formal, polite conversation. 'So you are a musician?' he said to Kay as they waited at traffic lights.

'Yes.'

'Do you play professionally?'

'I used to belong to an amateur group, a string quartet. We played at private functions.'

'You no longer belong?'

'I pulled out of the group — after the operation.'

'And will you return to them, now that you're recovered?' he wondered.

'I don't know. They found a replacement cellist.'

'Will you join another ensemble?' His

questions seemed relentless, detached and assessing.

'I don't know.'

'How will you maintain your expertise if you don't?'

'I won't,' she admitted. 'I'll lose it.'

He raised his eyebrows.

'I'm glad I'm not on the witness stand when you're cross-examining,' Kay commented bluntly, determined not to be intimidated.

He gave a brief nod, no smile. He was silent for a time, guiding the car through the traffic with calm precision.

Eventually they drew up at a small row of shops on the edge of an affluent-looking estate whose 1930s houses were snugly ensconced in lawned, tree-decked gardens.

Majid unfurled himself from the car in a single elegant movement and walked around the front of the vehicle to open the passenger door. As Balbinder prepared to get out she swivelled back to look at Kay. There was a tiny pause. 'Goodbye,' she said.

Kay strained to hear warmth in her voice, a hint of an invitation to keep in touch, to meet again.

Majid and Balbinder walked together to a shop whose central door was flanked by windows displaying western clothes on one side and Asian clothes in the other. Both displays vividly colourful, seductively stylish.

In the doorway Balbinder turned to Majid and spoke briefly to him. He leaned towards her and kissed her lightly on each cheek, continental style.

Kay found herself staring at them, fascinated, hungry for shreds of clues to their lives and personalities.

Majid returned to the car. He did not invite Kay to join him in the front passenger seat.

Kay felt the omission as an affront. Anger flashed within. She stared at the back of his head. The sculpted contours of his skull beneath the thick black hair sent a lurch of electric sensation through her nerves.

'When does your train leave?' he asked as they drove into the hotel car park.

'I haven't booked a seat. I can go any time I like.'

He nodded. 'I shall go to visit my aunt at the hospital and I shall drive back to London after that.'

He sprang from the car and opened the door for her, just as he had done for Balbinder. But the courtesy did not make up for his coldness in drawing her attention to the fact that they would be making the same journey to London, and that they would be making it quite separately.

Kay had encountered blustering and hectoring and bullying in some of the males she had worked and played with. She had never been on the receiving end of such unruffled, clinical arrogance.

'Thank you for lunch,' she said, matching his cool. 'And for giving me the chance to make amen . . . to talk to Balbinder.'

He gave a brief nod of acknowledgement.

Looking at his hawkish features she had to admit to finding him undisputably fascinating. She recalled that Fi maintained it was always the bastards who played havoc with your better judgement.

She swiftly reminded herself that fleeting sexual attraction was of supreme irrelevance in this situation. She reminded herself also of the reason behind her search to find her donor's family. Of the chilling dream that had taken such a strong hold on her imagination.

As Majid prepared to bid her a polite and cool farewell, she placed her fingers on his arm. 'Majid,' she said, 'how was Parvinder killed?'

The muscles around his mouth tightened. 'She was in a car accident. I'm sure you had already found that out.'

'Was she alone in the car?'

His features froze. 'Yes.'

'There was no one else involved in the

accident? No other car? No pedestrian?'

'No.' He looked at her with disdain. 'If you'll excuse me now, I must go back to the hospital.'

She tightened her fingers around his arm. 'Please listen. Since the transplant operation I've been having a recurring dream. I dream that the donor of my heart was murdered. I've tried to ignore it, to forget it. But the image keeps coming.' She braced herself, waiting for the inevitable crushing words of outrage and disbelief. He remained silent, his face impassive, his body tensed and stiff.

'Majid,' she insisted, 'I truly believe Parvinder was murdered. I have to find out. I have to do something about it.' She held her breath, waiting for his retaliation, as though she had hurled a weapon at him.

He withdrew his arm from her grasp and gave her a long steady look. 'Then bring me the evidence,' he said quietly.

16

Kay went to the local library and read up accounts of recent murder trials in the national press. She studied extracts from police reports on the conducting of murder enquiries. She bought a stack of recently published crime novels and skimmed rapidly through them, picking up clues on investigative techniques.

She discovered little that she had not already been aware of; that most murders are committed by someone close to the victim, that detectives start from the core and work outwards in their investigations, interviewing first family, then friends, then work colleagues. That in all murder enquiries the first forty-eight hours are the most crucial, whilst the memories of witnesses are still fresh.

'Maybe you're looking at things from the wrong angle,' Fiona suggested, glancing across the table at Kay, noticing the dark shadows under her eyes.

Kay was forking up chunks of tinned tuna spiced with Mexican salsa. An odd combination, but all she could find in the cupboard when Fi had called in. She looked up. 'Go on.'

'Maybe you need to be looking more closely at this dream that's been troubling you. After all it was the dream that started everything off. If it hadn't been for the dream, you probably wouldn't have bothered to go any further than writing to your donor's family and then simply calling it a day. The key must be in the dream. Yes?'

Kay laid down her fork. 'Yes,' she said slowly. 'Yes! So what next?'

'You need to find out if there are other transplant recipients who've shared your experience of disturbing dreams. Maybe there's some crazy psychologist or other weirdo who's made a study of this kind of thing.'

Kay felt an electric surge of excitement! 'Of course. Why the hell didn't I think of it before?' Her mind began to bound through possibilities. 'Fiona, you're a marvel.'

Fiona smiled. 'Glad to be of help.' She made a swift movement and pushed her plate away, clasping her hand over her stomach.

'Are you all right?' Kay asked.

'Just this wretched nausea.' She took a long sip of water. 'I'll be OK.'

'Have you decided anything yet?' Kay wondered hesitantly.

'Have I hell? I fooled myself I could be neutral. I told myself I could deal with this in a calm, adult manner, that a modern woman has a 'choice'. Absolute rubbish. One tiny biological event means my life will never be the same again.' She let out a sigh of furious frustration.

'It's like this. If I go ahead and have this baby, I could lose Hugo. I'd have to rely on my mother helping me out — God forbid. I'd have to go to work and have a daytime life of drudgery and then come home to a screaming baby and mind-numbing baby babble. Hell on wheels.'

Kay saw the pain and panic rise into Fiona's eyes. 'Oh, Fi!'

'For heaven's sake let's not talk about it. I'd just like to forget about it for a few minutes.' She picked up her fork once more with an air of determination. Kay pushed her own plate away. Her face wrinkled into a frown of concentration. 'Do you remember that mad composer Orlando Bird who wrote a solo cello sonata a couple of years ago? I played it once at a concert.'

Fi glanced up. 'Oh yes! A real latter-day hippie. Now he is weirdness personified.'

'Maybe. But it hasn't stopped him making himself the god of Classic FM and a mint of money with a disc he recorded of his latest, greatest work.'

'Oh, yeah, I know the one. Lots of echoing electronic keyboards. It's real mind-zapping, hypnotic, connecting-up-with-God stuff.'

'Fair description. Well he's deeply into the psychic and paranormal. I couldn't understand half of what he was on about when he came to congratulate me at the end of the concert.'

Fi's eyes twinkled. 'He could be just the person you need to speak to, he's bound to know someone who knows someone as Hugo would say.'

'Exactly.'

'How about it?'

'I'll phone him tonight.'

'Good,' said Fiona, grimacing at Kay's offer of a chocolate biscuit. 'I like people who can make quick decisions.'

'Fi,' said Kay sternly, 'You've got to make up your mind about this baby.'

'I have to exercise my modern woman's choice,' Fi said mockingly.

'Yes.'

'No. I have no choice.' She rested her chin on her hand, looking thoughtful. 'You'll be amazed to hear that I'm already totally enslaved to maternal feelings I never dreamed I possessed. I'm completely in love with this tiny being growing inside me.' She leaned forward. 'In fact I'm completely obsessed with the primitive, overwhelming desire for life.'

Kay felt a slow smile spread over her face. 'That's the best news I've heard for a long time,' she said.

★ ★ ★

Kay telephoned Peter. His response to hearing her name was friendly but guarded. Damn, thought Kay, once again bitterly regretting their meaningless grappling in bed shortly after her heart surgery.

'Don't worry about asking me how I am,' she told him. 'I'm incredibly hale and hearty!'

'Good! Great news!' She imagined his anxious expression, a wincing foreboding about what might be coming next.

'You remember I played one of Orlando Bird's pieces some time ago?' she said. 'I'd rather like to make contact with him, but he seems to have changed his phone number. Have you got the current one?'

'Yes, I think I have.' Peter's voice lightenened up several semi-tones now that they were on safely neutral ground. 'Are you sure you want to get in touch with him? I met up with him at a concert recently. He is quite crazy now.'

'That's no problem because I'd like to talk to him on rather crazy sorts of issues.'

Peter laughed. 'Hang on while I run through my address list.' Returning, he read out two phone numbers, together with the address of the composer's recently acquired country house which he described as being in the depths of East Anglia marooned on the edge of a sea of boggy reed beds.

'Now he's famous will I have to do battle with a ferocious secretary when I call him. Do you think I should write first?' Kay wondered.

'Just ring. He still works all on his own. There's just his smiley, roly-poly wife who makes fabulous chocolate cake and keeps his incense smouldering.'

'Ah, I'm getting the picture.'

'If you tell him you hear whispers from God when you play your cello and speak to him as though he were marginally more spiritually loaded than the Pope, he'll probably fit you in tomorrow.'

'Sounds like good advice.'

'And don't forget to mention his latest CD. It's in the Classic top ten this week.'

'How about if I tell him I've had a heart transplant and I'd like to talk to him about some of the feelings I've been having since.'

There was a pause. 'He'll probably send his classic 1959 Jaguar round pronto to collect you.'

It took Kay three hours to get from her London flat to Orlando Bird's house in the middle of nowhere. She booked a taxi to take her to the station, had a slow ride on a frequently stopping train, then hired another taxi to drive her between the low wind-torn hedges of a dead flat landscape which ended in a green sea of frail, waving reeds.

The driver of her taxi put on a whimsical expression as she paid him and looked towards the sprawling, ramshackle-looking house. 'Have a nice day,' he said, winking, then roared off up the rutted dirt track which could just about merit the description of a road.

The front door was half open. A voice called out, 'Enter,' in response to Kay's rattle on the huge brass knocker. As she moved through the doorway she left behind the sunshine of a late summer morning and stepped into the dim dusk usually associated with an unlit church. Peering into the gloom she saw the composer standing motionless, illuminated in a shaft of sunshine which streamed dustily from a thin window half-way up the staircase.

He was like a creature from another age, another world. His figure was long and emaciated, swathed in a huge purple shawl. His silver hair fell Jesus-like on to his shoulders.

Ralph would have dubbed him a cranky sixties hippie and steered well clear.

The composer breathed out a husky, barely audible, 'Welcome, welcome,' and shuffled ahead of her into a dim, low room where he lay back on a sofa.

Waving a long skeletal hand he indicated a bell on the piano. 'Ring that,' he told Kay. 'My wife will bring tea and cake.'

He stared up at the ceiling and began to tell Kay his life story. There was something about sharing his mother's labour pains as a child whilst she was giving birth to his sister. And how he always felt connected to nature when he was composing. 'Willow trees weeping into a dark pool,' he mused. 'I feel a real bond with willow trees.'

Kay wondered just what she had got herself into. She doubted if she would ever get a word in to seek Orlando's opinion on her own situation. She feared that the visit would have to be written off as no more than an interesting afternoon to put down to experience.

Mrs Bird came in with the tea and cakes. She was blonde and plump and businesslike.

She poured the tea and placed a cup in her

husband's outstretched hand as though he were a helpless invalid. Stroking the dome of his head she told him that she was about to collect the children from school and that she would not be long and she hoped he would be all right whilst she was gone. She smiled across at Kay. 'Don't let him talk too much,' she said. 'it makes him so tired.'

'She is my muse,' Orlando sighed as his wife left the room. 'She is Constanze to my Mozart.'

Kay felt her jaw drop. She had made a point of listening to Orlando's strange hypnotic music in preparation for the visit and she didn't think it was a patch on Mozart.

'I wanted to talk to you about my heart transplant,' said Kay.

'Ah, yes.' He folded his arms and closed his eyes. Seconds passed and Kay thought he was asleep.

'I've been having a recurring dream since the operation,' she said, wanting to speak her thoughts whether Orlando was listening or not. 'It's a very troubling dream and I feel that it's coming from the new heart I've been given. But everyone I talk to thinks that's a crazy idea and that I should pull myself together and simply put the dream down to drugs or post-surgery stress.'

Orlando's eyelids flickered. 'No one believes in anything any more,' he lamented. 'They don't believe in God, or in music. Everything must have an intellectual explanation.' He shuddered. 'People no longer look up to the sky in order to glimpse paradise.'

He talked on; developing these themes, playing with his ideas and offering them up in an endless variety of forms. Well, he is a composer, thought Kay.

'I wondered if you had any thoughts on whether a heart can carry ideas, thoughts that can transfer from one human being to another?' she asked bluntly when there was a gap. 'Or if you know of anyone who has made some kind of study on it.'

The question seemed mundane enough to be embarrassing, like asking him for his wife's chocolate cake recipe. It was hard to imagine that Orlando Bird was even aware of other members of the human race, let alone tuned in to their thoughts and imaginings.

'The heart is the fountain spring of all love,' he informed the ceiling. 'But life in the new millenium is heartless. Everyone is so hectic that we forget to hear the songs that come from our heart. Music must always come from the heart. And from God.' He took in a long, deep breath and waved his hand towards the hi-fi equipment. 'Press the button under the red light,' he told Kay.

Music issued into the room. Treacly, soulful, hypnotic music, based around just three notes. Kay, who loved the precision of Haydn, Bach and Mozart, tried to resist the soporific qualities of this offering from twenty-first century Bird. But the seduction was powerful. She felt her body relax, her muscles become heavy, the beat of her heart slow down to meet the languid insistent rhythm.

At the close of the piece she glanced across at Bird who lay with his eyes closed, an expression of beatific contentment on his face. 'There is no more to be said,' he told her. 'You may go now.'

* * *

'Did you get anywhere?' Peter asked when she telephoned him that evening.

'I think I was meant to get on a direct line to paradise, but I didn't quite make it.'

'No useful information then?'

'Zilch. But I did have an interesting time.'

'He's rumoured to have made a million out of *Willows Weeping*.'

'God,' exclaimed Kay. 'Obviously he's hypnotized half the population of Britain.'

* * *

A miserable, apathetic day followed during which Kay found herself trapped in inactivity and indecision.

Ralph phoned in the morning to say that he was going to take his new lady up to Scotland for a golfing holiday, that he was really sorry to have been neglecting Kay, that he was even more sorry his two favourite women still hadn't managed to meet.

'Enjoy yourselves,' Kay told him. 'Don't even think of feeling worried on my behalf. I need to think about getting myself ready for the Autumn term. New students, new start . . . '

In fact she did very little besides lie on the sofa watching cringingly bad 1950s movies and feeling uncharacteristically sorry for herself.

The stress of the past few days, of meeting Parvinder's family and weathering Majid's cool scorn, eventually caught up with her and she fell into a deep sleep, to be wakened around nine-thirty in the evening by the warble of the phone.

'May I speak with Kay please?' a bright female voice demanded.

'You already are.'

'This is Mrs Bird.'

Bird? Bird?

'Mrs Orlando Bird. My husband was

talking to me about you after your visit. You have had a bad time of it. You poor thing.'

Kay struggled into a sitting position, picturing the cosy, bossy wife of the eccentric composer. 'But I'm feeling much better now.'

'That's good. Now take my advice. Don't underestimate the value of good wholesome food and plenty of sleep. There are no better ways of coping with life's problems. Now then, my husband has asked me to give you the name of someone you might like to speak to. A good friend of his.'

'Really!'

'Do you want to get a pen?'

'I've got one.'

'The name is Dr Daniel Weiner. That's spelled W E I N E R. He's over here from the States. He's staying at the Dorchester hotel. Do you have that number?'

'I can look it up.'

'Yes, of course. Well, Dr Weiner is giving some lectures. He's giving a talk in London tomorrow and then he's going to Birmingham and Manchester and Edinburgh and so on.'

Kay found herself coming fully awake. 'What's he lecturing on?'

'The Symphony of the Cells.'

'I'm sorry?'

'That's the title of his lecture. Shall I spell

it for you? S Y M — '

'No, I understand now. Cells as in body cells, symphony as in musical composition for full orchestra.'

'That's right.'

'Is Dr Weiner a composer?' Kay asked.

'No, no, no. He's a professor of psychiatry.'

'Oh!'

'You really should go along to his lecture. He's a simply intriguing man. Wonderful speaker. You're bound to learn something fascinating.'

17

The venue of Dr Daniel Weiner's lecture turned out to be the faded ballroom of an Edwardian hotel in north London. Rows of incongruous-looking black plastic chairs stretched between the red flocked walls and gilded pillars. The room was rapidly filling with people.

Kay and Fiona sat five rows back from the stage on which Dr Weiner was soon to appear. Red velvet curtains were looped back framing a large screen on which the words Symphony of the Cells shimmered in glowing blue letters against a dark, star-spangled background.

'Looks like there's going to be a good turnout,' said Fiona. 'Your man must have a cult following.'

Kay scanned the audience, searching for anyone she might recognize; perhaps one of the many medics and paramedics she had come into contact with in the past few months. Or maybe the strangely matched Birds. So far there was not a familiar face in sight.

There was a ripple of anticipation as a

small, dark-haired man in black jeans and a sunshine-yellow shirt strode on to the platform, moved the centrally placed microphone to one side, and without further preamble began to speak.

Kay rapidly found herself fascinated by the monkey-faced Dr Weiner, lulled into security by his low drawling voice, mesmerized by the message he sought to convey.

He turned and gestured to the glinting screen. 'All living things are made of cells,' he said to his audience, speaking so quietly, so intimately, that people had to strain to hear him. 'And cells generate energy, they record information, they store up memories. For me the reverberation of energy in the cells of our bodies is a kind of music. The cells are like a million infinitesimal bells chiming out a harmonic celebration of life. A truly universal symphony.'

Fi gave a sigh. 'Oh dear.'

Weiner went on to explain to the audience that he had begun his career by studying biology and chemistry. He then completed a medical training and worked as a physician in a big urban hospital. He was drawn to the human aspect of his work and embarked on a training in psychotherapy. Whilst in his mid-forties he became suddenly ill. His heart began to fail.

'When I learned that my only hope for survival was a transplant, I was filled with horror and fear,' he told the audience. 'I was put on a waiting list for a transplant, but the likelihood of a suitable organ becoming available was tiny. I began to sink into a black, voidless despair and my only thoughts were of dying. I know that any of you here who have undergone a life-threatening illness will recognize those feelings.'

Kay stared at the speaker, fascinated. Yes, Oh, yes!

'It was at that point,' continued Weiner, 'that I began to listen to my heart instead of constantly going over the anguished debate in my brain. I became intensely aware of the strength I was able to draw from the doctors who cared for me, from my friends and my wife and children. If I focused on their humanity and on the feelings and energy flowing from their hearts to warm and help me, then I began to believe that in some way I would survive my illness, even though all the odds were stacked against me.'

The man beside Kay began to drum his feet on the floor. His face tightened, from his lips came murmured words of disbelief and derision.

No, thought Kay. We shouldn't hold out against this. We should listen and go with it.

'As a scientist,' explained Weiner, 'I used to be focused on obtaining evidence, on clearly definable, measurable phenomena. But once I became a transplant survivor I found myself seeing things differently. I began to search for the essential spirituality at the core of all our lives.'

The man beside Kay gave a loud sigh. She shot him a warning glance.

Weiner was still speaking. 'For me the heart is not simply a piece of splendid biological machinery, it is the mainspring of life energy which reverberates through every cell of our bodies and gives each one of us our essential individuality. For me the heart is quite simply the carrier of the human soul.'

A ripple went through the audience, a mingle of awed expectancy and hissing disbelief.

'Bollocks!' exclaimed Kay's neighbour.

Dr Weiner held up his hands. 'Please, don't make a judgement yet. I'm going to stop speaking now and let the facts speak for themselves. You are going to hear the remarkable stories of three transplant recipients. What you hear will astonish you. And afterwards I shall invite you to share your reactions with me. Challenge me with any questions that spring to mind.'

'You bet,' muttered the man next to Kay.

A woman from the front row climbed the stairs to the platform. Kay guessed her to be around thirty-five years old. She was wearing a bright yellow suit and black stiletto heels. She cleared her throat nervously before she began to speak.

'I had a heart transplant two years ago. After the operation, once I got well again, I began to notice changes in myself. My doctor knew about Dr Weiner and his research with heart transplant patients and suggested I go to see him. None of the other doctors and therapists I'd talked to seemed to believe what I told them, but Dr Weiner listened to me and helped me understand what had happened to me. He asked me to come and talk to you tonight so I could help other transplant patients to understand some of the strange things that can happen to *them*.'

Fi leaned across to Kay. 'He's been coaching her. Looks like this is a Weiner promotion exercise.'

'Ssh!'

'My husband and I had always been happy together,' the woman continued, 'although I'd never been very interested in sex. Gradually I started to want to make love as often as possible. I started to watch blue videos which I'd always disapproved of before. I got much more adventurous in my lovemaking. My husband couldn't work out what was happening.' Suddenly she smiled. 'He said he'd married an apple-pie girl and ended up with a siren.'

'Lucky man!' murmured Kay's neighbour.

'One night when we were in bed together, my husband started teasing me about my new sex drive. He told me I must have been given the heart of a tart.' There was a shocked silence. She cleared her throat again. 'I was very angry, and very troubled. Then I started to think hard about what he'd said and I realized I had to find out about my donor. I discovered that she was a beautiful girl who worked in a high class escort service. Gradually it came to me that my new feelings must have come from the new heart inside me. The memories from the cells in my donor's heart were speaking to me, showing me a new way of living. I feel I was really lucky to get such a lovely, warm, sexy heart. And now my life is so good, so much better than it has ever been before.'

The woman bowed her head, suddenly overcome with emotion. Dr Weiner stood close to her and put an arm around her shoulders. A man in the audience walked up on to the platform and gently led her back to her seat.

'The shagged-out husband, I presume,' Fi whispered to Kay.

'Don't!' Kay exclaimed fiercely. 'Don't joke.'

Now a man in jeans and a crumpled jacket climbed on to the platform. He was in his forties, a big, lumbering figure. He looked ill at ease, embarrassed.

'My transplant was four years ago.' He stopped. He was nervous, twisting his hands together. Dr Weiner smiled at him in reassurance.

'I was so ill before the operation,' he went on shakily. 'I was dying. Afterwards I felt as if I'd been caught in a hurricane. I felt this surge of new strength come roaring through me as though I were young all over again. I started having dreams that I was driving this high-powered sports car, racing down an empty motorway. Later I found out my donor was a student who crashed his father's Mercedes into a road bridge.' He paused to allow the information to sink in. 'I didn't use to believe in all that stuff about connecting up with the new heart inside you. I used to say, leave all that to the head shrinkers. But now — I know that it's true. You can't have a new heart put inside you without getting something of the person who had it before.'

'Yes,' whispered Kay, 'Oh yes!'

There was an excited buzz from the audience now. A good deal of shuffling and head bobbing. But nobody moved from their seat.

A second woman walked on to the platform. She was around forty, dressed simply in navy trousers and a white shirt. She stood for a while in silence. 'My daughter Amy had a heart transplant when she was eight,' she said eventually, speaking so softly that Kay found herself leaning forward in an effort to hear her better.

'Amy was given the heart of a girl the same age.' The woman stopped, pressing her fingers against her temples.

'Do you want to go on with this?' Weiner interposed gently.

She considered, nodded, straightened up. 'After the transplant operation Amy started to scream in her sleep. She told me that she kept dreaming about a man who was murdering a girl. The little girl who had given Amy her heart.'

The next pause was longer. Weiner got up and offered the woman a glass of water. She waved it away, turning again to face the audience. 'The donor's family were willing to meet me and I asked them how Amy's donor had died. They thought it had been a tragic accident, so I put Amy's disturbances down to all the dreadful experiences she had gone through during her illness. After a while I got so worried I took her to a child psychologist. Amy told the psychologist that she wanted to go to the police to help them catch the murderer. She said she knew what the murderer looked like. When a man walked into the police station and confessed to attacking the child he fitted Amy's description.'

A collective sigh reverberated through the audience.

'Amy described the man's face, the clothes he was wearing,' said the mother. 'I know it sounds impossible and bizarre, but it's true. And everything Amy reported was found to be accurate.' She looked up, scanning over the audience. 'Thank you for hearing me out,' she said. 'I'd like to tell you one last thing and that is that Amy is still alive, and the most precious gift God ever gave to me.'

Kay felt a tremor shoot through her body like an arrow of ice. Deep within her was a chime of resounding acceptance of the woman's words. And yet, how could it be true? Her surgeon had told her that transplant organs were never taken from murder victims because of the need for an autopsy. But maybe the circumstances had been very unusual, maybe the death looked like an accident at first, maybe it had happened in another country where the laws were different . . .

She let out a low groan, torn with the need to be rational and the urgent, irresistible desire to believe what she had just heard.

Fiona shot her a worried glance. 'You OK?' she murmured as the woman returned to her seat and the audience sat in tense, shocked silence.

The man sitting next to Kay suddenly sprang up, hardly able to contain himself. 'Dr Weiner, my name is Roach. I'm a cardiologist in one of the London transplant units with years of experience of transplant surgery and its attendant traumas and I can tell you that none of my patients have reported the dramatic psychological changes your patients describe. You've given us a very entertaining road show tonight but I must question your professionalism in bringing transplant patients here to tell their stories in public — and most of all I must take issue with you on certain scientific points.'

'Sit down!' shouted a woman three rows forward, squirming round and glaring at the speaker.

'No, no. Please continue,' Dr Weiner invited, leaning forward towards the speaker.

'What we have heard is very moving, very

persuasive. But that could be said of all human stories,' Roach observed. 'I doubt if you have provided us with any hard evidence. Where are your controlled or double blind studies? Where is your scientific proof that what we have heard tonight is nothing more than the emotional outpouring of people in a delicate psychological state following major surgery? No more than a lingering symptom of their illness or a side effect of the medication they have been prescribed?'

There was a ripple of applause, and loud opposing hisses of disapproval.

Weiner stood up, smiling patiently. 'Dr Roach, I too am a scientist. My scientific brain constantly asks me how I can be certain that the objections you so rightly raise are not valid. Maybe after lengthy research we will indeed find that the heart is nothing more than a beautifully designed pump, as I'm sure will be your current view.'

Roach inclined his head in acknowledgement. 'So you're not able to counter my objections.'

'I would not be here,' Dr Weiner said gently, 'if my heart didn't constantly remind me that it is filled with wonderful mysteries, a repository of memories resounding through every cell in my body. I would not be here if I were not convinced that the heart has a secret language all of its own, a language which the ancient healers have always known about — and which science may soon be on the verge of cracking.'

There was an expectant pause.

Roach smiled around at the audience with an air of triumphant disbelief. 'I rest my case,' he said sitting down.

A woman in nurse's uniform stood up. 'I find your comments about the heart being the carrier of the soul incredible. And also highly dangerous. If the national press got hold of the idea that one person's 'soul stuff' can go along with a transplanted organ into someone else's body, they'd have a field day. Some patients waiting for an organ might cry off, believing they would be a changed person when they came round from surgery. Other people might decide to donate their organs so as to gain a kind of immortality through cellular memory.'

Again Weiner smiled unperturbed. 'There is always a critical shortage of organs,' he countered softly. 'The increase of willing donors would be a resoundingly good thing, whatever the motivation of the donor.'

'Carry the card!' someone shouted.

The nurse stood her ground. 'I can tell you this, if I were a patient waiting for a transplant I'd be scared to death if I thought I was going to be invaded by another person's soul. And I suggest you would have been too, Dr Weiner, if professionals had been foolish enough to be talking about this kind of thing before you had your transplant.'

More shouts of approval.

'And what about the use of animal organs?' the nurse demanded. 'We now have the distinct possibility of pigs' hearts being used in human transplants.'

Weiner nodded agreement.

'So,' she continued, 'if a patient is told he's going to get a porcine heart, should he be worried that he might suddenly grow a curly tail and start grunting?'

There was uproar.

Dr Weiner raised his hands in an appeal for calm. 'He need not be worried. There is far more to a pig than its grunting and its curly tail. Don't forget we humans are already a part of the life-energy system shared by animals. We are a part of their cellular memories and they are a part of ours.'

'Absolute bunkum,' someone shouted from the back. Turning, Kay saw a scuffle break out near the caller. One man was struck in the face. Blood trickled from his nose.

Weiner appealed once again for calm. But the audience's attention was shattered. The seminar dissolved into disarray.

'Well!' said Fiona, as she and Kay pushed through the jostling crowd in the hotel lobby. 'What did you make of all that?'

'Astonishing. Incredible. Fantastic!' Kay was still transfixed from hearing the account of Amy's dream. The mother's low, intense voice echoed in her head.

'He's a crank,' said Fiona. 'A charming, persuasive crank.'

'Maybe.'

'Do you really believe his theories about cells having memories and the heart having a language?' Fiona asked.

'I don't know. All I can say is what he said makes everything I've experienced since the transplant fit into place.'

'Yes,' Fiona said thoughtfully, 'but is it evidence?' she demanded, as they emerged on to the pavement.

'No,' Kay agreed regretfully. She imagined Majid's response if she should present him with the personal stories they had listened to that evening. He would counter with all the points raised by Dr Roach. He would probably mention the issue of false memory syndrome and the unreliability of unsubstantiated personal accounts.

She knew that what she had heard this evening would hold no sway at all with Majid.

But it had been a crucial milestone for her.

It had given her the determination and courage to approach him and ask for the help she needed to further her search for Parvinder's murderer. Because she now knew without a doubt that it was murder that had marked the end of her donor's life.

18

Kay dialled the contact number on the card Majid had given her, then steeled herself.

There was mingled disappointment and relief to be answered by his recorded voice on a machine. The message was predictably brief and remote. She responded in kind, leaving just her name and number.

To her surprise he called back within the hour. She sat down with the phone in her hand and breathed deeply. To her greater surprise he said, 'I would prefer not to talk over the phone. I think we should meet.'

Her heart gave a little buck. 'Well, yes. When were you thinking of?'

'This evening.'

With any other man, asking in any other way, she would have interpreted it as a date. With Majid, it sounded like a summons for a reprimand.

And yet she felt enlivened, excited. He was a member of her heart family. He was important to her. She would get to like him. And he would like her. 'All right,' she said. 'Where?'

'I'll pick you up at your flat. Seven-fifteen.'

'Should I be casually dressed — or formal?' she enquired with faint irony.

There was a pause. 'Black tie,' he said.

He put the phone down, and Kay went to rifle through her wardrobe.

★ ★ ★

His BMW parked outside her house one minute before the agreed time. Kay admired the sheen of his black hair as he walked to the front door.

He clasped her hand between firm fingers. 'Hello,' he said.

She saw him scanning her room, his eyes swiftly assessing it, maybe trying to gain clues about Kay who had planned and arranged it. She saw his eyes rest for a few moments on the cello case before returning to her face.

As he took in her freshly washed hair and simple blue silk dress she felt a thin line of moisture break out on her forehead. 'Are you ready to go?' he asked.

'Yes.' She took up her bag and followed him to his car into which he ushered her with grave courtesy.

'Where are we going?' she asked after they had been driving for a few minutes in silence.

'To the birthday party of one of my legal colleagues.'

'You should have told me, I would have bought a present,' she said drily, realizing that beneath the correct and remote exterior he was the sort of man who had the capacity to surprise you more than most.

'There's no need, Kay. I brought some flowers on your behalf.'

She turned to look in the back of the car and saw a huge bouquet of bronze tiger-lilies wrapped in crackly cellophane. Well, well!

She watched his face in profile as he drove; the sharp cut of his bones, the steadiness of his dark brown eyes. She recalled the way he had said her name. It suddenly occurred to her that it had been a long time since she had felt truly happy. Sitting beside Majid in the softly pulsing car, looking out on to the streets of London glowing dustily in the evening sun, it was as though the gloom she had been staring into for so long had gently lifted, allowing her to see a brighter vision, a new future. A sensation of hope grasped at her.

'There are things I want to say,' she told him.

'Yes. And I do as well. Mainly to tell you that I'm sorry for my behaviour at our meetings in Bradford.'

'In the circumstances I think you behaved pretty commendably,' she told him.

'Balbinder tells me that I am cold.'

'She spoke very warmly about you to me.'

'She's a very forgiving woman.' He sounded pleased. He turned his head slightly and Kay caught his eye for a moment.

'Majid, I want you to tell me about Parvinder.'

He nodded. 'I knew you would ask me to do that.'

'I'm talking about her as a person.'

'Yes, I understand. That is part of the reason I invited you tonight. I can talk to you whilst I'm driving. I can tell you things I couldn't bring myself to say if we were sitting in a room facing each other.'

As they turned on to the M40 and left the city behind Majid began to tell Kay about his early life in Bradford and his father's vision for the future of Asian families within a British culture. He described the uneasy disparity between his father and his uncle Javed and the unhappy circumstances of Kulvinder's entry into the family.

'My uncle Javed was determined that his daughters would be brought up as devout Muslim girls. They were to be totally subservient to the wishes of their parents, they were not to mix with British girls, they were to leave school at the earliest opportunity and agree to the marriages which had been arranged for both of them with young men still living in Pakistan.

'When Mudassar was born, Javed made it very clear to the girls that they were of no interest or importance beside this much longed for son. For Javed the girls were regarded as little more than servants, whereas Mudassar had come straight from Allah, trailing divine glory. Mudassar embodied all Javed's hopes for the future. Nothing was too good for Mudassar, Mudassar could do no wrong.' Majid's tone had become quite heated. He checked himself and was silent for a moment. 'In fact he's a boy with little natural talent who's grown up to be arrogant, lazy and boorish.'

'There are plenty of English boys who get spoiled to bits and grow up very much the same,' Kay observed with a wry smile. 'Even now.'

Majid did not challenge this.

Kay reflected on what he had told her, trying to imagine Parvinder and Balbinder as they grew up. 'Was it the same for you in your own family?' she asked. 'Were you made to feel special?'

'Very much so. But my father was much more socially and politically aware than Javed, and he was prepared to be flexible. Whilst he treated me as the future head of the family, he managed to subdue his traditional Asian instincts and at least allow my sister to make friends with British girls he considered suitable.'

'But not with boys?'

'That was absolutely forbidden.'

'And no drugs, drink, smoking, free love.'

'Most certainly not.'

'What does your sister do now?'

'She's the wife of a rich Asian businessman. I believe she's perfectly happy. Some women manage to combine an outward acceptance of Asian docility with an inner western-style ambition that gives them a degree of freedom.'

'But Parvinder?'

'Parvinder wanted total freedom. The freedom that was so readily extended to her brother. The freedom that all the Yorkshire girls around her took for granted. She rejected all of the values of Javed and Kulvinder. And she was fearless. The threats and beatings Javed handed out to her as she began to grow up did nothing to alter her views or behaviour, they simply made her angry. He never managed to cow her. The two of them became locked in a battle of wills. The more he struck her, the longer he locked her in her room, the more determined she became to follow her own ideas. She used to shout at him that she would never submit to his demands, never bow to his will. And she never did, because Parvinder had an even greater will of her own.'

Instinctively Kay placed a hand over her heart. She pictured Parvinder as a girl of twelve or thirteen; beaten, shut away, maybe starved. Majid's words were calm and measured, but Kay knew that he was telling her about cruel and shocking violence.

'What about Balbinder?'

'Balbinder was rather like my sister. She saw all the injustices of our traditional system for women, but she found her own way to deal with it. Whereas Parvinder rebelled and defied, Balbinder used diplomacy and feminine charm to get to the place she wanted to be. And like my sister, she has found a good Asian man who values her and wants to care for her.'

'That's what she truly wants?'

'Yes, I honestly believe so. She's soon to be married to the man who owns the chain of shops in which she works.'

'Marrying the boss!' Kay smiled. 'That's always been a good move, whatever your creed or culture. Or your sex, for that matter.'

Majid looked grave.

'Tell me more about Parvinder,' she urged gently.

'When she was fourteen the staff at her school requested the medical officer to investigate bruising on her face. Javed had been careless — normally he only beat her on her legs and body. No one had found out because both Parvinder and Balbinder were excused from physical sports on religious grounds. The doctor, of course, discovered extensive bruising and cuts during the examination. This doctor was a courageous woman. She went round to the house and told Javed and Kulvinder that she had reported Parvinder's injuries to a Social Services officer. You can imagine the scenes that followed. Javed was outraged at what he considered the interference of a decadent society. And when Parvinder was taken away to live in a children's home his main concern was the shame that would be reflected on Mudassar.'

'What happened to Parvinder after that?'

'She went to a foster home for a while. It was not a happy time for her.' He paused. 'After a year she was returned to her own home. The beatings started again, but Javed was careful not to leave marks which could be publicly seen. Around the time she was about to leave school he booked her on a flight for Pakistan to marry the man he had paid out a substantial dowry to. Parvinder flatly refused to go; she went out and got herself a job in the kitchens of one of the big hotels in Bradford. When Javed threatened her with a knife one night, she wrenched it from him and turned the point on his throat. Naturally gossip soon reached Pakistan and the would-be husband pulled out of the marriage contract. A few months later Javed had a stroke and died instantly. Kulvinder and Mudassar openly blamed his death on Parvinder and made it known that they were going to cast her out of the family. Their words, not mine.'

Majid's face became grim. He changed down a gear, moved out into the fast lane and surged past the line of traffic that had built up in front.

'Mudassar had other words for her too. Immoral. Wicked. A slag. A western whore. He never attended much to his teachers at school but he certainly picked up the vernacular of his peers. There were times I could have killed him when he started his shouting.'

Kay glanced at the speedometer. They were doing over a hundred miles an hour. She sat quiet and calm, waiting for Majid to continue.

'Casting Parvinder out was something of a joke,' he observed. 'She had already moved into a flat with two other girls and was struggling to live independently.'

'God. How awful for her. For all of them.' Kay exclaimed.

'Yes.'

Kay glanced at him. She had imagined this evening as difficult and awkward. She had steeled herself to pump Majid for information, probably failing miserably. She had expected him to be cold and withdrawn. She had determined to try not to dislike him.

She reflected that reality was always different from projected imaginings. Sometimes completely so.

'Were you in love with her?' she asked. 'Were you in love with Parvinder?'

'She was much younger than me,' he said. He shot Kay a swift glance, creating a fresh tug of connection between them.

I'll take that as a yes, Kay thought.

'I want to know about *you*,' he said. 'Are you married?'

'No!' The bluntness of the question made her fizz with a curious adolescent excitement. 'Are you?'

'No. I'm a dry old bachelor.'

Heavens! thought Kay. He's even got a sense of humour.

'So,' he said crisply, changing the mood, 'when we last spoke you told me of your belief that Parvinder was murdered. Have you brought me any evidence?'

'No.'

'I thought not.'

Kay flushed. 'I can't forget about it, Majid. I can't just let the issue drop. I know my dream meant something. I know in my bones that something terrible happened to Parvinder. She bequeathed me the most precious gift anyone can give and I owe it to her to do all I can to learn the truth about the way she died.'

'You speak like a character in a TV soap opera.'

'Yes. OK, fine. And if I tell you how I was swayed by a lecture I went to earlier this week you'll think I'm not only gullible but crackers.'

'Tell me!'

'Oh God. I don't think I can.'

'Tell me!'

He listened blank-faced. When she had finished he was silent for a time. 'So you're trying to say that you believe the memories in the cells of Parvinder's heart have transferred to your own memory system and they're telling you that she was murdered.'

'Yes.'

'Surely the brain is the carrier of thoughts and images. Not the heart?'

'Yes. But the brain is not the sole carrier. Weiner believes that every cell in our body resonates with psychological energy.'

'Before Columbus scientists and geographical experts believed the world was flat.'

Kay sighed.

'You're talking of belief not fact,' Majid countered patiently. 'Of supposition, not evidence.'

'I know that. Of course I know that. I'm an educated person. I'm not stupid.'

'For you the belief is as powerful and convincing as any clear, measurable piece of forensic evidence?'

'Yes, it is.' She felt mulish and thwarted. She looked out of the window at the lush, green landscape. They had left the motorway and were travelling along a winding road with no room for overtaking. 'How long until we arrive at the party?'

'Another ten minutes.'

'Will you help me with this, Majid?'

He tapped his fingers on the wheel. 'If I can.'

'Will you at least tell me about the family Parvinder was staying with when she had her accident?'

He did not answer immediately. 'Most probably. After all you could no doubt find out yourself if you were tenacious enough.

Why should I withhold information of that kind?'

'I want to feel that you're helping me.' she exclaimed, horrified at the desperate tone in her voice.

He wrenched the wheel of the car and turned into the opening of an ungated field. He hauled on the brake and switched off the car's engine. He faced her square on.

'Kay, when you told me your suspicions of murder, I felt sick. Physically sick. I deal with accounts of violent crime every week of the year. But when I thought of Parvinder as a murder victim I felt my insides revolt.'

'Yes. I'm sorry.'

'You struck me as a sensible woman. Intelligent, reasonable, not malicious. I found it incredible that you could suggest such a thing.'

'Yes.'

'And then I began to think things through. I assumed that you would be well aware that most murders are committed by family members or friends. I guessed that you would be well aware of the jealousies and rivalries in Asian families, the potential for violence. It occurred to me also that you might have read a recent report in the press on the trial of an Asian mother who enlisted the help of her son to murder the daughter who had become pregnant.'

'No. Oh God!' exclaimed Kay appalled. 'I never thought — '

'You're treading in dangerous waters, Kay.'

'I accept that. And water is a strong element in my dream,' Kay told him. 'For weeks I believed Parvinder was drowned in a diving accident.'

A muscle flickered in Majid's jaw.

'Did she dive?' Kay demanded.

'Yes, she was learning scuba diving — amongst a number of other things. She was making herself as independent and western as possible. She was playing sports, running her own business organizing luxury parties, driving a fast car, enjoying herself with a rich, upper-class English boyfriend. She openly renounced all Asian family traditions and all ties with the Muslim faith. But she died in a car accident Kay. And Kulvinder and Mudassar were miles away in Bradford at the time.'

'I never suspected them.'

'Yes, you did.'

'All right. I thought about it. But then I rejected the thought.'

'Why?'

'Because I didn't want to believe it.' She stared down at her ringless hands. 'Because I wanted to love your family, not doubt them.'

He looked at her for a few moments and Kay was swamped with feeling. She was both elated and scared. She was filled with thoughts of Parvinder's murder, but through them filtered entirely different ideas of life and love. She knew she could have an affair with Majid, she was sure of it. A piercing, roller-coaster of an affair. Crushing, burning, liquefying sex. If he asked her to let him make love to her here in the car she would have no choice but to say yes, she was so attracted to him. But with Majid it wouldn't be just a roll in bed as it had been with Peter. It wouldn't be just a friendship with sex thrown in like it had been with Luke. It would be a real connection, a relationship. They would talk over each other's past, dig up old wounds, share the grief of loss. With Majid she could lose her loneliness and rediscover the old Kay. With Majid she could reconcile the loss of Kay's heart and the final acceptance of the heart that had once belonged to Parvinder.

She sat very quiet and still as the thoughts surged through her mind in a tiny second of revelation.

Majid reached for the ignition key. He turned to Kay. 'You're very pale,' he said. 'Do you feel well enough to go on? Would you prefer to go back to London?'

Damn you, she thought. 'No! I'm perfectly well. I'm looking forward to this party. I've hardly had any social life at all since the operation.'

He fired the engine and eased the car over the deep ruts of dried mud at the edge of the field and back on to the road. 'You're angry. Was I patronizing you?'

She looked at him and saw that he was smiling.

'Yes. I was very offended.' She laughed and the tension in the car eased.

They drove through tall iron gates and along a drive lined with lime trees at the end of which sat a square Georgian-style mansion.

'Wow!' said Kay. 'Your colleague must have a little stash besides his lawyer's salary.'

'He's the grandson of a supermarket billionaire. He's no need to work at all,' Majid said, bringing the car to a halt and slipping off his seat belt. 'He's a rather unusual man.'

He opened the door for Kay and took her hand as she stepped out. As they set off towards the house, he said, 'The family Parvinder was staying with when she died are called Cavendish. I have the address at my flat. If you want it you're welcome to have it.'

He spoke evenly, with no emotion. Handing it to her just like that — the possible key to a calculated murder.

He kept hold of her hand, his fingers dry and cool, linked with hers. They walked slowly towards the house like a calm, established couple.

19

Guests were sipping drinks on the terrace in front of the house. Waiters skated among them offering replenishments. A string quartet played Haydn. As Kay and Majid approached, a tall man with longish, white-blond curls detached himself from the laughing guests and came forward to meet them.

'Majid!' He clasped an arm around Majid's shoulders. 'Welcome, welcome! I was beginning to think you'd got lost, or maybe got a better offer elsewhere!'

'I'm sorry we're a little late.' Majid was once again in charming but unfathomable mode. He placed his hand on Kay's back, bringing her forward in order to make introductions.

She vaguely registered the blond man's name as Theo Lacy but was more alert to Majid's having introduced her simply as his friend Kay. She liked that.

'I'm Majid's junior counsel,' Theo explained to Kay. 'I sit in court at his feet. I watch, listen, learn and marvel.'

'A model pupil,' Kay suggested, looking

into Theo's eyes and noticing that they were a very pale, very unusual duck-egg blue.

'I hope so.' Theo grinned at Majid, who predictably gave nothing away in response.

A waiter glided up and offered champagne. Majid took a glass for himself and orange juice for Kay.

Theo watched Kay as she took the glass from Majid's hand. 'Have you ever seen Majid in court?' he asked with a touch of roguish provocation.

'No.'

'Well I can tell you that he's quite a showman once the wig goes on and he starts cross-examining. And not a shred of fear about skating near the edge.' He glanced at his senior who gave the faintest of smiles.

'Skating near the edge?' Kay was interested.

Theo leaned forward, his eyes twinkling. 'We had a Pakistani man in the dock last week. He'd defrauded the Department of Social Security of some very serious money.'

'Alleged to have defrauded,' Majid broke in mildly.

'He'd definitely done it,' Theo told Kay. 'Which was bad luck for him because Majid was prosecuting counsel.'

Kay smiled. She was enjoying herself.

Theo put on the intense expression of a

practised storyteller who knows how to entertain his audience. 'This man had shown himself to be an excellent liar, in fact I was quite envious of his skill because the jury were completely taken in. Until Majid set about him.'

'Oh dear,' murmured Majid, looking resigned.

Theo leaned closer to Kay. 'He challenged the poor chap about his choice to swear on the Bible. He put it to him that if he had sworn on the Koran he might have told a different story. 'Are you a religious man?' he asked him. 'Do you go to prayers every Friday? Will you now swear on the Koran?'' Theo's imitation of Majid's beautifully enunciated English was frighteningly authentic. 'The poor chap went completely to pieces.'

'I can imagine,' Kay said with feeling.

'Majid got away with murder,' Theo concluded, glancing wickedly at his senior colleague. 'He was so outrageously un-PC it was not true. No Brit lawyer would have got away with that line of questioning.'

There was a short, tense pause.

Got away with murder, Kay thought in horror. And for one terrible moment she looked at Majid with suspicious eyes.

No, she told herself. No, no, no!

'I am British, Theo,' Majid said quietly. 'You meant to say no Caucasian lawyer, perhaps?'

'I stand corrected,' Theo was contrite but not dismayed. 'Sorry Majid.'

'What was the verdict?' asked Kay quickly.

Theo made a gesture of cutting his throat. 'A triumph of British justice.'

Majid was frowning. A glance shot between him and his pupil.

'Come and meet the crowd,' Theo commanded Kay, taking her hand and pulling her gently along with him.

As Kay had guessed from the ambience and setting of the party, the guests were all beautiful people. Theo drew them forward, naming them and describing their occupations.

They were lawyers and bankers and landowners. And the women were wives. They were all country people. Their leisurely conversation made London and grime and crime seem a million miles away.

'Do you ride to hounds?' Kay was asked. 'Do you play tennis; golf; bridge?'

She kept smiling, shaking her head. 'No blood sports,' she said. 'No tennis or golf. But I sometimes go running.'

Theo put his arm lightly around her shoulders. 'You and Majid must come to stay for a weekend. I'll find a lovely quiet hunter for you and we'll go for a hack through the stubble fields.'

'Will I be confronted with panic-stricken foxes?' Kay wanted to know. 'Maimed and bleeding pheasants or whatever?'

'Not a one. Not if you don't want.'

'I don't.' She looked around for Majid. He was talking with a group of svelte lovelies with Knightsbridge ankles, his dark head an exotic contrast to their English-rose fairness.

'We're lovers of animals down here in the country, not barbarians. We kill them cleanly and kindly,' Theo said. He followed her gaze. 'And Majid can fare for himself with the Tory babes.'

'Is this an important birthday?' Kay asked him.

'Entering the fourth decade.'

She nodded. 'I'm not quite there yet.' And last year I was scared witless that I never would be, she thought.

She looked back at the gracious, symmetrical house and saw a huge dog come trotting out of the front door and stand poised, looking around it, searching.

Theo put his fingers into his mouth and whistled. The dog threw up its massive shaggy head and bounded up to him, leaping up to place its paws on Theo's shoulders, covering his face with hot, loving licks.

Theo pushed the animal gently away. 'Down!' he said and the dog subsided into a low position at his feet, motionless as a sculpture.

'What breed is he?' Kay asked, conversant with little more than Labradors or terriers.

'An Irish wolfhound.'

'Does he go hunting with you?'

'No, no.' Theo smiled tolerantly. 'He's a pet. And also a trifle mad. But then he's Irish.'

Kay patted the dog's head. 'What's his name?'

'Pilot. Like Mr Rochester's dog in *Jane Eyre*.'

'Oh yes,' said Kay remembering. 'But I assume you haven't got a mad wife locked up in the attic?'

'Not a one,' Theo responded smiling. 'How did you meet Majid?' he asked.

'Through a friend of a friend,' Kay said, having anticipated the question.

'Have you known him long?'

Is this an inquisition, she wondered. 'No, not long.'

'He's a most remarkable man,' Theo said.

'Yes,' Kay agreed, 'it didn't take long at all to discover that.'

* * *

Dinner was held in the dining-room. It was a formal affair served on a huge Georgian mahogany table set with silver and crystal which glittered in the light of the candles blazing from four massive candelabras.

Waves of braying conversation flowed up and down the table. The stock market, the merits of holidaying in India against the Caribbean, fillies in foal, the ghastly decline of the exclusiveness of Ascot and Cowes.

'The English upper classes at play,' Kay murmured to Majid.

He nodded. 'If you can't beat them, join them.'

'Spoken like a true Yorkshireman,' she laughed.

After dinner there was a choice of entertainments. Relaxing in the heated pool, floodlit tennis, dancing in the library where the carpet had been rolled back and a disc jockey was playing hits from the seventies.

Majid and Kay opted for the drawing-room where guests lolled on sofas drinking coffee and helping themselves to the variety of whiskies and brandies on offer.

Theo had taken off his jacket and loosened his bow-tie. Having checked that his guests were well topped up with alcohol he was lounging comfortably, smoking a cigar and chatting to a pretty brunette girl who was giving him her undivided attention.

'Let's have a little entertainment,' he said, taking a silver lighter from his pocket and rolling it through his fingers with the deftness of a gambler in a 1940s black and white film.

He bent towards Pilot who was crouched at his feet, watching his master with an intensity of concentration easily matching that of the brunette.

'Hey, Pilot. Look at this, boy.' Theo accelerated the movement of his fingers slithering the lighter between them, making it wink with light.

The dog raised his huge head, his eyes tracking the movement of the lighter.

Theo gradually slowed the progress of the lighter, his fingers skilful and sinuous. As the dog's eyes followed the flash of silver, Theo talked to him softly. He was reciting from Shakespeare's *The Tempest*: 'we are such stuff as dreams are made on'. His voice was low and rhythmic. Mesmerizing.

Kay felt Majid shake her arm. 'Don't go to sleep, Kay. Wake up!'

She gave a start, opened her eyes, shamed to have been caught drowsing in public. 'I'm sorry. I still get tired . . . '

She looked towards Theo and felt her eyelids heavy once more. The room was warm and comforting. Everything was soft and dreamy.

The weight of her shoulder rested against Majid's. He pushed her away. 'Wake up!' he repeated sharply.

She was jolted into full alertness. Glancing around she saw that several of the guests had their eyes closed, their mouths open, their heads drooping like broken flower heads.

She glanced questioningly at Majid.

'Just stay awake,' he said.

Theo stopped reciting. He put the lighter back in his pocket. He pushed the dog gently with his hand and it rolled over on to its side as though it had been shot. He looked around the company, noting that almost half the guests were in a state of apparent semi-consciousness.

'What have you been up to, Theo?' one of the Knightsbridge-ankle babes asked.

'Mesmerism, Harriet,' he said to her, smiling.

'What?'

'Mesmer was the inventor of hypnosis,' Theo told her. 'He lived in Vienna around two hundred years ago. A great friend of the Mozarts actually.'

'Know-all!' she chided him. She thought for a few moments. 'You've hypnotized them!'

she exclaimed, delighted, looking at the drowsing guests.

'Yes. It's simple, you see.'

'You wretch.'

'It won't do them any harm. Most of them are half-cut anyway.'

'How do I know they're not pretending?' Harriet demanded. 'You put them all up to it when you were planning the party.'

'No,' he said. 'I only just thought of it now. A little light entertainment.'

'I don't believe you!' Harriet goaded.

Theo looked around the company. 'Has anyone got a needle or a sharp pin?'

One of the men reached up to the carnation he wore in his buttonhole, extracted a long pin and offered it to his host.

Theo cleaned the tip carefully with a handkerchief and went to stand beside one of the seemingly sleeping girls. He took her wrist, slowly raised her arm and then let it drop. It fell with the weight of a stone into her lap.

'You'll feel no pain, Sarah,' he said softly, 'you'll feel nothing.' He picked up her hand, turned it palm up, then drove the pin into the flesh. There were gasps from the audience. But Sarah made no response.

He repeated the process with two other guests. Neither of them so much as twitched

278

when the pin punctured their skin.

'How will you wake them up?' Harriet enquired.

'I shall simply tell them that they will wake up to a certain trigger. And then I shall pull it.' Theo smiled around at his fascinated audience. 'Don't worry, I shall do nothing more alarming than click my fingers.'

'Try to put me under,' said Harriet. 'Try to *mesmerize* me.' She rolled her eyes suggestively. 'You won't have any luck. I've a will of iron.'

'Want to bet,' said Theo.

Majid spoke in Kay's ear. 'Shall we leave now? Or do you want to see more?'

Kay smiled and stood up. They slipped away into the entrance hall. Music from the disco drifted through the doorway of the library.

'I see what you mean about Theo's being unusual,' she commented.

'Yes.' Majid was looking thoughtful.

'You didn't approve of that little display of human manipulation did you?'

Majid shrugged. 'I'm instructing him in the practice of law. He's a competent counsel. What he does in his own home is his affair.'

'Spoken like a true diplomat,' Kay said. 'You don't give much away do you, Majid?'

'No.'

'Anyway, thanks for waking me up. I wouldn't have liked to have been one of Theo's sleeping beauties.'

He was watching her, his expression dark, maybe troubled. She was struck afresh by the quality of his attention. When Majid looked at her, he really looked. His gaze was a kind of scrutiny.

The lights in the library dimmed down and the music changed tempo.

'Will you dance with me, Majid?' Kay asked.

He took her hand and they moved together to stand on the polished floor where several couples were entwined, moving slowly to music almost as hypnotic as Orlando Bird's *Willows Weeping*. Coloured lights made a dreamy shifting pattern on the honey-coloured wood.

Kay felt Majid's arms move around her. They were the same height, able to look directly into each other's eyes. She found it achingly arousing. She looped her arms around his neck and allowed her cheek to rest against his. The music curled itself about them and she wondered if anything would ever again be as good as this moment.

'Are you tired?' he asked after a time.

'Yes,' she said regretfully.

'We'll go home.'

In the car he reclined the seat for her and she lay back, drifting into sleep as the car cruised down the motorway. The images from the past days fused together in a medley of bizarrely shimmering images. Orlando Bird, Dr Weiner, Theo Lacy and his mesmerized guests. The man in the mask, the eyes watching her, coming nearer. Terror roared through her nerves.

Her eyes snapped open. She made a noise in her throat.

'Kay?' he said.

'Was I snoring?' she asked, grasping at the security of the mundane.

'No, you were whimpering.'

'I'm not surprised. I seem to be inhabiting a very strange world at the moment, both waking and sleeping.'

'You sound worried Kay. Are you all right?'

'Oh yes. Absolutely fine — as I tell people several times a day. The thing is, before the operation I used to be so pragmatic, so down to earth and rooted in reality. And now look at me.'

'I can't look at you,' he said. 'It would put me off my driving.'

He said nothing else for some time and Kay decided she would have to make do with the last remark as an indication of his undying love.

'Would you like to come in?' she asked as he drew up outside her flat.

'Yes.'

'But you're not going to?'

'No.'

'I think you're right.' She felt a sudden leaden weight of dread. 'Will we go on with this? Seeing each other?'

'Of course. I'll call you very soon and give you that address you wanted.'

'Yes. Fine.' She fumbled with the door handle.

'Kay!' he said, leaning towards her as she turned. He put his hand on her jaw and tilted her face towards him. Carefully, as if she was very fragile, he slid his fingers into her hair and cradled her skull. She found her hands sliding under his jacket.

His eyes were shiny dark, peering into hers. Then he closed them and kissed her; a throbbing, connecting kiss.

'Just you be careful with me,' she told him as she got out of the car, her body aching with longing. 'I may seem hysterical and a touch crazy, but at heart I'm a very strong-willed woman.'

20

Kay woke at seven the next morning after a night of stumbling, incomprehensible dreams and wanted Majid to phone her *now*.

She went to the bathroom, counted out her tablets and ran water into a glass. The mirror threw back a picture of a chalkfaced woman with wild eyes and tangled hair.

And only last night she had kissed Majid and felt herself glow with life.

'Serves you right,' she told the hag in the glass. 'You wanted to see him to get information. Instead you fell for him, hook, line and bloody sinker. Never mix work with pleasure.'

She soaked in a warm bath, washed her hair, put on crisp, fresh underwear, black jeans and a white shirt, and sprayed herself with Miss Dior. Always be ready for the unexpected, she told herself. She pictured Majid's car drawing up by the gate, his lean brown body sliding out of it. She struck her forehead with the heels of her hands. 'Oh, for goodness sake!'

Grilling bacon and cracking an egg into the frying-pan she began formulating plans for her visit to the family who had been Parvinder's last hosts. Of course she couldn't actually proceed with it until Majid had given her the necessary information. She looked at the phone. Her heart bounded.

'Torture me,' she said to it. 'Don't ring. Never ring again!'

There was a banging on the front door. The frantic buzz of her entry phone. She looked at the video screen. Hugo's face shimmered there, distorted and agitated.

'Damn and blast,' she muttered, pressing the door release button.

'What?' she said to him rudely as he opened the door. Instantly she relented. His lips were trembling, his body shaking. He was on the verge of tears.

'Oh no,' she cried. 'Is it Fi?'

'She started bleeding a couple of hours ago. Blood everywhere. Sheets, carpets, bathroom floor.' He rammed his fingers through his hair.

'Where is she?'

'Hospital. I called an ambulance.'

'Oh, heavens, poor Fi. And poor you.' She pulled him inside the door. 'Sit down. I'll get you coffee, or something stronger if you want.'

He shook his head.

She went into the kitchen and made instant

coffee with plenty of sugar. 'Here you are,' she said to him. 'Drink it. What do you want me to do?'

'She wants to see you.'

'Did she say so?'

'No, I just know she does.'

'She'll want you Hugo. You should be there,' Kay said gently.

'I can't do anything. They took her away to do things to her. I was useless.'

'Look, let's both go. Right away.'

'Right.' He jumped up.

Kay grabbed her house keys and followed him. He set off like a madman, horn blaring, hazard warning lights flashing. The traffic parted like the Red Sea.

'Slow down,' Kay shouted at him. 'You'll get us killed.'

He braked, pulled over into the inside lane.

'Is it a miscarriage?' Kay asked.

'Yes. She never told me, Kay. She never said a word about having a baby.'

'Oh dear.'

'And I never suspected.' He stabbed the brakes and came to a screeching halt at traffic lights. 'I've been making love every night to a pregnant woman and sharing a bathroom with her. I must be the only man in the world with less sensitivity than a traffic cone.'

That sounded to Kay like Fiona's phrase-ology. 'Fi's always been good at keeping secrets,' she said.

'But she told you?'

'Yes.' Kay felt really sorry for him. 'There are some things women always tell each other. We're tied together by bonds of blood and pain.'

He sighed. 'Did she think of getting rid of it?'

'Yes.'

He shook his head in misery.

'Then she decided she couldn't do that. She really wanted this baby.'

'Why didn't she tell me?' He hit the steering wheel with the palm of his hand. 'Why didn't she trust me?'

'The usual reasons. She thought you might be angry, that you might ditch her. Not want the responsibility . . . '

'Ditch her! Fi! *I* was the one always waiting to be dumped.'

'Really?' Kay shot him a swift glance. 'I'm surprised. To be honest, I had you down as a possible Don Juan, a bit of a ladies' man.'

'What gave you that idea?'

'Oh, come on, Hugo. That morning you came round unannounced. Prowling round my flat, coming on to me as though you'd never given a thought to the fact that Fi's my best friend.'

'Yeah.' He looked flattened. 'Told you I was useless.'

'Well, maybe you had a dodgy childhood and your mother didn't love you enough and you can't help yourself,' Kay snapped at him. 'But I'll tell you this, if Fi manages to keep this baby and you let her down, I'll personally batter you to death.'

When they reached the hospital Hugo was shaking so much he reversed the car into a concrete wall in the car park and smashed a tail light. Inside the hospital's main building he became completely disoriented whilst trying to find his way round the labyrinth of wards and Kay had to seize him by the arm and drag him along to keep him moving in a straight line. Eventually they reached the gynaecological ward and were told that Fi's doctor was with her, but would see them as soon as possible. They were directed to sit in the visitors' room, which turned out to be a dim, cheerless box dotted with signs saying no smoking and reeking of the sour smell of stale tobacco.

Hospitals! thought Kay with a shudder. I don't want to be here.

Hugo sat in silence, his face grooved with lines of misery.

Kay opened a window and took gulps of fresh air. She went to sit beside the hunched Hugo. 'Women bleed and still keep the baby.' she said gently.

'If I believed in God, I'd pray,' he told her. After a time, he looked up and said, 'How are you Kay? How are *you* getting on?'

She smiled. 'I'm fine, Hugo. Absolutely fine.'

★　★　★

Back at her flat two hours later she checked the answerphone for messages. Just one message. She wound back the tape with shaking fingers. Her ears strained for Majid's voice.

'Kay sweetheart!' boomed Ralph. 'We're back from Bonny Scotland. The weather was bloody disgusting. Worse than winter. I've booked a table for three this lunchtime. Thought it was high time you met Isobel. We'll pick you up at twelve-thirty. No excuses.'

'Huh!' Kay exclaimed. Well at least a bombardment from Ralph and a meeting with the new woman would take her mind off the silence of Majid and the terrifyingly white face of the drowsy Fiona lying flat beneath tightly tucked linen, a line in her arm attaching her to a transfusion unit, her legs raised up on a block.

Kay had left Hugo sitting beside Fi, holding her hand and willing her to pull herself back into life. Apparently the bleeding had been so dangerously sudden and severe that without the transfusion Fiona could have died. The baby had had no chance. Its tiny life was over.

Thinking about it made Kay feel sorrowful, angry and then reckless. The lingering shreds of doubt about confronting the Devon family vanished. She would get their address and she would go to see them. And quickly. Tomorrow for preference. And if Majid had not rung her by six this evening she would simply go round to his flat and speak to him.

* * *

Isobel was a tiny, youthfully pretty woman dressed in a neat blue suit.

Kay smiled at her as they sat sipping pre-lunch drinks in a smart Islington restaurant and realized she was horribly nervous.

'I've heard such a lot about you,' Isobel said. She winced. 'Oh dear, that sounds like an awful cliché.'

'I'll lob one back,' Kay smiled. 'What's he

been saying about me?'

Isobel blinked. 'How ill you've been. How brave.'

'How increasingly stroppy?' Kay suggested mischievously.

'Too true,' said Ralph, half way through a large gin and tonic, unencumbered by any feelings of embarrassment or anxiety. 'She used to be a little angel when she was a girl. Fairly angelic as a young woman too.'

'Now I'm a tigress with terrible teeth,' Kay joked.

'I've heard that can happen to people when they've survived a terrible illness,' Isobel said seriously. 'They seem to respond to life quite differently when they get well again.'

Kay stared at the bubbles leaping from her mineral water. 'Thank you for saying that, Isobel,' she said slowly.

'Oh, I'm sure it's a very well-known phenomenon. Nothing original.'

'Maybe not. But it's a wonderfully clear and simple way of looking at things. I've spent a lot of time grinding myself down with rather more fanciful thoughts.'

'Oh, now come on, Kay. Let's not get heavy,' said Ralph. 'Keep things cheerful.'

'No,' Isobel told him with surprising firmness. 'Let Kay say what's on her mind.' She looked at her with expectant eyes.

'It's months since the operation,' Ralph said. 'Kay's been simply fine. No point in raking up what's in the past.'

'How do you know I've been fine?' Kay challenged him.

He stared at her. 'Well, I know I haven't seen as much of you as I'd have liked recently, but you always seemed . . . ' He flushed, suddenly disconcerted.

'I've never spoken to you about how I really felt Ralph,' Kay told him, 'because you don't like it when things get 'heavy'.'

'Well, here I am,' Ralph said helplessly. 'All ears.'

Kay turned to Isobel. 'After I had my heart transplant, I began to dream about a murder. Eventually it dawned on me that the murder was that of my donor. So I tracked down the donor's family and I'm currently trying to find out if my dream had any truth in it.' She took a long sip of her mineral water. 'In a nutshell,' she concluded with a wry smile.

'Good God!' said Ralph. 'Bloody bombshell!'

Isobel laid her hand on his arm. Delicate little fingers, tipped with pearly pink varnish. 'Just let her speak, Ralph.' She looked across at Kay.

'For weeks after the operation, I was in a state of indecision and tension. I got tired easily which meant 1 couldn't do very much. But once I started feeling better I became fired up with determination to find out everything I could about my donor and the way she died.'

'Why didn't you tell me all this?' Ralph asked, hurt and bewildered.

'You'd have patted me on the head and told me not to be a silly, over-imaginative woman.'

'True,' he agreed, taking a gulp of gin. 'True.'

'You said your donor was a woman,' Isobel said thoughtfully. 'so you know her identity?'

'Oh yes. She was an Asian girl from Bradford.'

'Good grief!' Ralph drained his glass and slammed it down on the table.

'Bit of a facer for you, Ralph,' Kay smiled. 'And no quips about my having a black heart.'

'Are you sure about this?' Ralph demanded. 'Don't the Muslim and Hindu lot have taboos about organ donation?'

'Yes, they do. Parvinder, my donor, was brought up a Muslim but she became Westernized, renounced the faith.'

'I'm surprised the family allowed it anyway,' Ralph said. 'They're the ones who make the decision.' Kay could tell he was shaken.

'None of that matters does it? It's just wonderful that you got a healthy heart,' Isobel said placatingly.

'Yes.' Kay agreed.

'This murder business,' said Ralph, catching the waiter's eye and pointing a jabbing finger into his empty glass, 'you're not seriously thinking of treating it seriously?'

'Yes, I am.'

'Good Lord!'

'Parvinder's cousin is helping me.'

'Two bottles of the Penfold Shiraz 1991,' Ralph barked at the waiter as he brought the fresh gin and tonic. 'And who the bloody hell is this cousin when he's at home?'

'He's a QC at a London chambers. He's very together, very cultured, and I've never once heard him say goodness gracious me!'

'He sounds very nice,' said Isobel. 'Come on, Ralph, stop looking as if you've swallowed something nasty.' She patted his knee and he placed his hand over hers.

'I think I'm in love with him,' Kay said reflectively, putting a seal of reality on budding emotions that had been too incredible to contemplate.

'Blood and effing sand!' Ralph blazed. And there was little more said until they were called to their table.

21

Kay arrived at Majid's flat with a Madeira cake she had baked and iced to fill in the intervening hours between lunch and her meeting with Majid at seven.

She held the cake out to him as he opened the door. He took it with smiles and thanks, placing it on a glass-topped table which was the sole piece of furniture in his entrance lobby.

His habitual courteous reserve was back in place, calm and impenetrable, as though the previous evening was over and forgotten.

Kay reached out a hand, pulled his head to hers and kissed him on the lips. His response was warm, protracted and anything but reserved.

She leaned against him. 'That's all right then.'

'There are things we need to discuss,' he said.

'Yes.'

Whilst Majid telephoned an order for a takeaway meal she stood by the window in his huge, high-ceilinged drawing-room, looking out on to the river, whipped up and pearly grey under a lowered sky.

Earlier they had argued a little on the phone about the venue of their meeting and the eating arrangements. He had not called her until four-thirty by which time her innards had been churning with tension and anticipation. Hearing his voice had made her weak with relief and furious with him for having the ability to stir her into such a ragged emotional state. He had suggested a meeting in a restaurant, but she had had enough of wearing her heart on her sleeve in public.

'I want to see your lair,' she told him. 'I want to see you in your natural habitat. And I want my own way.'

A pause. 'Very well. But what about food? I haven't eaten, and I don't cook.'

'We'll get something in. I've baked us a cake for pudding.'

'Then I can see you must have your own way,' he had said in a voice which gave no clue as to the expression on his face.

He came to stand beside her now at the window. 'The food will be here very soon.' He rested his arm lightly around her shoulders and pointed out the landmarks.

'I called Balbinder earlier on,' he said. 'Kulvinder is back home. Doing quite well, apparently.'

Kay felt the breath stop in her chest at the mention of that poor, sad woman's name. 'Thank heaven for that.'

'She's been referred to a consultant psychiatrist who seems very sympathetic. Kulvinder has actually agreed to cut down on her tranquillizers and to attend some therapy sessions.'

'That's good,' Kay said hesitantly.

'It's a minor miracle.'

Kay turned back to the room: shining oak floorboards, one gleaming Persian rug, white paint, barely any furniture. 'This is a long way from a tiny terraced house in a back street in Bradford.'

'Yes. That's what I wanted.'

'To get away.'

He nodded. 'Some people would find that very sad.'

'Abandoning your roots?'

'I suppose my roots are partly in Bradford, but also in Pakistan, the soil that nurtured my parents.'

'Do you go often to Pakistan?'

'No.'

You're very alone, Kay thought. Just as I have been since the operation.

'I'm going to be stern and cold this evening,' he said, his arm still around her. 'And I'm going to lecture you.'

'Right.'

'But first I want to give you this.' He handed her a folded sheet of paper.

Kay unfolded it, quickly scanning over the address and contact number of the Cavendish family who had been host to Parvinder at the time of her death.

'I've no right to influence you,' Majid said. 'What you do with that information is your choice. That's why I'm giving it to you now before I start lecturing!'

'You're going to try to make me change my mind?'

'I'm going to present you with information which is relevant to your plans to go and see this family.'

Kay looked at his solemn, warrior face and broke into a smile. 'Majid, do you ever take a break from being in court?'

His eyes lit with an energy that could have been humour. 'Yes. But not tonight, not until later.'

He took her hand and walked her across to a glass-topped table matching the one in the hallway, but double its size. On its surface were neat stacks of paper, a number of reference books, a laptop computer and a mobile phone — both switched off.

He spread one of the stacks of paper. Kay saw that they were extracts from American and British journals. She looked at the various headings: Human Memory — Facts and Fallacies; Emotions and Healing; The Challenge of Energy Cardiology. Those were just a few.

'The case I was on this morning was adjourned,' Majid told her. 'I took the opportunity to do some research at the British Library and on the internet. I had a look through Weiner's latest book, then found a transcript of his recent London lecture on his website.'

'Scarily impressive,' she told him, flicking over the closely printed pages. 'What did you make of Dr Weiner's cellular memory theory?'

'I'm reserving my verdict,' he said drily. 'But what he writes in his book fits very closely with your own account of what he said in the lecture, so clearly your own memory — the conventional type that's stored in your brain — is functioning very accurately.'

'That's good then. Maybe I'm not as crazy as I seem.' There was a buzz on the entry phone announcing the arrival of the food. Kay followed Majid to the kitchen and watched him unpack it. The room was immaculately clean and tidy, clearly a cooking-free zone.

'Where are the plates?' she asked.

He gestured to open shelves running along the back wall. Neat little stacks of china. All plain white. There were just four dinner plates.

'Are these all you've got?' she asked.

'Yes. If I want to entertain more than four people I take them to a restaurant.'

He was setting out a variety of fragrant spicy delicacies. Kay examined them with interest. She picked up a small fried ball which appeared to be made of mixed vegetables, minced and bound together with tomato paste and cream. 'What's the spice?' she wondered, sniffing at it. 'Fenugreek? A touch of coriander?'

'I'm afraid I've no idea,' he said. 'Fenugreek sounds likely.'

'I didn't think you'd choose Asian food,' she said. 'I thought you'd be into sophisticated, Londony nouvelle cuisine.'

'That's what I thought you would think.'

'Ah!'

'This is authentic Gujarati food,' he told her. 'It's prepared in a restaurant nearby owned and run by one family. All the ingredients are bought in fresh and cooked when you order them. Or so they tell me!'

Kay poked at minced aubergines tucked into vine leaves and spiced with chillies. 'I'm going to love all this.' She leaned back against the counter and looked at him, her eyes heavy and languorous, allowing herself to enjoy his harsh, dark beauty. 'Is this the kind of food Parvinder provided for her rich clients?'

'Yes, amongst other things. She was a very versatile and proficient cook.'

'And is this the kind of thing she liked to eat?' Kay arranged the vine leaves in a wheel shape.

'She had very catholic tastes. She was keen to try cuisine from all over the world. I think she had a particular liking for some traditional British dishes. Roast beef and Yorkshire pudding, duck and orange sauce.' He paused, thinking. 'And she loved steamed treacle pudding with custard.'

Hmm, the cellular memories had clearly become a little scrambled there, thought Kay, who very rarely ate roast meats and loathed custard.

He placed two glasses on the counter, then reached into the fridge and drew out a bottle of pale lager. 'It's low alcohol,' he said.

Kay took a glass and held it out. 'Did you order any extra chillies?' she asked Majid.

'No. Should I have done?'

'No, it's OK.'

'You prefer highly spiced foods, Kay?'

'I certainly don't choose to eat bland ones. Not since the transplant at any rate.'

He frowned. 'So do you think your tastes have changed since the operation?'

'Yes, I do. I started shaking Worcester sauce and bottled mayonnaise over my food, hankering after chillies and curry powder.'

'Don't pregnant women experience certain cravings? Isn't that connected with changes in body chemistry? You *know* all this, Kay.'

'OK, I've thought of the parallel of pregnancy cravings. But those are hormonal changes. They shouldn't apply to me.'

He raised an eyebrow. 'I assume you would have been told that it's likely that the biochemistry of your body might have been disturbed after major surgery?'

'Oh yes.'

Majid drew out a bunch of coriander leaves from the bottom of the bag. 'What do I do with these?'

'Garnish the food with them. Give me some scissors and I'll cut them up.' She saw him purse his lips. 'No kitchen scissors?' she chuckled. 'A sharp knife will do.'

'I'm not playing devil's advocate,' he told her, as they arranged the plates on the low coffee-table in front of the sofa and sat down to eat. 'I'm simply curious about the things you've told me.'

'And interested to examine the evidence.' Kay looked across at the journal print-outs on the glass table.

'Examining evidence is how I make my living.'

'I should have done more research myself,' Kay said regretfully. 'I am an academic after all. And the study of music has a lot more to do with logic and rules than many people imagine.'

'You've been focusing on your feelings,' he said. 'You've been listening to your heart as Dr Weiner would put it.'

'Is that wrong?'

'Of course not. What else would you be doing after your heart had been in danger of ceasing to function?' He poured more beer. 'Whilst I was reading these various articles I was imagining myself making a case for the validity of Dr Weiner's theory. Of finding proof to offer in a court of law.'

She put down her glass. 'Yes?'

'It would have taken a lot of ingenuity,' he said with a small smile.

'I accept that. A part of me thinks his theory is simply preposterous. But I've experienced some of the things the other transplant patients talked about, and when I heard them talking the other night, I felt a connection with them. And I felt enlivened and excited.'

'I would assume it was the account of little

Amy's dream that had the most powerful effect.'

'Oh, yes!' Suddenly her throat felt full. 'And at the same time I wondered if the mother's account was falsified, or at the least an embellishment of the truth.'

'There's a more detailed account of Amy's story in Weiner's book. It's emotionally powerful and persuasive, but far from convincing as a piece of evidence. The little girl's description of the killer followed the stereotype of film and TV criminals. Typically male, youngish, coarse features, wearing jeans . . . '

Kay sighed. 'When I calmed down from my excitement of first hearing the story, that occurred to me too. In fact I've reached the point when I'd feel much more comfortable to take the view of the sceptic.'

He looked steadily at her. 'Am I demolishing precious beliefs?'

She shook her head. 'It's not so much a question of beliefs, more being driven by images and sensations that refuse to go away and leave me alone.'

'Mmm.' Majid seemed unimpressed. He stacked the empty plates and dishes into a neat pile which he pushed to one side of the table.

'When I was a law student,' he said, 'we

went to the Institute of Psychiatry for a course of lectures on human memory. For criminal lawyers it's obviously a highly relevant subject. The lecturer played a number of games with us. Memory games. We had to read passages of fiction — they were synopses of Greek-style myths composed by the lecturer so that none of us were familiar with them. We had to memorize the stories and then recall them. We had to do that at varying intervals of time, with and without the interference of other stimulating input, such as reading another passage or listening to a recorded conversation on tape. What particularly impressed me was the extent to which we lost information on recall. Here we were, young, bright, motivated students, and yet we frequently couldn't recall a twenty-line story without losing some vital piece of information, without distortions creeping in, without an average of ten to twenty per cent condensation of the original. With ten minute clips from old films the effect was pretty much the same. I think our lecturer rather enjoyed our discomfiture at not doing better.'

'OK,' she responded, 'so none of us are as reliable and accurate in remembering things as we'd like to think. How does that apply to me?'

'Be patient,' he told her. 'I was merely setting the scene by reminding you that it is quite normal for memories to be incomplete or distorted. Our lecturer maintained that the brain was remarkably efficient as regards storing information. The problem is retrieving the information — getting it out of storage in the same form as it was when it went in.'

'Get to the point, Majid!'

'Very well. Let's consider so-called false memory syndrome. Let's ask why reliable, honest people would 'remember' something that turns out to be false?'

'Does that often happen? In court?'

'There are plenty of proven examples. People do, in fact, retrieve supposed memories that are later proved to be invalid because they could not have happened. For instance the accused person could not have committed the crime because on that particular day they were half-way round the world, or laid up in hospital with plenty of witnesses to confirm it.'

'So why do people remember falsely?' Kay asked. 'Simply to suit their own purposes — a kind of wish fulfilment?'

'I think that is part of it. But the clients I've personally been involved with have all either suffered a serious trauma or illness, have been recent recipients of a general anaesthetic, or have been treated by a therapist who uses hypnosis. There are probably other reasons also.'

Now she understood the thrust of his argument. 'I certainly come in the first two categories, but I've never been hypnotized, not that I know of. Although I was dropping off when Theo started twiddling with his lighter and talking in a dreamy voice.'

'Yes, but you were tired. And, of course, your dreams and altered feelings had all been troubling you long before last night. But the issue of false memory must surely be comparable to that of so-called cellular memory. Which is what you are claiming to be experiencing. Isn't it?'

'I suppose so.' She was silent for a time, thinking. Majid sat quietly, waiting.

'So if normal people have inaccurate memories and can sometimes remember things that aren't true, then memories which supposedly come from transplanted cells must be even more suspect?'

'That's exactly what I'm trying to say.'

'But Dr Weiner is not stupid. And he didn't strike me as a liar or a charlatan. Why would he promote this theory of cellular memory?'

'Kay, Weiner is an evangelist, appealing to emotions at the expense of reason. I'm confident that he believes his theory, even though he hasn't subjected it to any scientific testing. But remember, he conceived this theory when he was in a highly emotional state, coming to terms with a near-fatal illness, following traumatic surgery. Thus he's got a huge amount of personal investment in it. And don't forget he's being paid large fees for his lectures and his recent book is set to be a bestseller. Weiner's cellular symphony is going to make him a lot of money.'

Kay sat very still, considering.

'If I were cross-examining Weiner in court,' Majid said quietly, 'I would start off by asking how it is that a transplanted heart can provide memories when it is well known that the brain is the storage centre of our intellectual skills. People who lose fingers or limbs in an accident do not lose their memory. Whereas people who suffer damage to critical areas in the cerebral cortex invariably experience significant loss or distortion. How would he answer that?'

'He'd be in big trouble,' Kay said. She turned to confront him, one final appeal. 'But what about my dream of the man in the mask?'

'Oh, that!' Majid smiled. 'A dream is no more than a number of images from the unconscious. In essence another form of memory, subject to all the problems we've already talked about.'

There was a long silence. 'I accept all you've said to me,' Kay told him. 'But I still want to go and see the Cavendish family.'

'Then you must go.' He took her hand in his, slowly stroking her fingers.

'You'll be here for me — on the other end of the phone?'

'Of course.' She looked at him. 'What's the matter?'

'Something that's been troubling me; that I haven't been able to speak about.'

'Tell me. Anything!'

'In the hospital before Parvinder died I took her part, overruling Kulvinder and Mudassar. I played the advocate, I was cold and hard and ruthless.'

Kay frowned, not clearly understanding.

'I insisted that Parvinder's wishes about organ donation were carried out. For Kulvinder that was the most terrible betrayal. The ultimate desecration of her daughter's body and memory. For nights I couldn't sleep for thinking about it, the cruel single-mindedness I employed. I wondered if I could ever forgive myself.'

Kay took his hand and placed it over her breastbone, letting his fingers trace over the healing scar, feel the steady beat beneath. 'I wonder if I can ever thank you enough.'

It was hard to say who made the first move, but suddenly they were pressed hard against each other, kissing hungrily, their hands eager and exploring.

Majid pushed aside her shirt and bra, and ran his lips over her breasts and the healing wound between them.

They went into the bedroom and fell on to the bed struggling out of their twisted and entangled clothes. There was no time for awkwardness; Kay felt him instantly inside her, hard and sure and satisfying.

Later they woke and made love again, this time at leisure, taking pleasure in the slow examining of each other's bodies. They lay awake for hours afterwards, talking. He told her about Jennifer and she spoke about Luke.

In the morning he kissed her deeply before he left for work. Kay lay for a while in his bed, smiling in indulgent pity for all those people who had simply spent the night sleeping.

22

The Cavendish house was in a little corner of paradise, standing high on the cliff tops perfectly positioned for a breathtaking view over the huge sweep of Torbay. It was a white stucco house, set in a garden lined with shiny-leaved palm trees.

Kay arrived there in the late afternoon having taken a taxi from the small station in Paignton.

The August day had the feel of southern France, with a bright yellow sun blazing from a deep blue sky. A light breeze set the palm leaves rippling as Kay walked up the drive, her heart beating with the urgency of anticipation.

A woman knelt beside the edge of an oval-shaped lawn. She was dressed in blue jeans and a nautical T-shirt with stripes and an anchor, and was occupied in dead-heading roses with a pair of secateurs. As Kay approached she looked up, passing a hand over her forehead which was lightly beaded with sweat. She smiled.

'Hello there!'

'Hello.' Kay walked up close, forcing a

smile in response. She opened her mouth to say more and felt her throat close up.

'Can I help?' The woman's face showed no trace of surprise or suspicion. 'Are you looking for someone?'

'Mr or Mrs Cavendish,'

'Then look no further. I am she — the latter.' She stood up. She was thin and tall. Around mid-fifties. A thoroughbred with fine bones, golden tanned skin and chestnut hair in a gleaming swingy bob.

'It's rather difficult,' Kay said.

Mrs Cavendish looked interested. 'In that case, come in and have tea. I was just going to make some.' She smiled encouragingly.

Kay hesitated. She had not been expecting this. 'Well . . . '

'You're not a murderess or a Jehovah's Witness are you?'

Kay laughed.

Mrs Cavendish began to walk towards the house. 'Come on!'

She sat Kay down at the kitchen table, filled and switched on the kettle. 'Scones?' she asked. 'Clotted cream? It's organic.'

Kay nodded.

'I was feeling at a bit of a loose end,' Mrs Cavendish said as though they had been chums for ages. 'My friends are holidaying all over the globe, my housekeeper's packed up and left, and my son and my husband have been at a trade conference for the last couple of days.' She looked appraisingly at Kay. 'So it's good to have someone to talk to.'

Kay accepted tea and a scone. Her heart still beat a warning.

'Now, what were you wanting with me and my husband?' Mrs Cavendish reached for the cream and laid an egg-sized dollop on her scone.

'I was wanting to talk to you about Parvinder Nazar. I believe she was a friend of yours. My name's Kay. I'm the person who was given Parvinder's heart.' The heart was pumping furiously now, drumming like a panic-stricken animal. The truth was perhaps the hardest card to play in these circumstances but Kay had decided it was the only option. And, of course, she was telling only part of the truth.

Mrs Cavendish took a slow bite from her scone and looked Kay in the eyes. 'How absolutely astonishing,' she said evenly. 'And how wonderful.' She tilted her head. 'You're looking very well. Are you fully recovered?'

'Yes.'

'Good.' She looked at Kay some more. 'How simply fascinating.'

Kay took a swallow of tea. It scalded the back of her throat and she coughed.

'So, what can I tell you about Parvinder?' Mrs Cavendish's composure was almost more worrying than the hostile incredulity Kay had been bracing herself for.

'I'd just like to get a picture of what she was like as a person. I've thought about her so much.' Surely this was Mrs Cavendish's cue to ask if Kay had approached Parvinder's family. And if not, why not.

'Well, of course you'd like to know about Parvinder. What an astounding thing it must be, to be given someone else's heart. Apparently it can push some people right over the edge if they start brooding over it.' Mrs Cavendish spread more cream on a second scone. 'I can't recall if I read that in the papers or whether I came across it in one of those weird Channel Four films.'

'I think I've managed to keep reasonably sane,' Kay said.

Mrs Cavendish smiled. 'Splendid! I'm glad to hear that.' She sprang up. 'Hang on a minute, I'll get you some photographs. What better way to start?'

She reached into the drawer of an impressive oak Welsh dresser and pulled out a small album with a Liberty cover. 'I think these are the latest lot.' She laid the album in front of Kay. 'Have a flick through, help yourself, I'm just going to dig some meat out of the fridge or there'll be nothing for dinner when my two men arrive back. Why don't you stay on and join us, Kay? You could meet William. He'll be able to tell you lots about Parvinder.'

Kay watched her disappear through a door at the back of the kitchen, heard her footsteps tapping down stone steps. She ran her fingers over the cover of the album. A vague but leaden surge of dread seized her.

She felt for her mobile phone clipped to the belt of her cream chinos. Majid was only a few button-punches away. She held hard to the reassurance.

The pictures in the album were a chronicle of an idyllic holiday: sun, sea, sailing boats, picnics on Dartmoor, candlelit suppers in the Cavendish garden beside a glinting pool.

Parvinder's image sprang out from each shot; leggy in shorts, svelte and sexy in diving gear, her smile wide and red-lipped, her eyes flashing with life and challenge. Her features were not as regular as those of Balbinder; her jaw a little squarer, her forehead higher. There was a dark drama about her, some vivid individual quality which drew the gaze, arresting and magnetic.

Mrs Cavendish returned and busied herself unwrapping a leg of lamb. 'Pretty girl, wasn't she?' Reaching into the fridge she took out yoghurt and mint and began to mix a marinade. 'You can keep those snaps if you like, I've plenty more.'

Kay hesitated, unsure. 'Thank you.' She watched Mrs Cavendish's strong capable hands and wondered if they had performed the evil act of murder. 'How long had you known Parvinder?'

Mrs Cavendish stopped stirring for a few moments. 'We first met last January. It was my husband's sixtieth and William and I decided to throw a party, something a bit out of the usual run. I have a friend who told me about this wonderful Pakistani girl who organized super parties and even more fabulous food.' Mrs Cavendish scooped the marinade from the bowl with her fingers and began to work it over the lamb. 'So, we hired her.'

Kay said nothing.

'The party was a huge success. And everyone was knocked out by Parvinder, wanting to book her for their next bash.' Mrs Cavendish paused, she looked straight at Kay. 'It never does any harm to be young and beautiful where getting business is concerned, does it?' There was provocation in her tone, but the accompanying smile was gay and carefree.

'I suppose not.' Kay looked at Mrs

Cavendish's profile as she returned to her cooking preparations, seeing how she too must have been beautiful around twenty-five years ago. Had Parvinder's smouldering female magnetism been hard for her to bear?

'Anyway,' Mrs Cavendish continued, 'after the party William and Parvinder started — seeing each other. They seemed to get on like a house on fire.'

'You sound surprised,' Kay said.

'I was. I know my son — and Parvinder was not his type.' Mrs Cavendish laid the yoghurt-smothered joint of lamb in a roasting tin. She turned to Kay. 'You will stay for supper won't you?'

Kay felt a prick of panic. 'That's very kind but I couldn't impose on you. And anyway, I should get back.'

'Where to?'

'London.'

'You don't want to take one of those ghastly creepy-crawly evening trains. Stay here for the night.'

'Oh, no, I've booked into a hotel on the front.' Kay flushed, hopelessly wrong-footed.

'In that case,' Mrs Cavendish pointed out, 'you've no need to worry about getting back to London tonight.' Her gaze was clear and level. Got you!

Relax, Kay instructed herself. 'You win. I'd

love to stay for supper. But afterwards I shall insist on getting a taxi to take me to my hotel and not to put you to any further trouble.'

'You must please yourself, of course. William's always telling me off for my bullying ways!' Mrs Cavendish placed the roasting tin in the oven, then reached into the vegetable rack. 'Here,' she said cheerily, plonking a huge bag of freshly picked peas in front of Kay, 'no need to feel you're imposing. You can sing for your supper and shell this lot.'

* * *

Two hours later Mrs Cavendish and Kay were sipping white wine spritzers in the drawing-room. Fragrant scents of cooking came from the kitchen and the table was elegantly laid in the dining-room.

Kay had been treated like a long-lost friend; been shown around the garden, invited to take a swim in the pool, consulted about the wine to accompany supper. And all the time Mrs Cavendish — 'Do call me Hilary' — had chatted cheerily about her garden projects and the problems of finding a good housekeeper. She told Kay about her husband and William's joint business ventures, describing the chain of souvenir shops, the yacht leasing company, the scuba-diving school. The conversation had all been so effortlessly casual and friendly — and Kay had felt more uneasy by the minute.

When Hilary eventually went upstairs to shower and change Kay had considered calling a taxi and making a bolt for it. But apart from the considerations of churlishness and cowardice, she felt a growing curiosity about William.

There was the growl of a car's engine in the drive. Hilary turned and glanced through the window.

'Ah, at last my menfolk return!'

Kay waited for her to go out on to the drive and intercept them. Tactfully apprise them of her, Kay's, presence. But Hilary went on sipping her spritzer.

A big, silver-haired man appeared in the doorway. 'Hi, darling!'

'Hi!' Hilary mouthed a kiss at him. 'Good conference?'

'Absolutely bloody useless, but we got some good food and drink. And William met a few useful contacts.' The man was looking at Kay. Mildly curious.

Kay smiled at him, her lips stiff. Maybe Hilary collected stray young women like other women collected fine china.

'This is Kay,' Hilary said. 'She's staying for

supper.' She got up and moved to the door, patting the lapel of her husband's jacket on the way. 'I'll get you a drink darling, while she tells you all about herself.'

Kay began to get to her feet.

'No, no, please don't get up.' The man offered his hand. 'I'm Anthony, Hilary's better half.'

He sat down and stretched out his legs. 'God, I'm stiff from sitting in the car all that time. And terrified from being at the mercy of my son's driving. All loud pedal and no brakes. I must be getting old. Tell me about you!'

'I'm an impostor,' said Kay.

He made a sweeping, dismissive gesture. 'Not to worry. We have open house here. Anyone welcome as long as they're not carrying a fatal disease or are a member of the New Labour government.'

Kay gave him a quick résumé of the reason for her visit. More or less word for word what she had told Hilary. His response was as unruffled as that of his wife. He made polite enquiries about Kay's health, regretful remarks about Parvinder's death. 'A lovely girl,' he said more than once. 'A gem. Such a tragedy . . . ' he shook his head.

From the kitchen Kay could hear muffled shouting. A man's — presumably William's

— angry protests, Hilary's barely audible replies. She glanced at Anthony.

'William's still a bit raw about what happened. He took it really hard.' He got up. 'Doesn't look as though I'm going to get that drink unless I pour it myself. Won't be a tick. Another spritzer, Kay?'

She shook her head, straining her ears to track his footsteps as he left the room. But he made no attempt to intervene in the confrontation going on in the kitchen. She could see him in profile, standing beside the silver drinks tray placed on the table in the hallway. Returning to sit opposite Kay, he said comfortingly, 'It's a bit of a facer for William, your turning up like this. Bringing back old memories and so forth. He'll be fine in a few moments. Hilly always knows how to calm him down.' He leaned back and took a sip of his whisky. His eyes moved over Kay and she felt her insides tighten.

'We can none of us understand how it could possibly have happened,' he continued, frowning. 'Parvinder was an experienced driver, she went all over the place on business.'

Kay swallowed. 'Did the accident happen near here?'

'Only a couple of miles away. That was the puzzle. She'd gone out for the day diving with

William. And just an hour or two later her car was found smashed on the rocks under the Babbacombe cliffs just round the point of the bay.' He shook his head. 'Unbelievable. We were all absolutely stunned.' He took another sip of whisky, sighing. With regret? With pleasure at the quality of the Scotch? 'Still, life must go on,' he concluded. 'Isn't that so?'

Kay longed to leave, prayed for supper to be over. They're all in it, she thought wildly. And all I want to do is run away from them. As far as possible.

She stood up. 'Would you excuse me?' she said to Anthony.

'Of course. Are you sure there's nothing I can get you?' he called after her.

In the downstairs cloakroom she splashed cold water on her face and took deep breaths. Standing very still she could hear nothing from the kitchen but the faint clatter of crockery. The verbal battles appeared to have ceased.

Emerging into the hall she gave a start at the sight of a tall, athletic man hurtling down the stairs.

He skidded to a halt when he saw her and they stared at each other, struck dumb.

'I'm sorry,' he said. 'I have to go out. Sorry! Nothing personal.'

'It's all right,' Kay heard herself saying. 'You didn't know I was coming. You don't even know me.'

He stood poised on the stairs, taut and nervy, bouncing on the balls of his feet like a sprinter waiting for the starting gun.

Like his mother's, his face was that of a thoroughbred. Cheekbones that could carve wood, features in perfect symmetry bisected by a nose cosmetic surgeons would use as a blueprint for perfection.

His eyes darted to the front door, hungry for escape.

Kay made a small gesture, indicating that he should go ahead. She watched him wrench open the door, slither through the gap and swiftly vanish. Was this Parvinder's last love? Perhaps her one true love? Perhaps the man who ended her life?

Suddenly Kay was unsteady on her feet, reaching out and clutching at the stair rail for support. She closed her eyes. Iridescent balls of colour danced in front of her eyelids.

Hilary erupted from the kitchen carrying a tureen of vegetables. 'You need some food, my girl!' she told Kay. 'Come along, grub's up.'

Kay placed the food into her mouth and forced herself to chew and swallow. She kept glancing at her watch, willing the hands to creep around faster.

Anthony kept the conversation spinning along, quizzing Kay about her work, moving on to talk about politics and the arts, warding off any awkward silences with a flow of eloquence based on his own informed opinions.

The food began to do its work and Kay began to feel steadier. She reminded herself of the countless times she had been told the importance of eating regularly, of keeping her body chemistry stable. Hilary had been quite right.

Kay looked at Anthony and Hilary and saw two people who had been involved in a terrible tragedy, their son badly hurt, perhaps traumatized, by what had happened. Two people who were opinionated and possibly flawed by social snobbery. But nevertheless two concerned and basically kind people. Open and generous with their views and their hospitality.

Hilary drained her wine glass and held it out to her husband for a refill. She pushed away her half-eaten raspberry tart and turned to Kay, eyes glittering with speculation. 'Have you met Parvinder's family?'

'Yes.' Kay paused. 'Have you?'

'Not in the sense of being introduced,' Hilary's words were slightly slurred. 'They were there at the hospital on the day Parvinder died. We didn't actually talk to the mother and the sister, but the cousin came to speak to us after it was all over.'

'Majid?' Kay felt her nerves electric with sensation.

'He's a lawyer! A QC. Astonishing.' Hilary's face twisted with an emotion that was hard to read.

'He's a very able man, I gather,' Anthony said.

'Probably be a judge before he's forty-five,' Hilary said, turning to Kay. 'The judiciary are into fast-tracking blacks, positive discrimination and so on.'

'Darling,' said Anthony, leaning towards his wife, 'I think you're a tiny bit tight!'

'Never known it happen before,' Hilary grinned, picking up her glass and waving it at him. Her hand stilled. 'It was bloody terrible, that day in the hospital,' she said slowly. 'The sister was wailing and the mother was yelling and bawling. My God! I thought there was going to be a murder at the side of the deathbed.'

'Hilary!' Anthony was beginning to show concern.

'No, let me tell Kay the whole story. She wants to know these things. She's a right to know.'

Kay felt herself freeze.

'They put Parvinder on a life-support machine. Brain stem death, the doc said. Car got tangled in vegetation on the way down the cliff. She was thrown out, back of the head bashed against the rocks. Doc thought it was a miracle she wasn't killed outright, but apparently some folks survive despite all odds.' Hilary took a gulp of wine. 'Spirit gone, flesh still willing.'

'Hilary, darling!' Anthony was now seriously worried.

'Please,' Kay said urgently. 'I'd like to hear.'

Hilary was already continuing. 'Brain was dead, but everything else was working fine. The medics keep them alive, you see, while they argue the toss about whether they can take the organs. Once they get the go-ahead they whisk the donor into theatre and whip everything usable out. Eyes, liver, kidneys. They leave the heart till last.'

Kay let out a low groan.

'It was a desperately difficult time,' Anthony cut in. 'For Parvinder's family, for us . . . well, you can imagine.'

'I'll say!' Hilary cried. 'My God! That poor woman, the mother. I can still hear her screams. Like someone dying in agony. Like an animal in a trap. Blood curdling. And all the time that cold fish QC nephew was

325

working on her, laying down the law. Beating her down until she gave the go-ahead for her daughter to be cut up into pieces. Going against all her beliefs, her religion.'

'I'm so sorry about this,' Anthony said to Kay. 'Hil's been through an awful lot of stress — '

'If it had been my little piccaninny on the slab,' said Hilary savagely, 'I'd have killed him.'

★ ★ ★

In the calm of her hotel room Kay fumbled with her mobile phone, desperate to get into the voicemail programme. Eventually she heard Majid speaking to her, terse and urgent: 'Kay, please call me back as soon as you get this message.'

She sat on the bed, disoriented and exhausted, her mind whirling with dark, destructive visions. Slowly, slowly she began to come to her senses. Ever since the operation she'd been in the grip of her fantasies, the dreams and the sense of personal dislodgement. They had been constantly in her mind. Driven by her obsessive thoughts she had let her life drift into the shadows, forgetting her work, her music, nearly all of her friends, her family. If she had only made a positive move to close the gap, Ralph and Isobel would have been there for her, loving her, supporting her. But she had held them at a distance. Even with Majid, this new precious love who delighted her, she had been looking inwards, been using him for her own ends, distracted by her urgent inner world.

It's over, she told herself. All over. She recalled Raymond King urging her to seize hold of life, not brood over death. She had not wanted to listen. And now, at last, she could hear him.

When she made contact with Majid, she gave away very little. What was the point? He was too far from her. He could do nothing but worry. And she could already hear the anxiety in his voice, a message far more powerful and reassuring than any pretty protestations of love.

'I know all I need to,' she told him finally. 'I'm coming home tomorrow.'

23

Kay's sleep was dreamless and she woke to a sense of calm. Today she would return to Majid, she would write off the past few months to history and her life would take a new direction.

There was one last thing to do before she left the place in which Parvinder had died. And that was to visit the exact location of her death. Pay tribute, lay the ghost.

She called a taxi to take her to Babbacombe Point. As they climbed the long ascent to the head of the cliffs she recalled that Mr King had indicated she could well be able to drive again after her next check-up. It was an interesting thought, an exciting glimpse of a restored freedom. Although she had rather enjoyed her taxi rides, the unexpected, unconnected fragments of conversation with the various drivers.

Her driver this morning was quiet and preoccupied which suited her fine. Paying him she asked if he could call for her later on and take her to the station. They fixed a time and he gave her a brief salute as he drove away.

She hitched her long-handled travel bag over her shoulder and stood looking over the bay for a few moments. There was a light mist clinging to the sea which shimmered bluish-gold. A black tanker lay at anchor to the east of Brixham harbour and nearer to the shoreline was a small forest of sailing boats. It was still early and there was hardly any human sound or movement.

Kay turned off the road and joined the cliff path for walkers. Her sandals crunched on the sandy red earth. Below her the imposing red cliffs plunged down to the sea, their serrated flanks striped with parched vegetation. Cormorants and gulls skimmed them, plummeting into the sea like missiles.

The bay into which Parvinder's car had fallen was small and enclosed, a strip of fine sand bordered on three sides by dizzily sheer drops. The huge rocks at the cliff base were stacked together like a mountain range seen from the air, their jagged points like weapons.

Kay stopped at the eastern edge of the cliff and sat down on the prickly grass. How long would it take a car with a body in it to fall from the cliff tops to the rocks? How long would the terror last?

She recalled physics lessons at school, being taught that the further an object falls the faster it moves. There was some specific equation, some law of velocity in relation to gravity and the duration of the fall, but she had forgotten the specifics. The main thing was that the plunge must have been very swift, very soon over.

'Oh, Parvinder!' she murmured.

She sat for a time, looking alternately at the shift of the sea and the drift of the luminous sky, her eyes always returning to the force and power of the motionless rocks.

A woman came by with a dog. It snuffled around Kay, bustling and friendly. Its owner called it away, smiling in anxious apology.

Kay looked at her watch and was surprised how much time had passed. She reshouldered her bag and walked on, gradually rounding the bay and eventually discovering a place where a curve of cracked tarmac sprinkled with grass marked what must once have been a road. To the north, behind her, she could hear the faint growl of cars on the current coastal road.

Her heart quickened. Was this the actual place? Was this where Parvinder's car had made its death dive? She looked for signs. There was just tufted grass growing from pink earth, little lumps of red rock showing through.

She heard footsteps behind her. Another dog bounded forward, tail whirling, eyes full of greeting. A huge donkey of a dog. One she instantly recognized with a stab of shock.

She turned and saw Majid's colleague Theo coming towards her. Her nerves gave a single screaming jerk and then a curious sense of detachment took hold of her. Suddenly she understood her mistake of the night before, understood that the images which had stubbornly enfolded her since the transplant were valid after all. It was not an understanding of the whys and hows, simply a clear apprehension of the reality of an act of wickedness whose magnitude was unthinkable.

'Kay!' he called out. He came to stand close to her. 'I thought I might find you here.' He was smiling, low-key, friendly. Behaviour which was entirely normal, yet in these particular circumstances bizarrely eccentric.

Kay stepped back from him a little, her brain working hard to place pieces of information together to form some coherent framework. Theo and Majid. Theo and the Cavendishes. Theo and Parvinder.

'Why don't we sit down over here?' said Theo, gesturing to a wooden seat, placed so as to give its occupants an idyllic view of the bay.

She sat. Pilot walked up and stood beside his master.

'Down!' Theo told him softly and the dog gently subsided, settling on his stomach, front paws outstretched in the pose of a stone sphinx. Theo patted his wiry head. 'Stay!'

Kay looked on, blank-faced.

'I once put him on stay outside my wine merchants,' Theo said. 'I left by a back door and forgot all about him. He was still in the place I left him two hours later.'

'Impressive.'

Theo gave a faint smile of agreement. 'You'll no doubt infer from that little story that I like to be in control.'

She nodded. Fear crawled up the back of her neck.

'There's nothing to be afraid of,' he told her. 'I'm simply going to talk to you.'

'How did you know I was here?' she asked, keeping her voice low and steady. 'Did William call you? Or maybe Anthony. Or was it Hilary?'

'It was Majid who gave me the clue.'

'I don't believe it!' She was filled with dismay.

'Don't get upset, Kay. The clue came from my observations — there was no question of Majid's making private disclosures. I noticed that he was unusually distracted at yesterday morning's chambers' meeting and that, even more unusually, he had his mobile phone on

332

stand-by. He was called away to take an urgent call in the administration office so I took a look at the day's schedule in his personal organizer. Your name and mobile number were there ringed in red beside the Cavendishes' number. I was puzzled, intrigued. But it wasn't difficult to start making connections.'

How? she thought wildly, her brain in panic mode, skating madly through possibilities. How could he know anything about me? Majid would never have spoken about the transplant.

'I'm a good friend of the Cavendishes!' Theo explained. 'I was a house guest when Anthony had his sixtieth.' His pale eyes swivelled to Kay, interested to see her reaction, watch her make connections of her own.

'I gave Hilly a call right away after the meeting finished,' he continued patiently. 'I told her she might be having a visitor. And that if she did I would be very interested to hear about it. You hadn't arrived, of course, when I made that first call. Hilly was still sober then.'

Kay forced herself to breathe slowly and steadily. 'Does she get drunk every night?'

'No. She drinks a great deal, but rarely gets drunk. That's how I knew something was wrong when she phoned later on last night.'

'You've known the Cavendishes for a long time then?'

'Ever since I was a child. Hilly and my mother went to school together. She's been a kind of fairy godmother to me. I'm very fond of Hilly.'

Another dog walker rounded the point. A man with two border collies who set up a volley of excited barking on spying Pilot.

'Come here!' the man shouted uselessly as the two dogs homed in on Pilot, snapping at his muzzle, provocative rather than aggressive.

'Dead dog!' Theo said to Pilot who immediately rolled over on to his side as though he had been shot. 'Piss off!' Theo said softly to the collies who glanced up at him and started to back away.

The owner looked sheepish. He smiled across at Theo with an apologetic dogs-will-be-dogs expression.

Kay noticed that Theo completely ignored him, his total refusal to acknowledge the man's existence making him scurry away like a scolded child.

'Ask me.' Theo said quietly.

Kay jerked with shock. 'Ask you what?'

'The question you're longing to ask me. About Parvinder — the way she died.'

Kay stared down at her hands. 'Was it an accident?' Before he could reply she faced him head on. 'Did you kill Parvinder?' she demanded recklessly.

'That's for you to decide, Kay,' he said. 'Why don't I tell you my side of the story, and you can be the judge.'

She turned away from him, revolted. Also choked with fear.

'Don't you want to hear?' he asked. 'Don't you want to know what happened to Parvinder? What really happened?'

'Of course I do. Wouldn't you want to know about the death of the person who gave you their heart?'

'On balance, I think I would,' he agreed slowly. 'Well then, where to start? Motive, method or means?' He paused. 'It seems logical to talk about motive first. So let's think about William. Here he is; young, rich, athletic. Idolized by girls. You walk along the front in Torquay with William and female heads turn to look back as he passes. And yet he never keeps a girlfriend for more than a few weeks. Hilly's getting bothered about it. She's beginning to think something's wrong. And then Parvinder comes along and William falls for her. Heavily. She's beautiful, she's fearless, she's exciting. Parvinder makes you feel you can do whatever you want, kick against any rules — just as she herself did. She's warm and sexy. And she's tantalizingly exotic: black — I use the word in the fashionable, supposedly most politically correct sense — and foreign. Very much forbidden fruit.' Theo stopped at this point, swivelling his glance to Kay. 'You see Hilly and Anthony hold very rigid views on class, and even tougher ones on race. Anthony used to keep a framed portrait of Enoch Powell on the piano. And neither he nor Hilly were to be heard cheering when Mandela was set free.'

Kay felt a pain starting behind her eyes. 'So Parvinder is not a suitable partner for William?'

'Most certainly not. On the other hand there is nothing Hilly would like more than for William to settle down, get married and prove his sexual normality. You see, Hilly has suspected for a long time that William is inclined to prefer young men to young girls. Anthony takes the line of simply shutting out the issue as too horrible to contemplate and William obliges by keeping a string of girls going as a denial and a smokescreen. Hilly continually pushes him towards girls, but when he finally finds one he wants she's cruelly thwarted. Any girl except that one. A black girl from the slums of Bradford.'

Kay pressed her fingers over the throb of pain.

'Have you formulated any theories about motive yet?' Theo enquired pleasantly.

'I need to know more.'

'So, we have a young man who is desperately trying to deny his sexual proclivities, parents colluding with him and desperate for him to find a lady-love, and then the arrival of an irresistible girl whom his parents find utterly unsuitable to join the family.'

'But so far the motive for committing murder would apply to Hilly or Anthony,' Kay cut in, 'not you. Or were you simply the means?'

'The hit man?' Theo smiled. 'No. I'm a very selfish person. I'm motivated by my own primary desires, not a need to satisfy other people's obsessions.'

Kay felt her lips tremble as she spoke. 'Get to the point.'

'I'm thirty, Kay. I'm rich, I'm reasonably clever, I have a good career and even better social connections. I'm a catch. But I have no wife, no fiancée. I have never had a prolonged 'relationship' with a woman . . . ' He raised his eyebrows.

Kay looked into the strange, pale eyes. 'You're gay too!'

'Of course. I don't deny it. I'm not

ashamed of it. Oh, I don't go screaming around in leather trousers, picking up boys in gay bars and so on. But I am fully homosexual, I have only ever had good sex with a male.'

'So,' Kay murmured, 'you were in love with William?'

'I fancied him. A simple physical attraction. Sweet, sweet William. Twenty-five and never been kissed. Not until Parvinder came along!'

'You killed Parvinder because of your jealousy of William's attraction to her?'

There were a few beats of silence. 'There is that to take into account. Also my rage at the way in which she disrupted Hilly's and Anthony's delicately balanced life. I have great regard for them you see. After my father left they used to invite me to stay at holiday times whilst my mother went off with the latest new man.'

Kay pressed her fingers against her forehead. 'All right. You've explained motive. So how did you do it?'

'Parvinder liked danger. That's what fuelled her with the energy and drive to cut loose from her roots, make new friends without any thought of social rules. She liked glamour, she aspired to all the trappings of the rich Brits for whom she provided fabulous parties. Her head was full of thoughts of fine wines, fast cars, sexual freedom. She'd do anything, try anything. And she was a perfect subject for my party games demonstrating the effects of hypnosis.' He stopped. A dramatic pause.

Kay's mind raced. 'You hypnotized Parvinder?'

'Yes.' His eyes met hers. He raised an eyebrow.

As Kay's heart began to pound she steadied herself with more slow breathing. 'How much do you really know about hypnosis, beyond party games?'

'A good deal. I learned from a knowledgeable and experienced tutor. My fifth stepfather. He was a Harley Street psychoanalyst who liked to dabble in alternative therapies. He was impressively successful.'

'Your *fifth* stepfather!' Kay exclaimed.

'My mother got rid of my father when I was two. She's had five husbands since then. As many as Henry the Eighth had wives. But a few less than Elizabeth Taylor's string of husbands.'

Kay felt a moment of compassion, thinking of the young Theo, deprived of a father, cheated of maternal warmth.

'Besides teaching me hypnosis, my stepfather number five also pointed out to me that as an unloved and rootless child I might well feel anger towards my fellow human beings as I grew older.' Theo smiled. 'Perfectly accurate. But it isn't an anger that cripples me. I enjoy my life, I don't agonize about love or hate. I watch and I observe and I manipulate. That's where I get my most intense pleasure.'

Kay's fear surged up in a fresh wave. 'How did you kill Parvinder?'

'I haven't said that I killed her,' Theo reminded her. 'I'm simply relating what happened. You must judge.'

'Then tell me.'

'I first hypnotized her in a group session at Anthony's party. It was at that point where half the guests had left and the others were hiding away screwing each other, or sitting around half asleep. Parvinder loved it. The whole idea of what I was doing, wielding power over other people, manipulating them. But she wasn't at all afraid to allow herself to be put under. She asked me to give her some private sessions to cure her fear of dogs. Like a good many Asians she feared dogs because of their association with disease. Nearly all her rich clients had pooches and it was embarrassing to break out in a sweat every time one trotted into view.'

'So, you hypnotized her. How many times?'

'Three. It was enough. Enough to firmly fix a suggestion in her subconscious. I suggested to her that she would die early. That she would die as a result of reckless driving whilst being pursued by another car. She would feel terror, she would feel utter powerlessness. She would lose control of the car. I rather enjoyed my own inventiveness — '

'Stop there. I don't believe you,' Kay cut in savagely.

'Then choose not to.'

She raised her hands. 'All right, I'll go with it as a theory. Now tell me what happened. Tell me!'

'Parvinder was spending the weekend at the Cavendishes. William was teaching her scuba-diving. The season was just starting and the weather suddenly became prematurely warm. Perfect for diving. William took her out into the bay one morning and they dived together. He always went in first. He'd streak down to the anchor and then swim off a little way, teasing Parvinder, giving her a thrill of fear when she couldn't find him. I went out in a small motor launch and dived in a few seconds after her. I swam down the line to find her. I indicated that there was an emergency, that she should come to the surface with me. Of course it was very easy for me to manipulate her. She was like a puppet.'

Kay glanced at him, imagining him in a diving mask, realizing how his eyes would look within the black slits. She felt the compulsion flowing from him, the menace.

'We sailed back to shore and I explained to her that there'd been a call from Bradford to say her mother had been taken into hospital. Guilt about her mother was a very sore point with Parvinder, as you can imagine. She had rejected and disgraced her family but she was still tied to them emotionally. The plan was for her to collect her car parked at the diving school and to drive back to the Cavendishes where she would telephone home, pick up her things and plan what to do next. I would go back and alert William to what had happened.'

'Why didn't Parvinder phone from the car?' Kay broke in.

'Her batteries were flat. They were always flat. And I don't carry one of those infernal mobile gadgets.'

'Go on.'

'As she got out of my car to get into her own, I triggered the suggestion I'd planted previously. I recommended that it would be quicker to use the coast road rather than drive through the town. I told her to be very careful. I reminded her that the road had always been a *black spot*. Parvinder set off ahead of me. I trailed her, gradually increasing my speed. When we got to the point where the old road is partly sealed off from the new one, her car veered off towards the cliff edge. Within seconds it had vanished.'

Beads of sweat broke out over Kay's skin. She was flushed with heat and then suddenly cold. 'Did you see the results of the crash?'

'Of course not. A killer with any sense always makes sure not to be found where the action is. I drove straight back to the harbour, then went for a long sail.'

'Oh God!' Kay whispered.

'So,' Theo said, leaning back and tilting his head to the emerging sun, 'how do you judge me?'

'I don't know. I find it hard to believe you, it's all too implausible.'

'You don't think I killed her?'

'I don't believe the hypnosis story. I simply don't believe a person could be hypnotized into engineering their own death.'

'You believe I killed her, but by a different method?' His persistent curiosity was chilling. 'Maybe I simply ran her car off the road?'

Kay stood up, unwilling to engage in this conversation any longer. 'It doesn't really matter what I believe. All that matters is that she died.'

'Instead of you,' he said evenly.

Kay looked towards the head of the cliffs

and thought of the rocks below, reaching up like waiting arms. How easily Theo could overpower her and send her hurtling on to those cruel spikes.

'Do you want me to die too? You missed killing Parvinder's heart once, do you want to finish the job off?' As she spoke she felt a huge, primitive longing for life, a rage against danger and death. She prayed for another dog walker to turn up. With another person present she would have a chance of making an escape.

But here, alone with Theo she found herself strangely magnetized and powerless. A dark new idea engulfed her, leaving her breathless with fear. Had he somehow managed to implant a hypnotic suggestion in her, Kay? No, that was not possible. On the night of the party Majid had shaken her awake before anything could happen.

Theo was staring at her, reading her changing expressions. 'Why should I want to kill you?' he asked. 'To shut you up from running to the police with my story? I'm afraid they would not be at all impressed. There's no evidence to link me with Parvinder's death. And even if they arrested me the DPP would be highly unlikely to allow a case to be brought on the basis of nothing more than flimsy suppositions.'

'Then why come to find me this morning? You could simply have left things alone.'

'But you wouldn't have left things alone, Kay. You're determined, you're tenacious, you're intelligent — Majid wouldn't waste his time with an airhead. Eventually you'd have found out.'

He came to stand beside her. Pilot still lay as though dead beside the bench.

Kay flinched from him. 'Did you hypnotize *me*?'

'I didn't have the opportunity,' he said. 'But, don't forget, Kay, you carry the heart of a woman who was highly susceptible to my hypnotic suggestions.'

He *is* going to kill me, Kay thought. Fear came in a fresh wave, like pain which recedes for a time then returns in full force. As the spasm gripped her she was suddenly incandescent with fury.

'You killed Parvinder!' she shouted in his face. 'You did such a wicked cold-blooded thing for no other reason than sexual pique.'

'I didn't kill Parvinder for jealousy over sweet William,' Theo said softly.

'What?'

'I did it to avenge the honour of a much more noble and worthy man.'

Her senses stilled. Her mind was stripped bare of thought.

'I'm talking of Majid, of course,' he said. 'I'm surprised you didn't guess before.'

'Majid!'

'Yes. I've been infatuated with him ever since I first met him.'

'No!' she yelled at him. '*No!*'

'Don't worry? Kay. Majid never spares a thought for me. He's as straight as they come sexually. That's why he's been totally oblivious to my lusting for him. He's a most percipient man, but like many sexually confident males, he simply doesn't tune in to so-called sexual irregularity.'

'You killed Parvinder to avenge Majid's honour?' Her voice was hoarse with disbelief.

'She was a slag. A tart, a whore. She screwed around like all young Western women do in these liberated times. She shamed her family and betrayed her tradition. And she caused endless heartache. Majid was constantly driving up to Bradford to avert a new crisis, to keep the family glued together whilst one renegade member tried to destroy them.'

'You hated her.'

'I told you, I'm not driven by love or hate. Simply the wish to organize my world as I want it. And the killing wasn't premeditated. I did it that morning because the possibility arose. It was a whim, a testing out to see if possibility could become reality.'

He moved closer to her and Kay tensed.

'Don't be frightened,' he said to her. 'Your idea that I'm going to kill you as well so as to finally destroy Parvinder's black heart is highly imaginative. But I think I'm rather too fond of my own skin to want to take the risk.'

He's toying with me. He's pawing me like a cat with a half-dead mouse. She tried to think, to devise some means of getting away from him. She imagined herself tumbling over the edge of the cliff, clutching at emptiness. She heard her own screams echo in her head as she was projected into blackness.

She felt pressure against her legs and her hip bone. Fear rushed back more terrible than before, twisting her nerves into a mesh of dark dread.

She looked down and saw the face of a large black and gold dog. A companion joined it. A carbon copy. Two muscular long-legged Dobermanns, their tongues hanging out wet and red.

She stepped back from them. She had once been badly bitten.

'They're just pets,' Theo said. 'They're not going to hurt you.'

Kay found herself dizzy with all manner of terrors beyond belief. She held herself rigid.

Then suddenly the dogs threw up their heads, catching a new scent. Their interest in her was rapidly replaced by the discovery of the slumped Pilot. The dogs flung themselves towards him, stiff with excitement and intent.

'Down! Stay down!' Theo yelled, as Pilot began to raise himself.

The Dobermanns were growling now, low primitive rumbles reverberating through their taut, honed bodies. Pilot pulled back his lips. The Dobermanns pounced.

Suddenly the air was filled with the sound of rampant, unleashed savagery. Pilot was pinned to the ground, his throat torn at and punctured by his assailants' teeth.

He struggled to free himself, eventually managing to get to his feet. All three dogs rose on their hind legs, united in fury like some crazed mutated creature with twelve legs and three tails. The bodies thrashed against each other, yelping growling and screaming.

'Christ almighty!' Theo waded in to rescue his pet. He hauled on one of the Dobermann's collars but the dog made no response. The squirming mass of muscle catapulted from one spot to another and Kay dropped to the ground, curling into a ball to avoid being hit or crushed.

A man was approaching, waving his arms. 'Goliath, Hercules!' He yelled the names over and over.

Theo was still in the fray. He was gradually being edged towards the head of the cliff. Somehow he managed to pull Pilot free from the skirmish. The Dobermanns swung around in rage, desperate to regain their prey.

Involuntarily Kay shut her eyes tight. There was one blood-chilling howl and a sudden shocking silence.

And then the air was filled with a man's keening cries. 'Oh, God, Oh, God, Oh, God!'

Kay sat up, trembling violently. The owner of the Dobermanns was standing at the cliff edge. The dogs were all gone. Theo too.

★   ★   ★

The rescue services found all four bodies lying amongst the rocks. Kay was gently steered into an ambulance and taken to hospital. She kept herself very calm, very still. A film ran constantly in her head; pedalling legs, flailing arms, hands clawing out to grasp at scraps of vegetation.

When Majid came much later she buried her head against him and wept as though all the veins and pipes in her body had burst.

He held her in a strong clasp as he listened

349

to her wild, halting story. He heard her out as she blamed herself for all manner of imagined wrongs: interference, provocation, the engineering of a tragedy.

When she was quiet, he said gently, 'You judge yourself too harshly. Because of you, a strange kind of justice has been done.'

24

It was six months later and Kay and Majid were awaiting the arrival of friends for supper.

Kay was in the kitchen. Various fish, meats, vegetables, cheese, yoghurt and spices were spread around her. Beside them one of Parvinder's cook books lay open, well-fingered and stained with specks of cooking oil. Kulvinder had pointed out the books to Kay on her first awkward, tongue-tied revisit to Bradford. On the third visit she had given them to Kay. And on the fourth she had allowed Kay to kiss her cheek as she left.

'You're in your element,' he told her, handing her chilled Pouilly-Fumé, and marvelling that pulling slimy grey bits from a squid could make someone so contented.

'I'm cooking, and people who I love are coming to eat the results. And you are already here.' She turned. 'You are always here. Pure happiness.'

He kept his arms around her as she tossed chopped onions into sizzling butter. 'You could have invited Ralph and Isobel too,' he

351

said. 'We don't have to keep them a separate item.'

'I know. I simply prefer to contemplate an evening where I don't need to keep holding my breath.'

Majid smiled.

'He'll come round,' Kay said. 'He already likes you, he can't help himself. It's just that sun-tanned look and the exotic background that bugs him. And the thought of caramel-coloured grand-kiddies. Which is one issue on which he and Kulvinder are in complete agreement.'

Majid found Ralph's booming and fumbling attempts to come to terms with an Asian partner for Kay both touching and amusing. Ralph's carefully rehearsed and edited racist jokes were especially entertaining. Particularly when Isobel blushed deep pink and ticked him off.

The entry phone buzzed and four heads appeared on the video screen. Balbinder and her entrepreneur fiancé, Fiona with Hugo, who, following the loss of Fi's baby, had been banished into the wilderness to consider his position and had then come flying back the minute she gave him the signal.

Kay looked at the four smiling faces. 'Ebony and ivory, as Ralph would say.'

'Smut and butter,' Majid commented drily,

recalling childhood days.

Later he watched Kay as she served out a meal designed to suit all tastes. He watched the swift movements of her short-nailed musician's fingers, the way the light formed a halo around her pale, long hair. He had never expected to find such happiness.

She no longer spoke of the dreams and images which had troubled and haunted her in the months after her illness. He assumed they had faded and eventually died. After Theo's death they had talked endlessly about the origins and meanings of the unexplainable concepts that had invaded her consciousness. And gradually they had both accepted that there are secrets of the human mind and heart which elude explanation.

He judged too that memories of the real-life horror on the cliff tops above Torbay had receded, and that her life, both personal and in her work and her music, was rich and steady and satisfying.

She looked up and smiled at him.

And suddenly it came to him that in years to come some trivial remark, some small innocent-seeming incident, could cause a reopening of wounds, a reliving of anguish. She would need understanding and patience and unconditional love. And he would be there for her.